HIGH PRAISE FOR
JOYCE HENDERSON!

WRITTEN ON THE WIND

"Joyce Henderson sweeps you into the old west with a no-holds-barred style! *Written on the Wind* is filled with action, suspense, and romance. Don't miss it!"

—Tina Wainscott, bestselling author of *In Too Deep*

"Henderson uses the potent culture clash theme to the best of her ability, incorporating Comanche customs and mores into her love story to add depth and historical accuracy. This is what Native American romance is all about, and Henderson delivers a great story with marvelous details."

—*Romantic Times BOOKreviews*

"Well developed supporting characters and good pacing are part of this book's success. A great opening chapter with just the right amount of tension throughout keeps the reader turning those pages...a wonderful second book for this new author."

—*Affaire de Coeur*

"A story sure to please fans of Western romances.... Not only does *Written On the Wind* sparkle with wit, humor, and a wonderfully written style of prose, but Ms. Henderson also manages to convey the emotional struggle of the Native American and the white man."

—Romance Reviews Today

MORE PRAISE FOR JOYCE HENDERSON!

WALKS IN SHADOW

"A powerful story of a strong-willed woman trying to maintain her independence and find love."

—*RomanticTimes BOOKreviews*

"This action-driven romance is straight from the old west. *Walks in Shadow* has enough grit and love to tame the western romance reader's thirst."

—Roundtable Reviews

"In her debut novel, Joyce Henderson's knowledge of horses and Indian heritage shines through in this very well-written story with realistic characters and good dialogue."

—Romance Reviews Today

"This exciting Western romance will thrill sub-genre fans....Joyce Henderson provides a strong tale."

—*The Midwest Book Review*

"I am grateful to Joyce Henderson for writing *Walks in Shadow*, a completely different type of Native American romance."

—Romance Reader at Heart

UNDENIABLE ATTRACTION

She seemed to linger on the precipice for a moment; then, her golden eyes opened. Staring up at him as if in a trance, her perusal traveled over his hair, his face, dropped to his lips, then went back up to his eyes. His body hummed as if her hands caressed him everywhere her gaze lingered.

"You said that wouldn't happen again," she quietly admonished.

"I know, but I..." He wanted her. That was certain. But from all accounts, she detested him. Except when she was in his arms—like now, this moment. Something in her eyes drew him.

He tiptoed along his own precipice, telling himself he was nothing if not honest. He took the plunge. "I want you."

JOYCE HENDERSON

TO THE EDGE OF THE STARS

LEISURE BOOKS NEW YORK CITY

A LEISURE BOOK®

December 2007

Published by

Dorchester Publishing Co., Inc.
200 Madison Avenue
New York, NY 10016

ISBN 10: 0-8439-5996-7
ISBN 13: 978-0-8439-5996-3

The name "Leisure Books" and the stylized "L" with design are trademarks of Dorchester Publishing Co., Inc.

Printed in the United States of America.

10 9 8 7 6 5 4 3 2 1

Visit us on the web at www.dorchesterpub.com.

ACKNOWLEDGMENTS

My love and thanks to Sandy Carmouche, my friend and fellow writer who has always been there when I needed a laugh...or a kick in the butt. And thank you to Prudy Taylor Board for teaching me, so many years ago, the basics of how to write for publication.

TO THE EDGE
OF THE
STARS

Chapter One

SAVAGE

Kalen Barrett stared up at the letters burned into a half-timber suspended over the gated ranch entrance. She pulled back on the reins. "Whoa, boys." The big brindle-colored horses responded, and the wagon creaked to a halt.

She glanced at Uncle Jed snoring next to her on the high seat, sleeping off another night of drinking in a Waco saloon. She'd accepted long ago that he would never change. But he was her only kin, and she loved him, weaknesses and all.

Having driven the wagon most of the day in the sun's glare and heat, she'd undone the top buttons on her shirtwaist, seeking whatever small relief possible, if only the wind to cool the sweat between her breasts. Her leather gloves stuck to wet hands.

Kalen surveyed the whitewashed rail fence that crisscrossed open pastures for perhaps a mile across the shallow valley. She'd never seen so many different-sized paddocks. Dozens of horses of every color and size, heads lowered as they cropped stubbly grass, filled many of the paddocks. Others lipped up scattered hay thrown over shoulder-high fences.

Lifting her floppy black hat, she shaded her eyes from the sun already in its western descent. Across the valley on a slight rise, tin roofs glinted. Other buildings nestled beneath towering oaks.

"They call this the Savage Ranch, but it's one of the most peaceful lookin' places I've ever laid eyes on."

Slapping the reins against Jack's and Jim's broad rumps, she clicked her tongue and drove through the open gate. "Hup, boys, I hope to get to the main house before supper."

Uncle Jed snorted, resettling his shoulder against the buckboard's backrest. Kalen's mind wandered to the oft-pondered question, *What am I goin' to do with him?*

She sighed. *Fake it.* She'd secured more than one job for both of them in the past few years by passing him off as ill. "Somethin' he ate didn't agree with him," or "He has a festerin' tooth." Like as not, she wasn't believed, and sometimes she'd done the work of two to maintain employment for both.

Less than a half mile after passing beneath the gate sign, Kalen again hauled in the horses. "Uncle Jed." She nudged him hard. "Wake up."

He cracked open a bloodshot eye and moaned, then wiped a hand down his beard-stubbled face and pushed himself up. "What?"

She pointed. "Look at that foal. Distressed, I think."

Jed Barrett might have spent half the time roaring

drunk, but the other half he was first-rate at handling horses. Coming fully awake, he crawled down off the wagon, holding on until his legs steadied. He peered at a foal curled up on the ground inside the fence.

Another horse stood several feet away, grazing. The dam, no doubt, and from the looks of her bag, she hadn't nursed the foal for a long time—maybe not at all since birth.

"Don't be sittin' there, girl! Hand me the rope. You start arubbin' the little guy's coat. I'll catch the mare."

Kalen set the brake, flipped the reins around it, jumped down and picked up the lariat coiled in the wagon bed. She and Jed edged between the rails. Jed built a lasso noose as he walked toward the mare. Kalen knelt next to the foal and crooned, brushing her hand over his soft coat. Though his eyes fluttered open, the colt didn't have enough energy to lift his head.

"Come on, little fella. We'll get your mama over here to feed you."

With the flick of his wrist, her uncle laid the rope over the mare's head. She whinnied but didn't resist when he pulled her in and led her across the paddock. He tied her to the fence and got the twitch out of the wagon bed.

Jed laid his calloused hand on her withers, rubbed over her back, gradually making his way down her flank. She jumped and danced away when his fingers grazed her swollen bag. Nodding her head up and down, she snapped her teeth and tried to nip him.

"Easy, girl. I'd say it's been awhile since she foaled. You see the afterbirth anywhere, Kalen?"

She hiked her chin. "Near the fence behind you. It looks dry, Uncle Jed. Is her bag feverish?"

"Uh-huh. Can you lift that foal by yourself?"

"I'll manage."

Jed pulled the mare's tender upper lip through the chain loop attached to the wooden handle. "Sorry, girl, but that boy of yours gotta eat or he's a goner." He twisted the handle, and the chain squeezed her lip. The mare went dead still.

Though not big, the colt was dead weight. He weaved and tottered from weakness as Kalen guided him the few steps to his dam's side.

Beads popped afresh on her brow as she struggled to hold the colt on his feet and guide his muzzle toward the milk-laden bag. When he finally latched on to a teat, she grinned. "Got it!"

As the colt hungrily jerked milk into his mouth, the mare kicked, barely missing Kalen and the colt. Jed applied more pressure on the twitch. After a time, he gradually loosened the chain, murmuring nonsense words of encouragement to the mare.

She would settle down once the pressure inside her udder diminished. It would be unlikely she'd balk again when her baby wanted to eat.

"I'd say this is her first foal, Kalen. Check her bag. See if it's still burnin' hot."

She reached past the foal's head, carefully laying her hand against the mare's bag. "Warm, but not too bad. The nursin' is relievin' her."

After a few minutes, Jed removed the twitch entirely, and Kalen eased her hands from around the colt's belly. Still pulling for all he was worth at his dinner, he quivered a bit on his spindly legs, but he didn't fall.

No matter how many times she had seen it, the miracle of birth always brought a warm feeling to Kalen's heart. This brown-on-white foal, a near perfect replica of his mother's colors, looked healthy enough, and he'd no doubt be fine after feeding several times.

She looked over the mare's back toward the house, still far in the distance. The place looked so well kept, surely the Savages must check their stock regularly. Though the little guy had been in trouble, his mama looked well-groomed, and she certainly hadn't missed any meals.

Kalen leaned back against the fence as her uncle cleared the mare's hindquarters,

"What the devil are you doing?" a terse voice asked.

Kalen gasped and spun about to find a young woman sitting atop another brown-and-white pinto. The girl's blue-black hair, parted in the middle, was braided and woven with leather and turquoise beads. A blue, man-style shirt topped buckskin trousers tucked into knee-high boots. Thick lashes fringed wide-set, dark eyes. High cheekbones framed a straight nose over a wide mouth. The words had been abrupt, but her generous lips looked as though it wouldn't take much for her to break into a smile.

Jed recovered first. "We saw this here foal in trouble, so we stopped to see that he ate."

The girl was definitely Indian, and her uncle

didn't have much use for them. His tone and expression made that vividly clear.

Well, he'd have to get over it. Kalen had learned that the owner of the Savage ranch was a half-breed, his Indian father dead fifteen years, his mother still very much alive.

Kalen slipped back through the fence. As she straightened, a horseman rode up next to the girl.

"What's going on, Blair?" His eyes appeared black, his skin darker than hers, but there was a definite resemblance.

The man looked about her own age, in his midtwenties, the woman younger. While she rode bareback, he sat on a black, tooled-leather saddle with silver inlay. A lot of silver.

She didn't know who these people were, but chances were good they lived here, so she decided to speak up. After all, she'd come for a job. "The foal looked like he hadn't eaten since birth. Uncle Jed . . ."

Offering an apologetic smile, she again removed her hat and ran her fingers through tousled chestnut curls. "Sorry." Indicating her uncle, she said, "This is my uncle, Jed Barrett. I'm Kalen Barrett. We're lookin' for work."

The girl smiled, befuddling Kalen. If she had been blessed with a sister, she would have wished for one as lovely.

"I'm Blair Savage." She glanced at the man next to her. "My brother Cameron. As for a job, you'll have to see Taylor."

"Taylor?" Kalen asked.

"Our older brother. He runs the place."

"I don't know, Kalen," Jed said.

She pivoted toward him, alarmed at what he might say next. "Well, I do know. We need work, and we need it today, Uncle Jed. We'll find Mr. Savage."

Cameron said, "If he's finished working in the ring, you'll catch him on the front porch this time of day nursing a scotch and water."

Jed smiled affably. "A man after my own heart." Under his breath he added, "Even if he is Injun."

"You're a girl!" Cameron exclaimed in surprise.

"Oh, for heaven's sake, Cameron, of course she's a girl!" Blair chided.

He smiled contritely. "Sorry, but your scratchy voice and short hair . . . Well, I just thought . . . Maybe you have a cold?" he asked hopefully.

"No," Kalen said. "This is my regular voice, Mr. Savage. But don't think a thing of it. A lot of people mistake me for a boy."

"*Mister* Savage. Don't bust your buttons, brother." Blair rolled her eyes as she dismounted and faced Kalen. "Go on to the house. If Taylor isn't there, he soon will be."

"Hold it, Blair. Where are your manners? They could meander for an hour looking for the gate to the house. I'll check the foal and keep an eye on the mare for a bit. You ride with them to the house."

"Are you sure? I usually handle Starduster."

"Well, today I will. She's a horse, for God's sake, not a person!"

"Wait a minute." A sly smile curved Blair's lips.

Bemused, Kalen and Jed watched the exchange between brother and sister.

"You think if Taylor hires more people, you'll be relieved of some chores!"

"Oh, for . . ."

"Never mind." She laughed, then turned to Kalen and Jed again. "Keep on this road for about a mile. There's a branch to the left through the fences. If I haven't caught up with you, that'll take you directly to the front door."

She faced her brother. "Starduster is *my* horse, Cameron. I'm going to take a look at the foal; then I'll follow these folks."

Kalen and Jed had barely moved out of earshot of the pair when he muttered, "Damned Injuns. I don't know. Maybe we better move on."

"Uncle Jed, we need this job. The Savage Ranch is the biggest spread for miles."

"But . . . Injuns?"

"Dadburnit!" she erupted. "Indians they may be, but they can buy and sell us ten times over! They pay wages, and we need 'em. Come down off your high horse and think for a change!"

Though contrite for flying off the handle, she didn't retract her statements. Sometimes he tried her last bit of patience with his drinking and senseless dislike of Mexicans and Indians.

She'd already lived through enough heartache where Indians were concerned and moved past mindless hatred. Uncle Jed had been livid and still harbored bad feelings about what happened to his brother and sister-in-law.

While Kalen was at another homestead visiting a friend, her folks had been killed in a raid, the house torched. As hard as they'd tried, she and Dr. Mulvaney had been unable to save her brother. While she clasped his hand and prayed, six-year-old Dillon had slipped away on a long sigh after three weeks of pain.

Why couldn't it have been her? Dillon was so sweet. Why wasn't she home to share her family's fate? At age ten and all alone in the world save for her uncle and aunt, she'd asked the questions time and again, but it was her lot to survive and remember.

Moving in with Aunt Livvie and Uncle Jed had been a comfort. Her buxom aunt had a heart as big as all outdoors. Jed "nipped at the bottle a bit," as Livvie so quaintly put it, but she was there to pick him up, dust him off, and send him out the door with a warm hug and lingering kiss for another day of work.

Until one evening Jed came home and his Livvie wasn't at the door to greet him. When Kalen walked in an hour later, he lay dead drunk on the floor, weeping inconsolably, his arms wrapped around Olivia Barrett's body. It was left to Kalen to ride for the undertaker. Dr. Mulvaney blamed her beloved aunt's death on her bum heart. Aunt Livvie had slipped away when no one was about.

Now they had to have jobs, and, by the good Lord's grace, they would get them on this ranch if there were any to be had. She didn't care what the Savages' heritage was. They paid wages. That was good enough for her. Uncle Jed would just have to live with it. Simple as that.

Three-quarters of an hour later, drawing the wagon to a halt, Kalen scanned the house. A lone woman sat on the wide porch, and Blair and Cameron galloped in just as Kalen jumped down from the high seat.

She removed her gloves and stuffed them in her back pocket. "Please, Uncle Jed, let me handle this," she said quietly. To her relief, he stayed put, gazing about at the half dozen buildings, especially the long, low barn some distance from the house.

The Savages dismounted and carelessly tossed their reins over a hitch rail. Before Kalen took a step, Blair clasped her hand and practically dragged her toward the porch steps. Kalen noticed how much dirtier her hand was, the creases of her damp palms encrusted with dirt.

"Mother," Blair said.

Kalen grimaced, self-conscious about her grubby appearance.

Looking in their direction, Miz Savage smiled. "You almost missed supper, Blair. Who's with you?"

"Folks looking for work," Cameron offered as he came abreast of Kalen and his sister. Though Blair stood a couple inches taller than Kalen's own five feet five, Cameron must have been near six feet.

Kalen reluctantly trotted between them as they climbed the three steps to the lovely lady seated in a rocker. Though her silver-shot, dark hair was swept back in a bun encircled by a blue ribbon, the style didn't render her face severe. On the contrary, like Blair, she was breathtakingly stunning and regal.

"Ma'am." Kalen extended her hand, dirt and all.

The lady smiled again as her blue-eyed gaze wandered in the general direction of Kalen's face. Then it hit her.

Miz Savage was blind.

Kalen stuck her hand in a back pocket as a blush crept over her cheeks. She mentally scrambled to cover her embarrassment. Though Miz Savage hadn't seen her, her children had. "Sorry to intrude at this hour, ma'am."

"Not at all, my dear. I'm Lael. Welcome to our home." Her head cocked as if listening for something no one else could hear. "You have a distinctive voice. I suspect you are a lovely girl."

"You suspect wrong, ma'am," Kalen retorted without thinking.

Blair's laughter drew her mother's attention. "More like a travel-stained ragamuffin, Mother. But she probably cleans up well." She grinned at Kalen.

Rather than taking offense, Kalen felt a warm glow inside. She had enjoyed the banter between the siblings, and now Blair teased her as if she were a longtime acquaintance.

"Blair?" a deep voice questioned. The screened door opened to a tall man with a glass in his hand.

"Just the man Kalen and her uncle need to see." Blair gestured. "My brother Taylor."

Kalen's breath caught and she barely heard the rest of the introductions. Butterflies took off helter-skelter in her stomach. Unconsciously, she smoothed her clothes and licked dry lips. A handsome man by anyone's measure and taller than Cameron, Taylor Savage's sable hair slicked back from a broad brow. He had his mother's gorgeous blue eyes, but his were alert and deeply unsettling. A half smile flashed pearly white teeth against skin darker than that of the other Savage children.

"Miss Barrett," he acknowledged absently.

She had the distinct impression his fleeting smile was insincere. Too bad. He was very handsome when he smiled. She felt deserted when his attention focused on her uncle still seated in the wagon.

"I think Kalen saved Starduster's foal." Cameron took a seat beside his mother.

Taylor Savage's glance landed on her again, scattering her wits. "Uh, no. It was Uncle Jed. I just do what he tells me."

"You lifted the foal by yourself. I saw you," Blair said.

Kalen took a step back when Taylor's gaze traveled over her. Clearly, he didn't believe she was capable of such a feat. When he directed his skepticism toward Uncle Jed, her hackles rose, and she said flatly, "He's prob'ly forgotten more about horse care than you know."

Expression patronizing, he lifted a brow and strode past her and welcomed her uncle. "Mr. Barrett."

Kalen grimaced at her own audacity and prayed they wouldn't lose the job before they'd secured it. After a short time, Taylor Savage walked back to the porch, ignoring her as he passed.

"Cameron, is the room in the back of the cook shack habitable?"

"Well, the window needs a wash, and the floor hasn't seen a broom in a long time."

"See to it, then. And find a cot. The kid can sleep there." He assisted his mother to her feet, a clear dismissal of Kalen and her uncle.

"Till later," Miz Savage said graciously as she tucked her hand around her son's arm.

Without looking back, Taylor ordered, "Get moving. Supper's on the table."

Kalen's mouth gaped. She looked down at herself and stilled, hands unconsciously twisting her battered hat. At twenty-five she was no kid, but he had dismissed her as he might a troublesome child.

Keeping her reactions in check might prove a greater challenge than controlling her temper when dealing with the gorgeous, arrogant son of a so-'n-so.

Chapter Two

"Uh," Blair said quietly, "he does run the place, Kalen. And he's got a lot on his mind."

Realizing that Blair had seen her indignation, she clapped her hat on. If she intended to work here, she'd better curb both her temper and gut reactions to her boss.

After showing them where to take the wagon and leave their horses with the ranch hand trusted to care for them, Cameron led her to the small room she would occupy. Though dusty, the room was totally bare, so it wouldn't take much to clean it up. Before disappearing for the night, Cameron returned with a cot and a lantern.

She divided her belongings and Uncle Jed's, handing him a clean change of clothes to take with him. Since the care of his clothes would fall to her, she kept the soiled garments.

As soon as she made the cot with her own bedding and tidied up as best she could until morning, she joined Uncle Jed with the other hands, eight in all, at the supper table. Ranging in age from about twenty to God only knew, they stared at her as if she were from another planet. She still wore her travel-stained cotton shirt and trousers, as grubby as any one of them after a long day's work.

The men would get used to her presence soon enough. If they had a problem with her, too bad. She'd do her work well enough to please the boss or die trying. If he accepted her presence, then the men had no say in the matter.

Two of the younger hands were obviously Indian. Uncle Jed didn't say anything, thank God, but he'd wedged himself between two others rather than sit next to either one.

Shrugging off their curiosity, Kalen dug in when the cook plunked a plate in front of her, overflowing with pork and beans and a large chunk of butter-slathered bread.

After supper, Tom, the bunkhouse cook, gave her a bowl to keep in her room for quick washup if she didn't have time for a full bath. Though he appeared curmudgeonly, he nevertheless thought of her comfort. Seeing that the men's accommodations had the only so-called bathroom, finding a bit of privacy would be tricky. But somehow she'd manage.

Kalen sought her bed early, pausing long enough to fill the bowl from the water well at the back of the stove. Though he had only a few dollars, Uncle Jed stayed at the table to play poker with four others. The rest melted away toward the sleeping quarters, although a couple lighted rolled cigarettes and walked outside to loiter next to a fence. Prob'ly jawin' each other with tall tales.

Ranch hands were the same everywhere: some good, some bad, some heavy drinkers, others teetotalers. But they all had one thing in common: most could spin yarns deep into the night.

Kalen rinsed her face and hands, swiped a wet cloth between her breasts and called it enough until she could soak properly. Crawling between the sheets, she groaned with relief when she stretched out flat on her back.

She was plumb tuckered after driving the wagon for ten hours, then having the pressure of asking for work . . . again. That never got easier, but she'd gotten good at it. Since Uncle Jed had fallen behind on payments and lost his small farm to the bank, the two of them had worked on four ranches in the past two and a half years.

Kalen grimaced and shifted on the cot. It was unlike her to bed down still covered in grit. No help for it this evening, though.

She brushed a tear from the corner of her eye and blamed it on exhaustion. It did no good to feel sorry for herself. Uncle Jed's drinking would send them packing from ranch to ranch as long as he lived and she traveled with him. That was a given. She could not, would not abandon him to sink into total drunkenness. The thought of him dying alone somewhere, sent her into a funk she had to fight past to even breathe.

Though past time to sleep, she couldn't turn off her mind, and thoughts of her new boss slithered beneath her defenses. No doubt about it, Taylor Savage was a handsome man. Powerfully built, he towered over Uncle Jed.

The men in her family, at least those she could re-member, were short and slight of build. Uncle Jed was only a few inches taller than her.

All the Savages were handsome. Gracious de-scribed Miz Savage and, Kalen suspected, kind as the day was long. All had various shades of dark hair. In the few minutes she had seen Taylor, his hair had gone from slicked straight back to a slight wave as it dried.

Willing herself to stop filling her mind with thoughts of him, she closed her eyes and drifted. But the last image that lingered was of that brief smile of his.

Despite her best efforts, her stomach took a nose dive when she again thought, *Devilishly handsome.*

Following supper, the Savage family gathered in the parlor until Lael said she wanted her bed. Taylor im-mediately crossed the handmade rag rug and of-fered his arm. She could find her way upstairs, but her eldest never failed to escort her to the base of the stairs.

"Taylor, before you retire, would you stop by my room?"

"Of course, Mother. Do you need something?"

"No, son, but I'd like to discuss something in private."

An hour later, after donning her night rail and wrapper, Lael listened to the quieting household.

"We should breed Comanche Moon tomorrow," she heard Taylor say as he and his brother crested the upper hall.

"Which mare?"

"The black-and-white pinto Barkley left with us two weeks ago. She's come in season, so there's no time like the present."

"See you *mañana*."

Closer to her door, Taylor said, "Eight o'clock, Cameron, not ten."

Her happy-go-lucky son laughed and closed his door. Lael smiled at the exchange. Poor Taylor. He worked harder than anyone and had assumed adult responsibility at such a young age. They might not show it to his face, but both Cameron and Blair admired him and loved him without reservation.

A light tap sounded. "Mother?" Taylor opened the door.

"Come in, son." She heard one step, the rest muffled when he walked onto the oval braided rug, and felt rather than heard him draw near. He sat opposite her at the small round table next to the south-facing window. She had raised the sash earlier to enjoy a slight breeze that stirred warm air.

"What did you want to talk about, Mother?"

Lael inhaled the pleasant scent of leather that hovered in the air when her children were near. "I don't usually interfere with your decisions, but I find this time I must."

"Oh? What decision is that?"

She smiled and groped for his hand. He took her fingers in his. "Don't be defensive. It's simply that I don't think you thought through the situation."

"I'm not defensive, Mother, merely curious. What situation?"

She patted his hand, then reached for the teapot Doreen had brought a little while before. "Tea?"

"No, thanks. I had a brandy with Cameron just before we came up."

From long practice, Lael filled her cup and set the pot aside. Taking a sip, she played for time, though determined to have her say. "Dear, I think Miss Barrett should be invited to sleep in the house. In the spare room."

"She's a kid, Mother. I thought she'd feel more comfortable near her uncle."

She laughed. "It amazes me that though I'm blind, I see more than you do!"

"What do you mean?" He sounded genuinely puzzled.

"Taylor, she's not a child; she's a woman. I can hear it in her voice. How do you expect she'll find enough privacy to bathe? You know there's only one tub in that small room adjacent to the men's sleeping quarters."

Silence reigned. Lael squeezed his wrist. "Trust me on this, Taylor. Miss Barrett would be far better situated if she had her own place to attend her toilette."

"Maybe," he said slowly, as if thinking hard.

"No maybe about it, dear. I suggest tomorrow you tell her she's moving in down the hall from Blair." She paused. "Or, if you prefer, ask Blair to speak to her."

"I can do it. I just don't know if it's necessary."

Lael released his wrist and patted his hand. "Speaking from a woman's perspective, Taylor, it is necessary."

Their first workday on the ranch, foreman Nolan Woodruff set the Barretts to mucking stalls. While cleaning a mare's hooves, he watched the Barrett girl out of the corner of his eye. She moved twice as fast as Jed. That really didn't make a lot of difference in his book. Sometimes the measured approach was better; a body could work all day that way.

Arms crossed on the top stall rail, Taylor asked quietly, "What do you think?"

Nolan had worked for Running Wolf Savage even before he'd married Miz Lael in a white man's church and long before the young'ns were born. Treated almost like a member of the family, he took personal pride in how Taylor and Cameron had turned out. Though Wolf's oldest boy was now his boss, Taylor had leaned heavily on his expertise when he'd been a whippersnapper, just taking over. The boy still valued his opinion.

"I've kept an eye on 'em most of the mornin'. She's a quicker person by nature, I'd say. But the old boy knows what he's doin', Taylor. I think he can be trusted with the stock, doctorin' and such. I saw him checkin' the mare's legs in that stall afore he moved her out of his way. He's got a steady hand when a horse is on the end of a line."

Taylor studied Jed Barrett for a moment. "He's a drunkard, Nolan. What if he's soused some morning and mishandles a horse?"

"It's up to you, but we're shorthanded. I'd give 'im a chance. I'll eagle-eye 'im before he leaves the bunkhouse of a mornin'."

The network of broken veins across Barrett's nose and cheeks screamed a bad drinking habit, but despite that Nolan still thought the man good at what he did . . . at least when sober. And if he didn't miss his guess, that slip of a girl knew more about horse care than she let on. She'd take up the slack if needed.

He flicked a glance over Kalen Barrett. Hell, with her curly hair shorter than his mane, understandably, his first impression had led him to believe her a boy, right up until she mouthed off. Then he had noticed the curves beneath her travel-stained clothes. And damned if she hadn't gotten her back up and taken an instant dislike to him.

Nevertheless, he had been drawn to her. Still was. But he wanted peace in the house, and he would do most anything within reason to satisfy his mother, so . . .

Kalen couldn't make out their words, but she knew Mr. Savage and Mr. Woodruff were talking about her and Uncle Jed. From the glum look on Mr. Savage's face, she didn't think her uncle was coming out on top in his estimation.

When Taylor Savage started toward them down the corridor between stalls, her heart sank. *Here it comes.* He'd prob'ly send them packing. As he neared, she straightened to take the bad news head-on.

"Mr. Barrett?" he called.

Putting a free hand to his back as he straightened, Uncle Jed leaned on the shovel and faced Savage. "Young fella?"

Not very respectful, but that was Uncle Jed's way. He didn't mean anything by it.

"I'm sure you can manage in the bunkhouse, Mr. Barrett, but after further thought, I expect your niece would be more comfortable in the main house. She'd be down the hall from my sister. You have any objection?"

Though Barrett's brow creased questioningly, Kalen's eyes flew wide, then narrowed. "Mr. Savage, maybe you'd be better advised to ask me about that."

To cover his inexplicable reaction to her, he scoffed, "Men are usually the head of a household, kid. You may not have a house, but he's your elder."

It wasn't easy, it surely wasn't, but Kalen curbed her quick retort. "Mr. Savage, I'm not a kid. I make my own decisions. I'm perfectly comfortable in the room assigned to me."

"Kalen, maybe he's right."

"No. I prefer to stay where I am, Uncle Jed." She fought the urge to fidget under Savage's assessing gaze.

Then he shrugged. "Suit yourself."

As he turned and walked away, she closed her eyes and wondered at her stubbornness. Oh well, not far a river flowed behind the barn. She could bathe there as long as the heat lasted. If Uncle Jed held true to form, likely they'd be asked to move on long before a chill arrived in the air.

Chapter Three

Morris Peabody, whose sole job was to exercise horses, pointed east. "Y'all'll find the compost pile 'bout a mile thataway, Miss Kalen."

She saluted the friendly, freckle-faced ranch hand and slapped the reins on the horse's rump. Shortly, the pungent smell of the compost announced she'd driven in the right direction.

Nose wrinkled, she brought the wagon to a creaking halt and tied the horse to a post. With an hour left before noon vittles, she had plenty of time to empty the soiled straw and manure. Lifting the pitchfork, she set to work, serenaded by noisy crows scrabbling in the odious piles, pecking up undigested seeds and other *delicacies*.

Despite the men's initial wariness, all were now friendly, or still shy, toward her. And praise be, Uncle Jed hadn't taken a nip for a month. Best of all, today he and Mr. Woodruff had gone out to a pasture together to check on an ailing horse. From their overheard conversation, both agreed the gelding had a bad case of colic.

It warmed her heart that Mr. Woodruff was willing to give her uncle a chance. It hadn't taken long for most other ranchers to give up on him. She'd already begun devising plans to thwart their firing. Depending, of course, on how much she continued to like it here.

Mr. Woodruff directed the hands in everything that needed to be done on a large ranch like this one, leaving the Savages free to work exclusively with the horses. She grimaced as she forked up the droppings and pitched them into the pile already several feet high and spread over a quarter acre.

These past four weeks had been filled with learning the routine. Now, she pretty much knew what was expected of her. She'd squeezed in a bath in the river several evenings after the men had bunked down for the night. Wrinkling her nose, she knew for sure she smelled every bit as bad as the droppings. As soon as she finished here, she'd enjoy another soak. Vittles could wait.

"Don't you ever take a bath, kid?"

Kalen flinched, almost pitching herself after the load of crud that flew up from the pitchfork. It rained down and just missed landing on top of her.

She rounded on Taylor Savage. "I could have fallen on the fork tines and killed myself!"

He leaned forward, propped a forearm on the saddle horn, and thumbed back his hat brim. "I doubt that, brat."

She stepped back. "Brat?" *The nerve of the man.*

"I've told you, *Mr.* Savage, I'm a grown woman. Stop treatin' me like a snivelin' child!"

"Sniveling you aren't, but you've got the same short fuse Cameron had at ten."

Was that laughter in his eyes? "So now you're comparin' me to your brother?"

He studied her from head to foot, then back again, slowly. She resisted the urge to squirm beneath his close scrutiny, especially when his eyes darkened and sparked fire.

"No. I hardly think I would compare you to my brother." He snugged down his hat, wheeled his mount and rode away.

His words left her uneasy, restless. She blinked and exhaled a breath she hadn't realized she'd been holding. Rubbing her chest, she took several breaths to assure herself she still could. *What was that all about?*

Perplexed, Kalen finished unloading the wagon. Stowing the pitchfork in the bed, she hopped onto the high seat and headed back to the barn. Part of it was her own animosity, no doubt stemming from his arrogant behavior. *That* was clear.

If not necessarily liked, most of the men respected Taylor Savage. She'd noticed a couple harbored the same enmity toward him as Uncle Jed. Still, they took the wages he paid and kept their mouths shut.

If it weren't for occasional Indian trouble in the North, folks might forgive and forget the Savages' heritage. After all, they trained the best mounts ranchers could buy and steadily sold them to the highest bidders.

* * *

Taylor rode toward number forty-four paddock where Nolan said he'd be treating a gelding. Unconsciously surveying the stock, he mulled over his most recent encounter with Miss Barrett.

Prickly little thing.

He sighed. Nothing new there. Her uncle had eyed him with something akin to a sneer until he had offered employment . . . on a trial basis. So far, Nolan assured him Jed remained sober. At first, Taylor had figured the girl's claim that Barrett's expertise rivaled his own was boasting to get his goat. Now he suspected the man knew horses from the inside out.

Today he had meant only to tease her some before again offering the bedroom next to Blair's. But the little lady didn't take to him. Consequently, he'd blown the opportunity to appease his mother. Bad luck, that.

Though Lael Savage had married an Indian, thereby suffering white society's slings and arrows, she remained a stickler for proper protocol. Already perturbed that a girl bunked so near the ranch hands, when Cameron let it slip that Kalen bathed in the river, fresh sparks flew . . . all directed at him.

Okay, he had messed up. His mother's displeasure bothered him. On the other hand, he didn't give a damn what other people thought of him. He had long ago given up trying to please the white man. He lived the motto, "survival of the fittest," and he survived very well. Had even gained a modicum of respect from the very men who, though willing to purchase his stock, shunned him if he occasionally turned up at social gatherings. His acceptance into the Indian village whence his father had come was enough for his peace of mind.

He scratched a stubbled jaw, thinking he would have to ask Blair's assistance. Surely she could convince the girl to move into the house.

Approaching the paddock, all thoughts of Kalen and his mother fled as he spied Jed Barrett jogging, leading the blanketed, protesting horse. If the gelding had colic, all the medication in the world wouldn't help unless he stayed on his feet and had moderate exercise.

Taylor pulled in his mount next to Nolan. The older man glanced up at him, then returned his attention to Barrett.

"Going to be able to walk off his bellyache?"

"'Spect so. Jed and me agreed he prob'ly just overate."

"You need me for anything?"

Not taking his eyes off the gelding, Nolan shook his head. "Jed's doin' fine. Ain't you breedin' that filly of Kutzner's this afternoon?"

"Yes. Waiting for Cameron to get back from Anderson's Trading Post."

Kalen left the dinner table stuffed and blinked rapidly to ward off the urge to curl up somewhere for a nap. "Just like a fattenin' hog," she chided herself. As she passed the stallions' barn, a commotion drew her through to the other side, where she remained in the shade to watch.

Braced each side of a powerful black-and-white stallion, Cameron and Taylor gripped the head stall and lead ropes to hold him in check. Pawing, tossing his head, trumpeting, the stud wanted nothing more than to get at the cross-tied mare. Diego Guadalupe held her and talked, with little success, in an effort to soothe her. She fidgeted and squealed in counterpoint to the stallion's frenzied snorting.

"Now."

At Taylor's one-word directive, he and Cameron allowed the leads attached to the head stall to slip through their fingers, maintaining only questionable control. The stallion lunged up on hind legs and draped his massive body on the mare's back. She squealed again when he stretched forward and snapped his powerful teeth on her withers while he pumped his hindquarters.

Within minutes, the stallion snorted his satisfaction as he danced back a step and came down heavily on all fours. He praised his own performance with a toss of his head and another snort.

"Thinks he is the cock of the roost." Taylor grinned at his brother over the stallion's back.

Behind Kalen, another stallion answered with a kick to his stall gate and a whinny. Like so many of their Comanche brethren, the Savages favored pintos or paints, and this impressive tricolored specimen obviously wanted part of the action.

Her gaze traveled over Taylor's and Cameron's powerful shoulders. It took a lot of strength to hold a stud in check with an in-season mare in mounting distance.

With an eye for good horseflesh, she studied the magnificent stud. If ever she owned a horse of her own, she hankered for a stallion. Most, like all four of the Savages' studs, seemed to breathe fire. High-spirited, yet manageable by the right person. Except for the breeding, she knew she could handle any stallion on four legs. Not bragging, she thought, just experienced, and until proven wrong, she'd continue to believe that.

Kalen slipped away before the men knew she was there. Mr. Woodruff hadn't assigned her to exercise horses yet, but she'd sweet-talked Morris into it a couple times. Maybe she could do so again this afternoon.

The soft, measured *bong, bong* of the grandfather clock in the parlor downstairs stopped at eleven. Taylor yawned and stretched, closing the ledger he'd hunkered over for the past two hours. He figured his notes to himself as well as the tallies would be there the next time he got around to them.

Before she'd lost her sight, the ranch books had been his mother's purview. Nolan had kept them up after a fashion for a couple years; then, at age twenty, Taylor took over. Necessary, but not his favorite part of ranching. Absently, he twiddled the pencil in his fingers, tapping the desk. It was about time, past time, he thought, for Blair to take over.

He turned down the lamp's wick, deciding he would speak to her about it tomorrow. Besides carrying her weight with feeding the stock, she helped around the house. Maybe he could relieve her of some chores and add the books to her work. She wouldn't be pleased about that, but the Spirits knew, *he* certainly hated bookkeeping.

His room plunged into darkness as he turned down the lamp wick. He rolled his shoulders, walked to the window and lifted the curtain aside. The breeze slipping beneath the open sash had cooled considerably the past couple of nights. Fall was on the way. During the dark of the moon, like tonight, stars glittered cold and clear in the heavens.

Time to turn in. He started to lower the curtain, then realized a faint glow stretched across the ground from the direction of the breeding barn. Though Nolan rarely involved him or Cameron in night birthings, Taylor decided he should have a look. The only mare close to dropping a foal had never given birth before. Sometimes, the first birthing was tricky.

As Taylor entered the barn, he heard Nolan and Jed talking. Pausing, he went no farther, preferring to watch. He'd see for himself how well Jed Barrett was doing.

Barrett motioned his niece over from where she stood just inside the stall gate. "The foal is wedged pert-near sideways, Kalen. Think you can turn 'im?"

Taylor's eyes widened at Barrett's question. Surely her uncle didn't expect that slip of a girl to . . . He couldn't hear her retort, but she rolled up a sleeve and washed her arm in a bucket.

"Uh, Jed, you think that's a good idea?" Nolan gave voice to Taylor's concern.

"She can do just about anythin', Nolan. The girl's a natural."

Kalen smiled at her uncle's praise. Without hesitation, she stepped to the mare's hindquarters, spoke in soothing tones, and buried the length of her arm in the mare's birth canal.

Astonished, Taylor stood still as a petrified tree.

Perspiration popped on her brow, but by the Spirits, Kalen turned that foal. The next thing he knew, the mare moaned as she lay down, and the colt spilled out onto the straw.

Sometimes grown men, himself included, barely had the strength to manage such a feat. Considering how he felt, Taylor curbed his laughter at Nolan's gape-mouthed expression.

Deceptively strong for her size, Kalen Barrett. Were she Indian, she'd undoubtedly earn the name Stout-hearted Woman.

He stepped into the light and knelt next to the newborn lying wet and shivering on the ground. Palomino. And a filly. He had begun to wonder if they'd get nothing but colts from Creation's seed. Pleased, Taylor brushed his hand over the foal's small head. Just what he'd hoped to get out of Belle. He had perfected breeding to pintos and paints; this was his first effort at branching into other colors. Still, no guarantee he'd achieve it with the next breeding he chose.

"Good job, Miss Barrett. You know more about handling horses than you let on."

She blinked amber eyes, obviously startled by his praise. "I . . . I do what Uncle Jed has taught me."

And then some, he thought. Even flustered, Kalen Barrett was loyal to a fault to this drunk. Well, that was her business.

Remember . . . She does not like you one bit. Keep that in mind, old son.

Chapter Four

"I need to speak to you."

Startled, Kalen gasped and sank below the surface. She came up sputtering, wiping water from her eyes. Blair stood next to the piles of clean and dirty clothes Kalen had heaped on the bank. "What are you doin' here?"

"I just told you. We need to talk. Mother insisted we do it today."

Treading water, beginning to notice the chill, Kalen scowled. Miz Savage wanted Blair to talk to her? Trepidation shivered up her spine. "Turn your back so I can get out and dress. It's cold."

Blair chuckled. "That's one of the things I intend to talk about."

She smiled as if that solved Kalen's problem. Not exactly a problem, but Kalen wasn't used to parading before others less than fully clothed. She tried again. "Blair."

"What?"

"Please turn around."

Blair erupted into full laughter this time. "My stars! We have the same equipment, Kalen. Besides, you're wearing a chemise."

Definitely less endowed than Blair, Kalen knew her chemise clung to her body revealing almost everything. "I still want you to turn around. And do it in the next month, please. I'm turnin' blue."

She allowed her feet to sink, barely touching bottom on her toes.

Blair relented. "Oh, all right. Your lips *are* beginning to look blue."

If her teeth weren't clamped so hard together, Kalen was sure they'd shake right out of her mouth. Grabbing the linen she'd brought along, she quickly dried her arms and back, then shrugged into a clean shirtwaist.

As she bent to retrieve her clean underdrawers, Blair asked, "Are you decent?"

Kalen hastily pulled up her trousers. "Yes, you can turn around."

Eyes practically dancing out of her head, Blair laughed again. "I'm sorry. You aren't used to teasing like we do in my family."

She didn't look sorry, but since Blair didn't have a mean bone in her body, Kalen accepted the apology in the spirit it was given. Guess she'd just have to get used to Blair's ways. "I'm sorry for my reaction, too. I just . . ." She fluttered her hand.

Blair glanced skyward. "We better get home before dark." She fell into step with Kalen. "Actually, that is kind of what I wanted to talk to you about. Moving into the house."

Scanning Blair's face, Kalen faltered, but the girl

never paused. Kalen walked quickly to keep up. "I'm perfectly comfortable off the tack room, Blair."

A crow flew from the foliage overhead. Both girls ducked as if expecting an attack; then Kalen laughed. "Are we spooked, or what?"

Blair lowered the hand she'd clapped against her chest, her gaze following the bird's flight. "Well, he needn't have scared me out of a year's growth!" She searched the deepening shadows. "Coyotes roam this time of day, along with the occasional bear."

"Never encountered a bear. Just as soon not."

"Amen." Blair picked up the pace and returned to her cause. "Kalen, Mother is really upset with Taylor for putting you next to the tack room."

Fallen leaves crunched beneath their boots. "Good heavens, why? I can't tell you how many spare rooms just like that one I've called home in the past couple of years."

"That's all well and good, but you work for the Savages now. Mother has fought to maintain propriety from the day she married my father." Blair glanced sideways. "It didn't please many folks when she began keeping company with Running Wolf."

"Running Wolf. What a wonderful name. Your father?"

Blair nodded. "Mother called him Wolf. Once he settled on this land, he refused to budge. He adopted a white man's name thinking it might help him fit in better."

Kalen nodded, fascinated. "What was his Christian name?"

"Cameron. I think my father had a sense of humor. He picked Savage as his surname because that's what the white man called him." She smiled.

"Your brother's a junior?"

"No. My father was simply Cameron Savage. Cameron's middle name is Joshua, after my mother's younger brother. He died when he was only five." Seeing her questioning glance, Blair added, "Scarlet fever."

"Oh. I'm sorry."

"That was a long time ago, Kalen. My brothers and I never knew him. Though the Taylors, Mother's family, live south of San Antonio, we don't know any of them, either."

"You don't know . . ." Her brow crinkled. "Miz Savage gave her firstborn her family name, yet you don't know them? Why?"

The back of the two-story house came into view. Blair paused, reached down and picked up a fallen leaf. After stripping it to the spine, she stuck the stem in her mouth and looked at Kalen. "Mother believes her father or her brother Ben shot my father."

Kalen's eyes flew wide. "Tarnation! Her kin shot her husband?" She wagged her head. "Surely not, Blair." She couldn't bring herself to believe such a thing. "Indian or not, he wasn't out raidin' or causin' trouble. He was your daddy. Your mama loved him. They just couldn't have!"

Blair's mouth twisted wryly. "You'd think. But Mother said, after the shooting, her father was by her side by the time she gained her breath and her wits. Too coincidental for Mother."

Kalen scrunched her eyes questioningly. "By her side?"

Blair settled into the loop of a rope swing suspended from an oak's limb and idly pushed herself in a circle. "Mother and Running Wolf often rode tandem." A deep sadness dimmed her dark eyes. "Somebody shot Father out of the saddle. The impact of the bullet sent him flying backward. With mother seated behind him, he landed on top of her."

Stunned, Kalen's mouth dropped open; then she repeated, "Your grandfather or uncle wouldn't chance hittin' your mother, Blair."

The girl stared off the way they'd come and shrugged. Kalen searched her distant eyes and sad expression. Hiding her feelings, Kalen thought. Indians killing her parents had been heart wrenching for Kalen. But to have your own kin murder your father . . .

"Maybe," Blair allowed. "Then again, Mother believes they'd rather have seen her dead than married to an Indian."

"But she had three children!"

"I doubt that mattered. I've heard enough slips out of Nolan to know what they thought of her and her Indian husband giving her family name to their firstborn." Blair swept her arm. "They buried Father out there . . . somewhere. Mother knows. Nolan does, too, but they've never revealed the location to anyone." She paused, thoughtful. "Well, maybe Taylor, but no one else.

"About a year after Running Wolf was shot, his stallion died." She smiled sadly. "Ghost Dancer was pure white. Mother believes the horse mourned his master's death so fiercely, he willed himself to death. I was only six, but I remember her words.

'Ghost Dancer's happy now. He's carrying Running Wolf through eternity.' "

Blair extended her legs and leaned back, allowing herself to spin again. Her braids dangled behind, nearly sweeping the ground. "Nolan and a couple of my father's Indian friends loaded that magnificent animal on a wagon and took him out there." She hiked her chin in the general direction of the river. "He's buried close to my father's grave."

"You said no one else knows."

"No one alive. Both warriors joined him in the Spirit World. They died in a raid five years after my father's death."

Kalen suppressed tears of sympathy for Miz Savage, for this family. "How terrible for your mother to have lost her love. To have never seen him and his beautiful stallion."

Blair dropped her feet and stilled her motion. "What?"

"She's blind. It only—"

"Since shortly after that day, yes. Kalen, you assume Mother has been blind from birth?"

"Well, yes."

"No. And I don't fully understand it," Blair added quickly. "The fall knocked Mother unconscious. Though she doesn't think she was out for long, when she opened her eyes, her father was pulling my father off her."

Kalen put her hand to her mouth, sorrow coursing through her.

When she failed to say anything, Blair continued. "Apparently, Mr. Taylor said something like . . .

'He's dead, Lael. Now you can bring your bastards home.' "

"Dear God!" How horrid that must have been, Kalen thought. And now Blair refers to her grandfather as if he were a passing acquaintance. Not worth her time or thought.

Blair's shrug belied the deep sorrow in her eyes. "Mother picked herself up. Her father didn't even help her. Nolan was there by that time, and she turned to him. I'm not sure how it all went from there, but Nolan helped Mother bring my father's body home."

Blair stared off into the distance, talking as if in a trance. "I should remember, but I don't. My father was buried according to Comanche custom before the sun set on his death. The next day," Blair's voice caught, "Mother followed Nolan to the site."

She fixed Kalen with anguished eyes. "Mother awoke the following morning to darkness. She hasn't seen a thing since."

If tears rained in a heart, Kalen felt certain they fell inside hers. She'd never heard such a heart-wrenching tale in all her born days. Yet, confused, she couldn't suppress her questions. "Your mother wasn't injured?"

Blair shook her head.

"Then why is she blind?"

Blair wiggled from the rope swing's loop and stood. "According to the doctor, physically Mother can see; she just doesn't want to face life without Running Wolf."

"But she does! Every day."

Blair nodded. "Still, I think if it weren't for us,

Mother would happily give up the ghost." Thoughtful, she bit her bottom lip. "Taylor was away at school. When Mother wired him about Running Wolf's death, Taylor didn't wait for permission, but came right home. He's managed the ranch ever since."

Eyes wide with wonder, Kalen said, "But he would only have been . . . how old?"

"Seventeen. Cameron was twelve, and I was five. I guess that's why my memory is hazy. As I said, I don't recall all the particulars when Ghost Dancer died a year after my father, when I was six. Kind of think I blocked it out. All of it."

"Blair!"

Both glanced toward the house. Doreen, the cook, held open the back door. "Supper's ready!"

Blair waved. "Be right there." She turned to Kalen. "Care to join us?"

Kalen recoiled as if burned. "No!" She gathered her wits. "I mean, I'm sure Tom cooked enough for me, and if I don't show, Uncle Jed will worry."

As she turned away, Blair caught her arm. "Think about what I've said, Kalen. Mother would be far more comfortable having you in the house. Even though you work rings around a couple of the men, you *are* a woman. You would have your own room and a tub in a room down the hall." She chuckled. "Think about that the next time you step into that cold river."

Standing in his bedroom, peering through the lace curtains his mother favored, Taylor watched Blair and Miss Barrett part company. As Blair approached the back door, the Barrett girl looked up, her gaze roaming over the house.

The hair on his nape rose, but he stood far enough back from the window she couldn't see him in the darkened room. He studied her. Tried to figure out what it was about her that interested him so much. When she didn't know she was being observed, she seemed so vulnerable. Maybe that was it. Thank the Spirits she wore loose-fitting shirts. Unfortunately, the boy's trousers cupped her trim backside far too invitingly.

Her uncle must be almost as difficult to live with as some children. Miss Barrett carried quite a load for one so young, her day-to-day existence tenuous at best. She had been forced to develop a thick skin. A pity.

Taylor tunneled his fingers through his drying hair and sighed as he looked down at himself. His body seemed to have a mind of its own. He glanced up to see Kalen Barrett disappear around the side of the house, headed toward her room.

For his peace of mind, it might be better if she stayed right where she was. But then his mother would be . . . not angry, just . . . disappointed. He shook his head, unable to figure a way to make everyone happy. The best solution would probably be to ask Jed Barrett to take his niece and move on.

He gazed out at the gloaming and grimaced. Sure as Father Sun rose in the morning, Nolan would question him if he fired an experienced hand.

Nolan was the closest thing he'd had to a father since Running Wolf's death. During those first years, while his mother adjusted to her blindness and he worked to keep the ranch going, Nolan had been Taylor's steadying crutch.

The man had never failed him. He'd stepped back to foreman without a word of protest when Taylor took the lead in running the ranch. Theirs was an easy give-and-take relationship.

So far, Jed had steered clear of the bottle, so what grounds did he have to fire him?

Well, it's like this, Nolan. The Barrett girl piques my interest. I'm as randy as Creation when he's about to mount a mare. When Kalen's near, I think about bedding her. He snorted, picturing Nolan's disgusted expression if he said such a thing. Yeah, that would be some conversation.

Chapter Five

Though not hungry, Kalen made a brief appearance at the supper table. Then she carried the one pur-loined ladder-back chair from her room to sit out-side as darkness deepened. A nice time of night.

Cicadas chirped; occasionally, a horse whinnied somewhere in the paddocks. Lantern light flickered on in the big house where the Savages probably gathered around the supper table. She tipped the chair against the wall and closed her eyes. Drawing in a deep breath, she smelled the dust in the air, faintly overlaid by the chicken and dumplings cook had served this evening.

Then she heard it. A flute?

The mournful sound sent a shiver up her spine. Sweet strains from a violin joined the flute. The melody came from the house. She dropped the chair's legs to the ground, stood and walked closer to the fence that separated the house from the out-buildings.

She crossed her arms on the top rail and listened,

a smile lighting her face. How lovely! Whoever played was very good.

A step nearby brought her head around. Mr. Woodruff touched his hat brim in salute. "Been a spell since I heard music comin' from the house. Taylor's been too busy, I guess."

She didn't know why it surprised her, but it did. "Mr. Savage plays . . . What? The flute, violin?"

Woodruff mimicked Kalen's stance, crossing his arms atop the fence. "It's a wooden pipe his pa made for him when he was knee-high."

"And the violin?"

Woodruff cocked his head and listened a moment. "It's the missus. Blair plays, too, but she sounds . . . different." He shrugged. "I don't know how to explain it."

Kalen nodded. "It's called touch. My Aunt Livvie played the Autoharp. Even if a half dozen played, I could always pick her out from the others."

"Miss Kalen, how you gettin' on here? Miz Savage called me to the house yesterday. Wants you in the spare bedroom." He scratched his stubbled jaw. " 'Pears to me, after thinkin' on it, she's right. You bein' a young lady and all. Well . . . maybe it'd be better all 'round if you did move into the house."

Not from her perspective. Taylor Savage was too unsettling. She saw enough of him during the day. Miz Savage, on the other hand, so refined and gentle, gained her druthers with sugar rather than salt and apparently wielded more power than even the men realized.

Maybe if she ignored the proddin', they'd forget about it, Kalen thought. Rather than argue the point with the foreman, she placated him. "I'll think on it, Mr. Woodruff."

A week later, one of the mares was far worse than Uncle Jed could handle. He sent Kalen to get permission to call in the horse doctor.

It galled him to have to seek help from outside. With no formal schooling, no one expected him to know everything there was to know about a horse's ailments. But logic didn't keep him from being short with her.

Kalen looked everywhere for Mr. Woodruff, Blair and Cameron, and finally, Taylor Savage. Not a one was to be found. Though baffled, she was also vexed. So far she'd avoided giving either Mr. Woodruff or Blair an answer about moving into the big house. Now, she had to speak with the very woman she most wanted to evade.

"Horsefeathers." Scowling at the screened door, she climbed the steps and knocked. Just as she was ready to knock a second time, Doreen's voice carried from inside. "I'm comin'!"

When the woman peered through the screen, Kalen smiled. "Is Miz Savage around?"

Doreen pushed the screen open and invited Kalen in with a welcoming smile of her own, blue eyes atwinkle. "And where else would you be findin' her?" Doreen's voice carried the hint of a brogue. "This way. In the parlor."

Boot heels echoing with every step, Kalen's gaze wandered over the impressive entry and parlor. She paused at the oval rag rug, the largest she'd ever seen. Twelve feet long and nine feet wide if it was an inch.

"Miz Savage, the lass is here to be seein' you."

Lael Savage sat before a dead fireplace, her pretty lavender skirts spread around her. She glanced up from her needlework as if she had been focused on the correct spot to insert the needle. Her unseeing eyes zoomed right to Doreen, then shifted to Kalen when she spoke.

"Ma'am, I'm sorry to bother you."

"Not at all, Kalen. Please." She pointed to another chair angled beside the fireplace. "Have a seat."

Kalen looked down at her dusty denims and boots, hesitating to even step on the rug let alone sit in the mohair-upholstered chair. "Ma'am, I just left a paddock. I'm too dirty."

Doreen gave her a little shove. "Never you mind, Miss Kalen. I sweep up after the bairns mornin', noon and night."

"Doreen, would you bring tea, please?"

"Not for me," Kalen said. "Uncle Jed sent me, and he's expectin' me back real soon. I couldn't find the others."

"The others? Oh, you mean the children."

Somehow, Kalen couldn't think of Taylor Savage in that light. 'Course, the lady was his mother. Only natural, Kalen guessed, for her to think of the strappin', tall man as her child. "Mr. Woodruff is nowhere to be found, either."

Miz Savage beckoned again. "Come, sit a minute."

Reluctantly, Kalen stepped onto the handmade,

shades-of-brown rug. She brushed the seat of her pants before perching on the cushion, once again scanning the room, taking in the lovely porcelain angel figurines on the mantel. The pale yellow-tapestried walls lightened the room, in direct contrast to the small, dark wood tables that sat beside every chair and on each end of the sofa that faced the fireplace. Between the tall, lace-covered windows, bookcases climbed the walls, loaded with more books than Kalen had seen in her lifetime.

"You have a pretty home, ma'am."

"Why, thank you. We're comfortable here. What can I do for you?"

Distracted when a tall grandfather clock chimed the hour, Kalen watched the brass pendulum's measured swing. "Um, Uncle Jed says we need a vet'rinarian. One of the mares is down, and he hasn't been able to get her up."

Miz Savage stuck the needle in her work and laid it on top of a sewing basket. "The children and Mr. Woodruff have taken a half dozen horses to Bear."

Kalen cocked her head questioningly, then realized she couldn't communicate with Miz Savage with gestures alone. "Bear? I don't . . ."

"My husband's brother."

"Beg pardon?"

"Running Wolf's immediate family lives near here. Taylor supplies them with meat and horses." She paused as if waiting for Kalen's reaction.

When none was forthcoming, Lael continued, "I'm sure there'd be no objection to sending someone, or going yourself for a doctor. Which mare is it?"

"I don't know this one's name, ma'am." Kalen

shrugged, then reminded herself again to speak up. "The breedin' stock mostly look alike. She's big. Uncle Jed says she'll drop a foal any day now."

"That could be one of several. By all means, go. Do you know where Dr. Summers lives?"

"No, ma'am, but one of the hands can tell me."

"Or send Jasper Higgins. He knows." She chuckled. "More often than not, mares choose the middle of the night. Many times poor Jasper has made that trip in the dark."

Not as dark as your world, Kalen thought as she rose.

"Before you go . . ."

Oh, shoot, here it comes. She couldn't very well walk out, so she inquired, "Ma'am?"

"I have yet to hear that you're prepared to move into the spare bedroom upstairs."

"Uh, well," she equivocated. Her thoughts raced, but no convincing excuse came to mind.

"You'll be much more comfortable in the bed rather than the cot Nolan provided."

"Oh, no, ma'am. I'm snug as a bug in a rug." She squeezed her eyes shut at the simile. Sure enough, Miz Savage laughed and commented.

"That's my point, dear girl. No young lady on Savage land should sleep with bugs anywhere near!"

"That was just an . . . expression," Kalen said lamely, knowing at this point it wouldn't do a bit of good.

"I should hope so," Lael said. "When you return from your errand, ask one of the men to help move your possessions here."

"I don't need help."

"Oh, well, that's fine." If Miz Savage heard the sullenness in Kalen's voice, she ignored it. "I'll have someone to share supper with this evening. I expect the children won't be back until tomorrow."

With her usual speedy saddling, it wasn't long until Kalen was swinging up on a horse and riding west on the beaten trail. Jasper had said Dr. Summers's place was just behind Anderson's Trading Post.

Definitely unladylike, but had anyone been within earshot, they'd have gotten an earful of every expletive Kalen knew. What could she do? Not a cotton-pickin' thing. Miz Savage was as much her boss as Taylor.

From just inside her tipi, Graceful Bird watched Taylor Savage saddle his stallion. He and Cameron had spent two moonrises in One Bear's lodge. On this visit, Blair had chosen to dwell with One Bear's first wife. Mr. Woodruff, the man who worked for Taylor, had spent the past two evenings fireside, smoking pipes and gaming with her tribesmen.

Black eyes dimmed by resignation, Grace, as the Savages called her, ached for Taylor, but the warrior barely knew she lived.

That is not truth, she chided herself. As she was yet unspoken for, more than once Taylor had visited her tipi. It was not forbidden. But she knew in her deepest heart that he would never claim her as his mate.

Chief One Bear had spoken sharply to her a day before the last full moon. It was time she accept a mate to her blankets. Sighing, Grace crouched beside the embers kept glowing even in the heat of summer.

Her chief was right, but she did not want Slim Arrow, the only warrior who had spoken for her.

Though he would provide well, her heart did not warm when he was near like it did when Sound Of Wind looked in her direction. "Taylor," she whispered. Ever since Running Wolf passed into the After World, Sound Of Wind refused to be addressed by the name he had acquired during his vision quest. Even One Bear honored his white man's name.

A scratch sounded on her tipi.

"Enter."

Blair ducked inside. Grace liked this young woman very much. She only wished she could bare her heart to Blair. But it would do no good. Taylor Savage did not want her. She had never seen him express an interest in any maiden. Maybe it would take a white woman to bring fire to his eyes, his heart.

Hiding her despair, Grace picked up the new tunic she had made especially for Blair.

Her friend's dark eyes glowed with pleasure as she lifted the soft buckskin and inspected Grace's needlework. "It is beautiful, Grace. Mother would like for me to learn needlecraft like yours, but I never will." She shrugged. "I don't have the patience."

"When will you return?" Grace asked. Taylor Savage and his brother always accompanied Blair when she visited. Already Grace longed for his return.

"After the next full moon." A smile lit Blair's face. "Taylor and Cameron accepted One Bear's horsemanship challenge. Will you participate this time?"

Grace shook her head. She was not a horsewoman. Unlike all her friends, Grace found no joy in riding. A horse was simply a means of transport from one place to another. She did not own one, did not want the responsibility.

"We will bring two more horses to One Bear. Maybe one will take your fancy, Grace."

She shook her head again. "My uncle would not give a horse into my keeping, Blair. I do not know how to care for one."

"Well, that's easy—"

"I do not wish to learn." But she did look forward to Blair's return. Maybe Sound Of Wind would come to her tipi in the night.

Chapter Six

After Kalen turned in, Lael sat in the parlor, contemplating the young woman she was beginning to like. She wished she knew her better. Oh, to see her. Lael raised her face and looked straight ahead toward a window she knew faced the barns.

Kalen Barrett had not been happy to move in here, but Lael would not abide a young woman living in such close proximity to the ranch hands. Granted, as far as she knew, all were trustworthy. She didn't believe Nolan or Taylor would hire men who weren't. It was simply the principle of the thing.

"Miz Savage?"

Lael turned to Doreen's voice. "Yes?"

"I'll be retirin' now if it's all the same to ye. Would ye like me to be walkin' upstairs with ye?"

"It's nearing ten, is it not?"

"Aye. Quarter to."

"I think I'll wait a bit longer for the children. Surely they'll be here soon."

At that moment, steps sounded on the porch. She

chuckled. "Good timing, that. Be gone with you now, Doreen. You've had a long day."

"Good night, then. Sleep with the angels, mum."

"Evenin'," Lael heard Doreen say as she passed . . . Blair, who acknowledged the greeting.

But they were all there. Lael could discern the different treads and looked toward the doorway to welcome her offspring home.

"You're still up?" Taylor asked.

"I wasn't sleepy, and I knew you would be home soon. Did you have a good time?"

"The usual," Taylor said.

Blair laid something in her lap. "Feel this buckskin, Mother. Grace made me another tunic. I really don't need it, but she insists on giving me gifts."

"She's a nice person," Lael allowed. She knew why Graceful Bird gave Blair so many gifts. The poor girl still pined for Taylor's attention and hoped to win it through Blair.

As Lael remembered, at fifteen Graceful Bird already had calf eyes for Taylor. Since Grace had yet to take a mate, Lael doubted the woman had changed.

Cameron dropped a peck on her forehead, and she heard the whisper of his body settling on the sofa. "Pour me one of those," he said.

"Brandy or whiskey?" Taylor asked from the sideboard.

"Brandy."

She inhaled a deep breath, mindful of the scents of leather and horseflesh that lingered whenever her children were near. Close by her elbow, she heard the clink of china.

"More tea?" Blair asked.

"I think I've had sufficient, dear." It was nice to have her family gathered 'round. Knowing their habits so well, she didn't have to guess where each one had settled.

Cameron sprawled on the sofa, taking up most of it with his long legs. Doreen had finally given up asking him to keep his dirty boots off the cushions. To give him his due, he usually brushed off the worst of the dirt before he left the room. Although, then it was on the rug. A no-win for Doreen.

Taylor sat on the far side of the fireplace in the chair Wolf had occupied . . . until his death. She drew a steadying breath and listened to Blair sink in her usual place, on the floor, her back propped against the sofa.

"We are going back next month, Mother, if you want to come along. We'll do a bit of racing," Blair said.

"Determined to break your necks?"

"*Au contraire, ma chère,*" Cameron mocked. "The Savage clan *extraordinaire* will win the day!"

Blair muttered over her siblings' laughter, "Oh, *brother.*"

"Anything I need to know about?" her eldest questioned.

"Kalen Barrett went for the veterinarian late yesterday. One of the mares was in trouble, and her uncle wanted Dr. Summers to see her.

"He stopped in before he left last evening. The two men got her up and walking, albeit slowly. When Kalen came in for supper tonight, she said the mare is doing fine."

Silence.

Lael's brow furrowed. "What?"

"What did you say?" Taylor asked.

At the same time, Blair blurted, "She's staying in the house?"

"Yes. I told you I prefer that arrangement."

Blair laughed. "I didn't think you'd pull it off, Mother. Kalen was very reluctant."

"Never let it be said Madam Savage doesn't have her way."

"Cameron!"

He chuckled. "It's true, Mother. You may manipulate people with a velvet glove, but you get the job done."

"I should hope so." She sniffed, feigning indignation. "It is, after all, my duty to see to the welfare of every soul on this ranch."

"And Taylor's duty?" Cameron asked.

He had uttered not one sound after his question. Lael turned her head to him . . . and waited. She could be as enigmatic as he.

"Mother's wish is my command," he finally said.

"Not quite. But I do appreciate you consulting me so often."

Not for the first time, Lael wished she could see Taylor's expression. She'd heard . . . something in his voice. Like his father before him, he was adept at hiding his thoughts and feelings. But when she could see, Wolf's and Taylor's extraordinary eyes had clearly spoken to her.

Blair stirred. "She's upstairs?"

"Yes. She wanted a bath before retiring." At that moment the chimes announced ten o'clock. "She went up at nine. It has been quiet for a while now. I suspect the girl is asleep."

"No wonder," Cameron said. "She does the work of two."

"She is a hard worker," Taylor agreed, "for one so young."

"Young?" Lael tilted her head. "She doesn't sound like a child to me."

"She might be nearly as old as Blair," he said.

"Hogwash!" Cameron blurted. "She's my age."

"How do you know?" Blair challenged.

"Something she said. I don't remember, exactly, but she's at least twenty-five." Lael heard him snap his fingers. "I know! Remember when Wildcat was captured and sent to prison? Well, she said her folks had died just prior to that."

"So?" Blair challenged again.

"You were too young to remember, but Kalen said she heard the news on her birthday, her *tenth* birthday."

"That grubby little waif is twenty-five?" Taylor asked.

"She wouldn't be so grubby if she didn't work so hard," Blair said.

"That's the gods' truth," Cameron interjected.

"Let's not exaggerate," Taylor chided. "She does no more than other hands."

Blair hooted. "Open your eyes, Taylor. If it wasn't for her, her uncle's work would go half done. Yeah, he can handle horses, but it's obvious he has wasted himself in drink."

Lael smiled. Blair was on a roll.

"Besides, since when does a woman have to do the work of a grown man on this ranch? I certainly don't, and don't plan to anytime soon."

"She's got you there, Taylor," Lael said, enjoying the banter. What joy to have her children so frank and playful in her presence. Cameron and Blair, anyway. Their openness helped her see far more than anyone suspected.

"When Kalen asked for permission to fetch Dr. Summers, she was careful to phrase the request as coming from her uncle, so that he was managing the situation." She shrugged. "I think she's savvier than anyone gives her credit for."

Silence.

Cameron finally spoke. "You are usually more perceptive, Taylor. Why is it you have a blind eye where Kalen Barrett is concerned?"

"I cannot be expected to watch every hand twenty-four hours a day, Cameron."

Lael tilted her head again. As wary of showing his feelings as his father before him, Taylor gave away far more in his defensive words than he would willingly expose.

Well, now, wasn't this an interesting turn of events.

She wondered if Kalen Barrett might harbor a mutual interest in Taylor. Maybe that is why the young woman had been reluctant to sleep in the house.

Lael remembered her first encounter with Running Wolf. The half-naked savage had scared her witless. Seventeen and riding alone, she had thought she could take care of herself.

But that day, One Bear and Running Wolf circled

her in silence. Running Wolf's glittering black eyes had held her captive as surely as if he'd tied her.

"Your name, woman."

Though fearful, she was equally shocked that he'd spoken in English. She stuttered, "La . . . Lael Taylor." Her mare sidestepped, tossing her head against Lael's sudden tightening of the reins. "Who . . . who are you?"

She hadn't known his name at the time, but One Bear backed off and watched as his brother circled her once more. The black-eyed warrior reined in close and looked deeply into her twilight-blue eyes. "Running Wolf," he declared, "your future mate."

Lael would never forget how her breath caught in her throat. How she'd believed him! And less than a year later, she had ridden off with him. Married in the Comanche way, they had followed their mating with a ceremony by a justice of the peace. At her request, the official had contacted her parents to let them know she was fine and would soon visit.

Happier than she could voice, she'd returned to her parents' ranch to introduce her husband, Cameron Savage.

After only one glance at Running Wolf seated on his stallion, her father had disowned her. "Never set foot near this family again, Lael. Not as long as you live with that savage."

Would Jed Barrett behave like that if Taylor offered for Kalen's hand? Lael knew as surely as she sat in her parlor that Taylor would indeed propose. She had no idea when, but the day would come.

Well, at least in his dress and manner, he appeared more white man than Indian. And had inherited her blue eyes. Taller and broader than his father, Taylor was undoubtedly intimidating, but not in the same way Wolf had been.

For her sake Taylor conducted himself like a white man . . . most of the time. If angered by someone, he'd don Indian leggings and moccasins to annoy. She knew he reverted to Indian ways when he visited One Bear's village. It came so naturally to him.

Cameron and Blair, on the other hand, were far more *civilized*. Much younger than Taylor, their father had little time to instill their Indian heritage in them before his death. Cameron had never gone on his vision quest as Taylor had.

Taylor interrupted Lael's thoughts. "We should turn in."

"I expect so. It is late." And it would put a stop to conversation about Kalen Barrett, she thought. At least for tonight. Taylor could avoid revealing his thoughts better than anyone she knew—other than One Bear.

As they climbed the stairs together, Taylor said, "Cameron, cut out two horses, a mare and a gelding, for Bear. Start working with them so they're ready to ride when we deliver them."

"When?" Lael asked.

"Right after the full moon."

"Mother, you just have to go with us. We'll be gone at least three days. One of them spent racing and showing off." Blair paused to give Lael a good night peck on the cheek.

"Sounds like fun." Lael tipped her head for good night kisses from both her sons.

* * *

Staring at the ceiling, Kalen listened to the quiet conversation in the hallway just steps from her door. Her shiver shook the bed. Something about Taylor Savage's voice zinged right through her.

Hallelujah. The whole family would be gone for several days. It was a few weeks off, but she could stay out of everyone's way until then, couldn't she?

Sure she could. She'd insist on taking breakfast with Uncle Jed, couldn't chance sitting across a table from Taylor Savage. Her brow furrowed. She'd worry about dinner and supper one at a time.

Even though Miz Savage had been most welcoming last night, Kalen didn't feel comfortable in this big house. She pulled the cover over her lower face and sniffed the sheets. Nothing like sun-dried sheets, though. She didn't know why, but a body rested better on a bed made up with clean bed linens.

Of course, it didn't hurt that the mattress was like a cloud floating across the heavens. She hadn't slept on feather ticking since leaving Uncle Jed's place. His few furnishings sold right along with the house and land.

She turned on her side, determined to stop her wandering mind. It inevitably snagged on Taylor Savage. Like he was the only fish in the Brazos.

Kalen scrunched her eyes closed, promised to listen to her usually sensible inside voice. After a moment, she flopped on her back again. Sighing, she threw back the covers and walked to the window.

Scanning the moonless heavens, Kalen marveled at how deceptive the lady of the house really was. Lael Savage knew what she wanted. Most important, she knew how to influence a situation to get her way. Miz Savage might look refined, even fragile, yet that straight spine of hers held a hint of steel.

Tarnation. She was a scruffy maverick compared to the Savage women. If Kalen had her druthers, she'd pack up her few changes of clothes and hightail it right back to her cozy little room. Unfortunately, it didn't look like she'd have that choice anytime soon.

Chapter Seven

Though everyone was grateful for the earth-nourishing rain, it made working horses hellish and Kalen's chores doubly hard. She'd waited an extra day, hoping the rain would let up, but nope, no such luck. It had taken nearly two hours to clear the wagon of the heavy, sodden mess. Miserably wet, she shoveled the last of the never-ending droppings into the compost pile.

As she stowed the shovel in the bed and swung aboard, she grinned wryly. If the sun shone day after day with temperatures high enough to melt iron, people complained. If a blue norther whistled in, their cussin' took on its own blue hue. She flicked the reins.

Pulling her hat brim low to keep the rain off her face, she felt water cascade down her back. She hunched inside the slicker she'd nabbed from the tack room. Not a cold rain, thank the Lord, just . . . wet. *Really* wet.

She parked the wagon at the back of the barn, unharnessed the stoic gelding and led him to his lean-to. At least the horses kept near or in the barn could shelter out of the weather. More than one mare had been brought in because of a young foal at her side. Those in pastures fended for themselves.

Hoofbeats inside the covered work ring didn't surprise Kalen. What did surprise her was the speed. The horse covered the ground at a dead run, Cameron atop the stallion's back . . . then not! Thinking he'd fallen, she already had one leg through the fence when Cameron reappeared atop the horse's back.

Holy smokes! He rode bareback, and had leaned over so far, she couldn't figure how the heck he'd regained his seat. How did he keep from slipping to the ground on the other side? Unnoticed, Kalen leaned on the fence, the damp, fecund soil teasing her nose.

Funny. Her belly didn't do that strange little dance when she looked at him. If it were Taylor out there . . . Not good.

Cameron was an excellent horseman, as were all the Savages, but his trick was phenomenal. Wheeling the horse to a stop at the end of the arena, he tugged his hat brim down. "Yah!"

His mount exploded into a dead run again. This time, he slipped over the side nearest her. He grabbed a bandanna off the ground, regained his seat, and waved it over his hat.

"The winna and new champion!" he bellowed.

Kalen grinned and broke into applause.

Cameron reined in, a sheepish smile on his face. "Didn't know anyone was around." He nudged the horse in her direction. "I'm practicing for the races at Bear's village. You're going with us, right?"

"Uh. No. Not that I . . . I'm needed here."

Cameron shook his head. "No. You'll go with us. We'll take several days to have some fun."

Not if I have anything to say about it. Rather than argue, she chose to ignore his comments. "What do you call that trick?"

"Don't know if it has a name. We do another one where we grab up a person at a dead run."

Kalen blinked. "That don't sound . . . possible."

"Come in here. I'll show you."

She shook her head. "If you mean to pick me up while that horse is runnin', I'm not hankerin' to break a bone today."

"I'll trot." He put his hand over his heart. "Honestly, I won't hurt you. Promise."

Was there ever a more stupid woman than she? Hopefully not. Lord help her, she wanted to see the trick. At Cameron's direction, she stood in the middle of the oval arena while he walked his mount to the end rail.

"Okay, Kalen, turn your back to me. Listen to the hoofbeats. As I get close, step forward, arms reaching toward the other end of the arena."

"Okaaay." She listened to the muffled hoof thuds. Closer, closer. Breathless, she extended her arms and stepped forward.

Cameron scooped her up, her legs dangling alongside the horse. "Bend your knees."

Awkwardly, she raised her knees, and he swung her in front of him. She plopped down on the horse's broad back.

"Oh!"

"At a run, the momentum carries you forward, and you can swing your legs quickly. You've got to be quick to win the race."

Kalen craned her neck around to see his face. "You're nuts! Now I *know* I'd end up with somethin' broken."

"Maybe," Taylor said from outside the arena. "But probably not. He's pretty good."

"Pretty good?" Cameron challenged. "If I can get Kalen to be my partner, I'll beat you. She's lighter than Blair."

Her stomach in a knot at the sound of Taylor's voice, Kalen sputtered, "No . . ."

At the same time, Blair questioned, "Are you insinuating I'm fat?" She stood beside Taylor at the fence, her expression vying between outrage and laughter.

"If the boot fits." Cameron wheeled the horse away to the far side of the arena.

"You *better* put distance between us, brother dear!"

Kalen didn't fear falling. Not only did she have a good seat bareback, but Cameron's strong arms enclosed her on each side. To be safe, though, she grabbed a hank of the coarse mane.

Cameron could tease, test, issue brash challenges all he wanted, but Kalen was determined not to be drawn into the siblings' friendly contests. Uh-uh. She meant what she'd said. At a run, that trick spelled broken bones.

Miz Savage's voice barely carried over rain beating on the tin roof. "Are you all here?"

Taylor swung around and strode over to his mother, who stood just under the roof's protection. Next to her, Doreen held an umbrella, a protective hand under her mistress's elbow.

Her brogue thick with concern, she said, "Yer mam's been cooped up these three days now, Mr. Taylor."

"Yes, I have," Lael Savage agreed. "Rain or no, I had to get out."

"Of course. Join us, Mother." Taylor clasped her other elbow. "Thanks, Doreen. I'll see her back to the house."

"You'll be needin' the umbrella, I'm thinkin'."

"No, dear," Lael said. "Taylor can find a slicker for me. You'll get soaked from here to the house."

"Go on," Taylor said. "We'll manage."

"Did I hear Kalen's voice?"

"Yes—"

Blair interrupted her brother. "Cameron's trying to sweet-talk her into partnering with him in pick-up-and-run."

As Cameron guided the horse toward his family, Kalen shook her head. "He can sweet-talk all he wants. I wasn't born yesterday. Besides, I won't be joinin' y'all at this village."

"Of course you will." Lael's pronouncement left little room for discussion.

Taylor suppressed a chuckle at the mutinous expression on Kalen's face. She had already learned his mother managed to get her way. It would be fun to watch her try to worm out of going.

And, the Spirits help him, he wanted her to go. He also wanted her to partner him, not Cameron. Not because she was lighter than Blair, not to assure his win, but because he had the damnedest urge to throttle his brother for having his arms around Kalen.

Nuts.

"We'll see," Kalen said in a small voice.

His mother waved a dismissive hand. "You have been working long days for weeks, Kalen. You deserve a break . . . right along with the rest of the family. You'll undoubtedly find Bear's village interesting. I did the first time Wolf took me there."

Taylor watched Kalen's expressive face. She appeared intrigued, but maybe not enough to spend time with his family. That sent a shard of disappointment to his heart. He really was losing his grip.

He'd decided long ago that if his father's line were to be carried on, it would be Cameron who mated. Taylor was as wary of white women as his Indian brethren. But the few Indian women who had shown interest in him didn't stir his blood. Graceful Bird came to mind. Nice, but not someone to spend his life with.

His gaze darted over Kalen's slender frame and dangling legs. How could he have ever thought her a boy? Inexplicably, she *was* his type, whatever that really meant. Prickly, opinionated, and downright rude. Toward him, at least. Those were character flaws in his estimation. But in her those very flaws amused him. None of this made a bit of sense.

A little demon took over in his head. He heard himself say, "I'll show her. But I'll pick her up, not Blair."

Startled, Kalen's eyes widened. He wanted to

laugh out loud, but suppressed the urge. Instead, he challenged her with a superior-than-thou grin. "You chicken?"

Sure enough, that got her back up.

"No, I'm not chicken. I just prefer not to play games."

"You miss all the fun in life," Blair said.

Cameron nodded. "We let off steam at gymkhanas several times a year."

Taylor persisted. "Nah. She's chicken." He bit back another chuckle dying to escape when she still ignored him.

"What's a gymkhana?"

"We dream up races and contests just for fun," Blair said. "Besides racing, the men compete in timed events like calf roping and bronc riding. A few women compete, too."

Kalen's brow furrowed. "That's work."

Blair rolled her eyes. "I hate to repeat myself, but you don't know how to relax and have a bit of fun at what we do best."

"She'll learn," Lael said confidently.

Taylor eased through the fence. "Get down, Cameron. I'll use your mount. Kalen, stand in the center like before."

She slid from the horse's back, amber eyes wary.

"Do exactly as Cameron instructed. Only when *I* catch you around the waist, swing your legs up immediately." He paused to needle her a bit more. "Unless you really are chicken . . ."

Kalen glared at him, then stalked to the center of the arena. "Whenever you're ready," she tossed over her shoulder.

"Taylor, perhaps you should demonstrate first with Blair."

Disappointment claimed him. He wanted ... *Never mind.* "Maybe you're right, Mother. Come on, Blair."

Briefly, Kalen's liquid-gold eyes held his gaze. Then she turned on her heel and hastened outside the fence. He didn't know if it was relief at escaping close proximity to him or trepidation about the ride.

Blair took her place. Taylor bore down on her at breakneck speed. As smooth as moving air, he leaned, cupped his arm around her waist, and lifted her. She whipped up her legs to straddle the gelding's back as he swung her in front of him.

Still at a good speed, the end of the arena coming up fast, Taylor and Blair leaned as if one body, and he reined the gelding to the side. They followed the fence line for a short distance until he slowed to a trot. In front of his mother, he reined to a halt.

"See?" Blair said. "Easy."

"For you to say," Kalen grumbled.

"Kalen."

"Yes, Uncle Jed?" Relief flooded her. *Bless him,* Kalen thought, though anxiety pricked her at the set line of his mouth.

"Time for vittles."

"Comin'." She flicked a glance at Taylor and Miz Savage. "I promised to noon with my uncle. 'Scuse me, please." Not waiting for acknowledgment, she hustled off.

"Listen to me, girl," Jed said as they barely got out of earshot. "Them young'ns is Injuns through 'n through. You steer clear of 'em, you hear me?"

"I hear you. They are also our bosses, Uncle Jed, and they deserve our respect." She stepped in front of him and pressed her hand against his chest. His flannel shirt smelled of dampness. "You don't have a bit of trouble takin' their money."

"Ain't got nothin' to do with how *I* feel 'bout Injuns. What's got into *you*, girl? You forget how your ma and pa died? How little Dillon suffered?"

She gritted her teeth, held onto her temper, and kept her voice down. "No, I haven't forgotten, but that was a long time ago and had nothin' to do with the Savages. They're as civilized as any white ranchers we've worked for, Uncle Jed." She snorted. "More civilized than some, I'd say."

"Don't make a lick of difference."

"Yes, it does! And I'm tired of your attitude."

He glared at her. "*My* attitude? Seems to me, you come flyin' to us when Injuns—"

"Yes, I did. I was young; Dillon was hurt. Dyin'. I've always appreciated how you took us in. But *that* has nothin' to do with the situation we're in now. Times have changed. Can't you see that?"

She sucked in a controlling breath, wiped the rain off her face, and continued to the mess at the end of the bunkhouse. Even through wind-whipped rain, she smelled apple pie. "I'm hungry. If you want me to take vittles with you, please stop talkin' bad about the Savages. Miz Savage is as kind as Aunt Livvie."

"I ain't sayin'—"

"Yes, you are!" Hands clenched, Kalen tipped her head skyward and got face-slapping heavy rain for her efforts. Swiping at the water, she glared at her

uncle. "Miz Savage married an Indian. Far as I can
tell, she loved him. Her children bear his blood, but
hers courses through 'em, too."

"Well—"

"No *well* about it. The Savages are tryin' to fit into
Texas just like you did when you moved here from
Louisiana."

"Ain't the same," he groused.

"I think it is. Now stop jawin' me 'bout this. Unless you're ready to move on." Her heart constricted
at the idea, but she pressed him. "Are you?"

He cast her a half-sheepish, half-defiant look.
"No, I ain't ready to move on. I'm gettin' on just fine
with Woodruff and some of the boys."

Some, she thought, knowing which two he ex-
cluded. Though the two young men undoubtedly
had Indian names, Mr. Woodruff called them
Nathan and Clay.

Weary to the bone from arguing with her uncle,
she sighed. He wasn't about to change. More's the
pity.

Chapter Eight

A scant two weeks after the falling out with Kalen, Jed fiddled with the lead rope of a tricolored paint he'd taken to the house for the Savage girl to gander at. Somethin' about ridin' her in a race.

"You are welcome to go with us, Mr. Barrett," Lael Savage said from her seat on the front porch.

Her offer caught him off guard. "Go where, ma'am?"

"To One Bear's village. There will be games and races and a barbecue."

Was she joshin' him? He wouldn't go near them Injuns. "Uh, thanks. Right kindly of ya to ask, but I got plenty of work here with Nolan."

"Of course. He mentioned he can't take the time, either." She shrugged. "I just thought since Kalen will be traveling with us—"

"'Scuse me?" First he'd heard about it. And if he had anythin' to say, she weren't goin' nowheres with these folks. Leastways not without him. "She ain't said nothin' to me, ma'am."

"Oh, well, perhaps it slipped her mind after we spoke of it in the arena."

"Mebbe so." He vowed to find that contrary miss and give her a talkin' to. Not like Kalen to keep things from him.

The screen door opened and the young Savage girl walked out, eatin' a piece of pie. She stuffed the last bite in her mouth and licked her fingers, then wiped them on her buckskin trousers and smiled.

"Thank you, Mr. Barrett." She assessed the mare as she came down the steps to brush her hand along the mare's flank. "She's a mess. Been rolling in the mud, I'd say."

Jed grinned. "I found her doin' just that, missy. She'll wash up good, though." Jed caressed the black-spotted muzzle. He liked horses a heap better than he did most folks. "This girl's got good lines."

"Yes, she does," Miss Blair agreed. "And she's going to run lickety-split for me."

"Which mare is it, Blair?"

"Moonrise. The one Uncle Bear gave us out of that black-as-a-cave stallion of his."

"Black or brown and white?"

"Tri, Mother. Moonrise is more white than anything, but her papa shows up in the black circle around each eye." The girl chuckled. "She's so muddy, it's hard to see the faint brown markings on her flanks."

"Looks like God run out of paint," Jed said.

Both women erupted in laughter. "How apt," Blair said. "You're poetic, Mr. Barrett."

Heat suffused his neck and ears. *Poetic?* Miss Blair

was daft. "Uh, don't know 'bout that, missy." He scratched the mare's jowl. "You sure this is the one you want me to clean up?"

"Yes, if you would, please. Just get the worst off. I'll do the rest." The girl shot a glance at her mother. "Even though I was very young, my father taught me along with my brothers that if I want to ride, the animal's welfare is my responsibility."

Jed wondered how savvy a damn Injun could be and how much the girl's pa could have taught her. She must've thought it mattered to her ma, though, so he didn't argue the point. Instead, Jed nodded and saluted the missus before he remembered she couldn't see. He led the mare toward the barn's hitch post where he could pour buckets over her, washing off the worst of the mud. Then he'd do what she said: Leave the rest to her.

Midmorning ten days later, Jed found himself slapping reins over the rump of a horse, the missus sitting beside him on the buckboard. He couldn't figure how he'd got talked into it but here he was, headed to that damn Indian village. Didn't make a lick of difference what he'd said; Kalen got her back up and decided she was goin'.

It was him and Kalen, the missus, her young'ns, and them Injun boys, Nathan and Clay, who worked on the ranch.

Up ahead Kalen rode one of the Savages' frisky paints. Unconsciously, Jed's chest expanded with pride. His niece was full of sand, and he'd taught her well. By-gum, she could handle any bullheaded horse she mounted. Sure, Kalen had taken some hard falls, but she always crawled back on and rode the horse's stubbornness into the ground.

He glanced at the quiet woman beside him. What a waste, he thought. She sure was a purty thing, but she'd bedded an Injun. Widow or not, that ruined any chance a white man would court her.

Miz Savage sat straight, her body swayin' graceful-like with the wagon's motion. Her frilly bonnet shielded her face some, but the parasol she held better protected her. The punishin' Texas sun was hotter'n an iron skillet settin' in campfire coals.

Jed tipped back his hat and brushed sweat from his brow. Resettling the hat, he asked, "Ma'am, you know how far this here village is from your spread?"

"Just under ten miles, Mr. Barrett. We should be there before suppertime." She looked into the wagon bed as if she could see. "I can smell the lunch Doreen packed for us. I expect Taylor will call a halt soon."

Her unseein' direct gaze was disconcertin' as the devil. Far away. Like she was lookin' right through a body.

"I don't know about you, but I'm thirsty, and I could stand to step down for a stretch."

She'd no more than gotten the words out when Taylor Savage spun his mount and raised a hand. "We'll eat and rest under those trees." He pointed toward a stand of oaks no more than fifty feet from the trail. "Loosen the cinches and let your horses drink before you hobble them."

As Jed turned the horse, Savage rode toward the wagon. "I'll help you down, Mother."

Figurin' her ridin' next to him made the missus his responsibility, Jed found hisself sayin', "No need. I'll do it, young fella."

Savage gave him an assessing look, then dipped his chin and rode off toward the oaks.

After driving the wagon beneath some branches, Jed drew the horse to a halt and wiped his dry lips on his shirtsleeve. What he'd give for a snort about now.

As he climbed down and skirted the back of the wagon, Jed cautioned hisself to stop thinkin' that away. He liked workin' for Nolan, but one drink and Nolan Woodruff would hand him his walkin' papers. Somehow he had to keep his cravin' at bay.

Though Kalen had balked at movin' into the big house, she'd settled in, some. And this past week, Nolan put her to exercisin' horses along with Jasper. Jed figured, hoped, he could slap back his cravin' so's Kalen could work at what she did best. But, God, it was hard.

"Here ya go, ma'am." He reached up and clasped the lady's elbow to let her know exactly where he was, surprisin' hisself. He'd figured out how to help her without intrudin' on her own ability to get around. Miz Savage done right well for herself.

Dusk, another time of day that Kalen favored. As they rode along the outskirts of the Indian village, she gazed around, curious and . . . surprised. Wooden structures outnumbered tipis three to one. Smoke curled skyward from chimneys as well as a dozen conical tipis. At first she thought the one long, low building might be a general store, but Blair rode up next to her and quickly disabused her of that thinking.

"We'll have supper in the council building with Uncle Bear's family and the elders," she said.

Kalen looked back at her uncle, who'd drawn the wagon to a halt. He glanced around, appearing as apprehensive as she felt. She'd had no luck convincing Miz Savage that she'd be intruding on family time. Now, her greater fear stemmed from worry about Uncle Jed's behavior.

"Ride over there, outside the village, kid."

"Wha . . . what?"

Taylor had circled back to block her and Blair's way. "Over there." He pointed toward a herd of horses the likes of which Kalen had never seen. There must have been five hundred head. And not one fence in sight.

"Tarnation! Who owns all that stock?"

Cameron joined them and the four rode on, leaving Uncle Jed with Miz Savage just as a tall, dignified Indian approached the wagon. Kalen said a silent prayer.

"Oh, about half of them are Uncle Bear's." Blair explained. "The rest belong to various warriors in the tribe."

"Warriors?" Kalen didn't like the sound of that one bit. She peered over her shoulder. "Who is that man?" Though she detested the anxious tone in her voice, she couldn't help it. She'd die if her uncle insulted one of these people. Shoot, both of them might die . . . in the literal sense!

"Uncle Bear," Blair said. "He'll see that Mother and your uncle are settled in the lodge house."

A shiver ran up her arm when Taylor suddenly covered her hand with his. She blinked at him, surprised he had ridden so close to her unnoticed.

"Get down, kid. I'll pasture your horse with the herd."

Kid. She narrowed her eyes but said nothing as she slid to the ground. Would he never look at her as a woman? *And what difference does* that *make, Kalen Barrett?*

Unsettled by his clear-eyed gaze, she looked away and stepped back to put distance between them. As Blair dismounted, Kalen asked, "Why don't the horses wander off?"

"Sometimes they do, but they always come back."

Kalen watched Taylor and Cameron ride in among the mostly pinto and paint horses, dismount, then strip bridles and saddles from the backs of the Savage stock. Content as if in their own pens, the four horses mingled. Then the gelding she'd ridden whinnied and charged away. Ears back, a pregnant mare nipped at his heels and drove him apart from the herd. Stopping, she tossed her head, swished her tail and returned to the herd.

"What's wrong with her?" Kalen asked.

Blair laughed. "Nothing, just flexing her muscles. She's apparently the main mama in that herd."

"I don't understand."

Taylor and Cameron joined them. Each slipped a saddle from his shoulder to the ground on one side as he dropped a second from his other hand. Bridles clinked against the leather.

"You girls take your gear to Grace's tipi. I imagine that's where you'll stay," Taylor said.

"And Mother?" Blair asked. "She usually stays there as well."

Taylor shrugged. "I don't know. She may choose to visit with One Bear's women."

Women? Kalen came to attention. One Bear had more than one? She would not ask Taylor about that. Instead, she brought the conversation back to her poor gelding. He stood off like a leper, all by his lonesome. "Why won't that mare let my horse in with the herd?"

"Cantankerous. Like her rider," Taylor quipped.

Blair and Cameron burst into laughter as Kalen gaped at him. Cantankerous? She'd show him cantankerous!

"Taylor! Stop teasing her," Blair admonished, still smiling.

Kalen frowned. "Funny way of teasin', if you ask me."

She spied the glint in Taylor's extraordinary eyes and watched in amazement as he broke into a smile.

Kalen forgot how to breathe. In all the weeks she'd worked for them, it was the first time she had seen him smile. The transformation was spellbinding. Warmth seeped through her. She shook her head to clear it, dropped her gaze to the saddle at her feet, and busied herself picking it up.

"Welcome," a quiet voice said behind her.

Kalen spun around. Too much was happening too quickly to suit her. A pleasant-faced young woman stood a few feet away. It took a moment for Kalen to realize the newcomer's attention rested solely on Taylor.

"Hello, Graceful Bird," Blair said. "This is Kalen Barrett. May we bunk with you?"

Graceful Bird. A lovely name. Her hair was cropped at her shoulders, the tresses exceptionally shiny. At first glance, because she was so short and chubby, she might be mistaken for a child, until one looked into her knowing eyes. She could possibly be a few years older than Taylor.

Kalen noticed a small tattoo on her temple. Squinting slightly, she discerned its shape: wings.

Finally, the woman focused on Blair and smiled. What a shame, Kalen thought. While her teeth were white, two were missing. Which meant she'd probably gone hungry while growing up.

Graceful Bird placed her hand on her heart. "I would be honored to have your company in my lodge, Miss Blair." Her smile faded as she dipped her head at Kalen and stopped short of speaking directly to her.

Kalen shivered. She had the distinct impression the woman disliked her on sight. Could she be as unreasonable as Uncle Jed? It sure made her uncomfortable to think she'd have to sleep where she wouldn't feel welcome.

She and Blair followed Graceful Bird to a tipi. Curiosity piqued, Kalen dropped her saddle next to Blair's by the opening, then ducked inside behind both women.

The interior was surprisingly spacious, and the beaten ground looked swept. A small trunk sat close to the sloping wall near a few cloth-covered pots.

"Please. Sit." Graceful Bird pointed to robes lying on each side of the small central fire.

"Thank you for having us, Grace," Blair said.

"You are welcome in my lodge, Blair."

No, not a good situation, Kalen thought. Blair didn't seem to realize one was welcome, one was not.

Chapter Nine

The next morning, Kalen assured herself that she had a good seat bareback. Confident she could compete in the races after Blair had explained them, two of them, anyway. Kalen was determined to ride exactly as the Savages did, without benefit of saddle and stirrups.

"Blair is ready?" One Bear asked.

A few feet from Kalen, Blair sat as relaxed as if about to take a stroll across the arena. She tugged down the brim to secure her hat, then nodded.

One Bear dropped a red bandanna. "Go!"

Kalen watched in admiration as Blair's mare exploded over the line. As the end of the course loomed, Blair leaned back and slightly to the side, turning her head to look over her shoulder. Her mount pivoted on its back legs, then stretched out at the run back to the starting point.

Blair's light touch on the reins amazed Kalen. She had only to look in the direction she wanted to go, and the horse seemed to run the course for herself.

"Fifteen second," One Bear announced. "Clean. No fault."

"Not good enough." Cameron grinned. "Clay's got you by a full second."

"Do better, brother dear," Blair challenged right back.

Cameron rode up to the starting line. "Watch me!"

Kalen again marveled at the performance. She'd give her eyeteeth to know how they trained those horses to run with little urging.

Dust billowed around those milling at the line as Cameron thundered home. One Bear clicked the stopwatch and looked at the dial.

"Much *tzat*. Fourteen, three-tenth."

"Hah!" Cameron crowed as Nathan signaled from the other end.

"Hah, indeed!" Blair said. "You didn't catch Clay, and you stepped over the line, so I beat you, too."

Cameron directed a mock glare at Nathan at the other end of the arena. "I was not over the line. You cheated!"

"I no cheat!" The young Indian yelled back. His square-jawed face fractured in a huge grin.

"Out of the way, little brother." Taylor's horse muscled past Cameron's. "Let the master show you how it's done."

This time the tone of Taylor's voice left Kalen in no doubt that he was joshin' his brother. Her gaze roamed over the gathered villagers. Except for Cameron, the Savage women, Uncle Jed and herself, every other soul wore Indian garb. Murmurs surrounded Kalen in the odd tongue she couldn't hope to understand.

Children's laughter rose from near a tipi where a spirited game with sticks and a bladder-ball was in progress.

Again, her gaze returned to Taylor and One Bear. Both wore full skins, shirt and trousers. Quite a few of the men were clad in only breechclouts. Some women wore buckskin tunics that reached to their ankles; others wildly printed, loose cotton dresses over long skirts. The colors of the two garments clashed so badly, Kalen blinked at the frightful combinations.

Long tables had been set up near the big lodge, and now older women brought out large, steaming pots and eating utensils in preparation of a midday meal. Kalen's mouth watered as fragrance from fresh-baked bread overtook the smell of sweaty horseflesh. This keyhole race, as Blair had called it, was the last before they'd eat.

Her attention refocused on Taylor as his horse leaped forward into a flat-out run. Another exceptional show of horsemanship. His return sent those in his path scurrying.

One Bear clicked the stopwatch and peered at the dial. "Thirteen-five."

Nathan bellowed from the other end. "Two faults! Both side keyhole."

"I don't believe it!" Taylor exclaimed.

"Ha, ha, ha!" Blair chided.

"Two faults?" Cameron chortled. "That means you came in dead last, *big* brother."

Kalen surprised herself by saying, "I haven't had my turn yet."

Smiling faces, except for Taylor's, turned to her.

Expression skeptical, he shrugged. "Give it a go, kid. You might get lucky."

She narrowed her eyes, trying to discern if he was still joshin'. "Luck has nothin' to do with it, Mr. Savage. It takes a good rider."

What a load of bull. One had to be an *excellent* rider to compete in these races, but she refused to back down now.

She rode up to the starting line and mimicked Blair, settling her hat firmly. Her gaze skipped to the table where her uncle had taken up a position beside Miz Savage. Kalen hadn't spoken with him since before they left the ranch yesterday. Though he could be difficult, right now he gave her sorely needed support with a thumbs-up.

She grinned in acknowledgment. "When you're ready, Mr. One Bear."

Though not as tall as either of the Savage brothers, One Bear was a formidable, dignified Indian. A great deal of pride in his bearing, he stood poker straight, his buckskin-clad chest outthrust. No more prone to laughter than Taylor Savage, he appeared more grave than stern.

"The clock she run. *Caballo* no step on line."

She nodded. "I understand the rules, sir."

"*Tzat.*"

Kalen whispered to Blair, "What did he say?"

"Good," Blair replied.

"Ready?" One Bear prompted.

Kalen focused on her destination. "Yes."

"Go!"

She slapped the reins to either side of the horse's

withers and raced to the keyhole shape drawn in lime. Pulling back on the reins, she slowed the horse's momentum. He pivoted on his hind legs.

"Yah!" She kicked him again and leaned into his neck. "Go! Go!"

At the finish line, everyone scattered. She leaned back, tugged the reins, and the pinto came to a sliding stop. A cloud of dust covered Kalen head to foot. She waved her hand before her face and coughed, then looked at One Bear.

He wagged his head. "No *tzat*. Sixteen second."

"Oh, come on!" she wailed. "Surely I did better than that."

Blair and Cameron burst into laughter.

Taylor shrugged. "Win a few, lose a few, kid."

Kalen sucked in a breath and growled at him. "If you call me kid one more time, I swear by all that's holy, I'm goin' to . . ." She clamped her mouth shut on her temper. He might fire her if she told him exactly what she'd like to do to him. And what was it she really *did* want to do to him? Heat rose in her face.

Fazed not at all, Taylor simply raised a brow and gave her a mocking grin.

"My husband," Blanket Woman said, "eat now, *por favor*."

A similarly dressed woman holding a young child by the hand stood near Blanket Woman. Astonishingly, the children younger than three years old were stark naked. No one in the village took notice. She also noted that occasionally Comanches jumbled in Spanish phrases when attempting to speak English.

Kalen followed Blair's lead and dismounted. "Who is that with the little boy?"

Blair glanced at the two women and smiled at the child. "The boy's mother, One Bear's woman."

Kalen frowned. "I thought Blanket Woman was his wife."

"She is. He bought Arrora from Comancheros five or six years ago."

"*Bought* her?"

Blair nodded. "She had been captured in Mexico for sale as a slave."

"Oh, no." Kalen shook her head. "Slavery is no longer tolerated."

"In the white man's world. Mexican and Indian people look upon it much differently."

"How do you . . . How does your family tolerate such a thing?"

One Bear headed toward the tables, his wives a step behind.

"Honestly? We don't have a say in the matter, Kalen." Blair shrugged. "Besides, I think One Bear has stopped the practice in his band. Believe me, Arrora is much better off as his second wife than as a slave in another tribe. It might interest you to meet his *third* wife."

"Three!" Kalen's brows shot up. "Holy smokes." What she'd heard was true.

"It's not a common practice anymore, but men often take widows of fallen friends to wife."

"How do they all manage to get along?"

"It's their way of life."

"If I had a husband, I'd be sorely grieved if he so much as looked at another woman."

Taylor's graceful dismount captured Kalen's attention. That would certainly be true if she were *his* wife. *What are you thinkin'?*

Taylor removed the rope snaffle from his mount, and a slap sent the stallion unerringly toward the herd. The other riders followed suit.

A few minutes later, much to her chagrin, Kalen found herself seated directly across a table from Taylor. His mother sat one side of him, Graceful Bird the other.

"It sounds as though our Indian brethren are getting the best of you children."

"We have the afternoon to redeem ourselves," Blair said. "Kalen, will you ride Gretna Green with me?"

Hoping it tasted as delicious as it looked, Kalen ladled soup into a wooden bowl. "I might if I knew what Gretna Green is."

"I don't know, Blair," Taylor warned. "It's a fast, dangerous race. You better ask her uncle if he objects."

Kalen deliberately placed her spoon alongside the bowl. "I'm grown, Mr. Savage. *I* know I am. *You* know I am. Why do you continually insinuate I need my uncle's approval?"

"Yes, Taylor, why is that?" Miz Savage queried.

He shrugged.

Kalen cocked her head, surprised at his discomfort.

"Mother can't see your shrug," Blair offered two seats down.

"Because she's young, and her uncle will have to take care of her if she's injured." Taylor surveyed his family. "Satisfied?"

"Maybe." Blair spoke at the same time his mother copied his shrug. An enigmatic smile curved her lips.

Kalen inadvertently glanced at Graceful Bird, then lowered her gaze to avoid the venom that shot from near-black eyes. What was the woman's problem? Not once last night in her tipi had she spoken to Kalen. She'd find another place to bed down tonight, and they'd hopefully head back to the ranch tomorrow.

That presented another problem, but at least there Kalen could always retreat to her nice solitary room as soon as she finished a meal. And most evenings she'd try to cry off supper with the Savages and join Uncle Jed.

Moments later, Graceful Bird's smitten expression as Taylor and One Bear conversed answered Kalen's question. For some crazy-as-a-laughing-hyena reason, the woman was actually jealous of her.

True, Kalen found Taylor Savage attractive. Okay, more than attractive. But as her boss and part Indian to boot, he was completely unsuitable for her. Wasn't he? Absolutely. Besides, he barely knew she existed except to rag her, calling her a kid. Regardless, she found herself mesmerized by those long fingers of his curled around a tin cup.

Abruptly discarding the fantasy that wheeled through her mind about what those fingers would feel like on her body, what they might do, she stood. "I need to talk to my uncle." She stepped back from the table and addressed One Bear. "Thank you for your hospitality, sir."

Blair tugged her hand. "Kalen," she whispered, "don't thank the chief." She nodded toward Blanket Woman. "Thank her."

Flustered, Kalen did so, then left without further conversation. What made up proper manners with these people? She had no idea. Arguments with Uncle Jed notwithstanding, she felt far more comfortable with her own kind.

An hour later, Kalen once again positioned herself at the starting line. Blair was mounted next to her, and both held ends of a bandanna. Maintaining their hold, they were to ride hell-for-leather, side by side around poles and sawhorses in an arena-sized oval. Kalen doubted she and Blair could beat the times of the two other teams that went before them, but she was game to try.

"Kalen, you should ride inside," Cameron said.

She glanced back. "Why?"

"The outrider has to move a step or two faster on the turns. It's real easy to lose hold of the bandanna in the turns if you're not quick enough."

"I can do that."

"Maybe. But your first time at Gretna Green, I'd advise you to ride on the inside."

Kalen looked at Blair.

The girl shrugged. "Your call, but Cameron is right. It might be safer if you rode inside this first time."

Though mounted bareback, Kalen believed herself almost Blair's equal. "I'll stay where I am." Determined, she set her teeth.

* * *

Idling on his stallion at the opposite end of the arena, Taylor combed his fingers through Creation's long mane and wondered what all the palavering was about. When Kalen maintained her position, he knew. Cameron had lost that argument. He swore under his breath.

Fool woman. Out to prove herself. Well, his job was to watch for faults on this end of the arena. Blair rarely made mistakes when she rode with him or Cameron. Riding with a greenhorn, sister Blair was about to lose.

Along the side of the course, his mother sat on a chair One Bear had provided and, oddly, Jed Barrett squatted on his haunches beside her. Ever since he'd decided to come along and drive the wagon, Barrett had taken it upon himself to look after her. Wherever his mother was, Jed was close by. Strange, that.

Taylor knew for certain Jed had no use for him. He thought little better of Cameron and Blair, but he at least spoke to them. Didn't matter to Taylor. In fact, sometimes he flaunted his Indian blood before small-minded men like Jed. Went out of his way to antagonize them. His mother continually pointed out that flaw, but he persisted. Probably would all his life.

He came to attention when One Bear dropped the bandanna and yelled, "Go!"

The two young women burst from the starting line stride for stride. Kalen's horse brushed too close to Blair's leg, forcing her to rein out of the way.

"Move over, Kalen," he whispered as they thundered toward him. As though she heard him, she did. He released a pent-up breath.

Both girls reined left as they started into the curve. No problem until Blair got a step ahead and Kalen had to lean inward to maintain her hold on the bandanna. Then, she kept leaning, leaning, leaning.

"Let go," Taylor said to no one. "Let go, Kalen. You'll fall."

Blair turned her head slightly to see Kalen's exact position, and that was enough for Blair's horse to follow her lead. The pinto veered into Kalen's mount. Jostled from her seat, Kalen disappeared between the two horses.

A knot in his throat, Taylor was off his horse and running before Kalen's body cleared the horses' hooves. She hit the ground hard once, then a second time, her arms and legs flailing like a rag doll's. He slid to his knees, gaze racing over her still—her very still—form, and prayed. "Don't be hurt badly. I'll kill you if you are," he said irrationally, his eyes searching her again from head to toe.

"Kalen!" Jed cried as he, too, dropped to his knees and reached out.

Taylor exploded. "Don't touch her!"

Barrett glanced up, his hand hovering over Kalen's shoulder.

"Something might be broken." Taylor added in a more reasonable tone. "We shouldn't move her until we know."

"How you plannin' to find out if I don't check her?" Jed sneered.

For the first time in his life, Taylor pleaded.

"Please, Mr. Barrett. My mother has excellent hands.
She can quickly detect broken bones."

Taylor glanced toward his mother. She stood but
hadn't moved away from her chair.

"I'll get her." Jed jumped to his feet.

Everyone ran from different directions toward
him and Kalen, but Taylor stayed focused on her
face. "Don't you dare be hurt badly." His main
worry was that she'd been stomped by a hoof or two
before the horses bolted away from her falling body.

Before he could say more, Blair jumped from her
horse and knelt. "God, Taylor, Moonrise turned
right in front of her."

This was the only time in all the years he and his
siblings had trained horses that Taylor wished their
methods hadn't been so effective. Their horses understood body motions—leaning, turning, shifting
body weight. Such techniques had become second
nature, and their personal mounts responded exceptionally well.

"Is she all right?"

"By thunder, I don't know!" he blurted.

Chapter Ten

Lael heard the panic in Taylor's normally calm voice. Laying comforting fingers on his shoulder, she knelt by his side. "Direct my hands, son."

Taylor clasped them and placed one on Kalen's shoulder, the other on her thigh. The grit on the girl's clothes abraded Lael's palms.

"Her other leg is twisted back at the knee, Mother," he offered. "It could be all right, or it could be broken."

"Was she trampled?"

"I don't . . . think so."

"Me, neither," Jed said. "I weren't as close as your boy, missus, but it looked like she dropped straight down and bounced a couple times."

"Thank you, Mr. Barrett." Her hands moved gently on Kalen's shoulder, down the arm, then back to her shoulder.

"What?" Taylor demanded.

At the same time, Jed asked, "Find somethin'?"

She didn't answer, concentrating on following

the ligaments and shoulder joint again. Shifting, she forced Taylor aside. "Her shoulder is already feverish."

Moving down Kalen's body, Lael checked the straight leg, then the other one bent at an odd angle. "I better check this hip more closely. A break would allow her leg to bend back more than usual. Does it look like it does, Taylor?"

She heard his sigh.

"It looks natural, Mother."

Squeezing and probing around the top of the leg, Lael made her way to the knee. "Oh dear," she murmured before she could stop herself.

"Mother?" Taylor asked, his tone clipped.

"The knee is already swelling. A sprain, I think. I can't feel anything out of place. Straighten her leg . . . carefully."

She felt his movement beside her and the heat from bodies pressing in around them. "I think she will wake sooner if she gets more air."

"*Jaa*," One Bear agreed. "*Maheyah* . . . move off."

"Oooh," Kalen moaned.

"By thunder," Taylor muttered.

"Is she waking?"

"Not really. Her eyes are closed. But she probably felt me straighten her leg." He gave his mother more room. "You can check down the leg to her ankle now."

Moments later, Lael pronounced nothing broken. "Taylor, take her to Pieces Of Sky Eyes's tipi. She can treat Kalen if necessary. I'll stay with her."

"Who's this Pieces Of Sky Eyes?" Jed asked, voice gruff with concern.

"An excellent medicine woman, Mr. Barrett, and One Bear's wife."

"You said Blanket Woman is his wife."

"Yes." Lael grabbed Taylor's arm when she felt him begin to rise. "Wait," she murmured for Taylor's ears alone. She'd have to calm Mr. Barrett's fears before anyone would be allowed to care for Kalen.

Glancing to where Jed knelt across from her, she smiled. "Mr. Barrett, One Bear has three wives. Pieces Of Sky Eyes is his third and much revered by these people. She lost her first husband four years ago and agreed to marry One Bear."

"That ain't right, ma'am."

"Not in our world, to be sure. But when a man dies in the Indians' world, a close relative will often marry the dead warrior's spouse and care for her."

"Well—"

"Mother." Taylor's impatience fairly vibrated the air. She couldn't hold him back any longer. With a nod, she rose to her feet.

"Mr. Barrett, Taylor will carry Kalen to the medicine woman's tipi." Knowing her next words would not sit well with him, Lael smiled ingratiatingly. "I'm sorry, but you are an outsider and a white man. Pieces Of Sky Eyes will not allow you into her dwelling."

"Well, then, what's to say she'll do right by Kalen. My niece ain't goin' there, neither!"

Certain Taylor had already removed Kalen from her path, Lael stepped toward Jed's voice and extended her hand. "Please, it's only for one night. I assure you she will be well treated. To make sure, though, I will stay with her. Would you be kind enough to follow Taylor and lead me?"

Taylor hefted Kalen closer to his chest. Though unconscious, she nestled against him and sighed. The sound cascaded through his veins like water flowing over a waterfall. Unable to conquer his body's reaction, he ground his teeth and walked faster.

She fit him. Spirits of the *Nermernuh,* she did. He glanced down at her face pressed against his chest. Though covered with a fine film of dust, the rosy hue of her skin shone through. Her dark, sun-tipped lashes lay on her cheeks like a lover's touch.

Lover's touch. He groaned. *Banish that thought right now.*

No way could he ever consider this girl other than a hired hand. For starters, Jed Barrett would shoot him right between the eyes. And he'd never press his suit, anyway.

Would he?

Of course not.

He was known for his levelheaded dealings with white men. They might give him short shrift, but he always rose to the occasion and allowed his better qualities to surface. Not necessarily for his sake, but for his family's.

Yeah, he persisted in wearing Indian attire, and at times he needled men like Jed, but he'd learned proper diction from his mother. He would not jeopardize her well-being or that of Cameron and Blair.

Again, he looked down into Kalen's face, remembering the feel of her hand beneath his. Her shiver. He sucked in a shaky breath. Damn his soul to the white man's perdition, he could not quell his desire for this woman. A desire that had come out of nowhere. Perhaps he should deliver Mr. Turner's horse rather than have the man come here. Take himself away from Kalen Barrett and the temptation she posed. But that was weeks away.

Taylor paused at the tipi's entrance and waited for Pieces Of Sky Eyes to bid him enter.

One Bear's woman lifted the flap and motioned him inside. Though born a white, Pieces Of Sky Eyes had been captured while yet a suckling. Taylor didn't know all the particulars, but he knew she had been raised by the Comanche and had mated well.

Blond, with startling turquoise eyes, Pieces Of Sky Eyes neither spoke nor understood English. In fact, she spoke hardly at all, and didn't now. She only gestured where to lay his burden.

Come to think of it, Kalen was no burden at all. While she weighed next to nothing, he wondered again at her strength, remembering when she'd turned that foal. Astonishing.

He lowered her carefully to the buffalo robe. Staring down at her, he couldn't help himself; he cupped the side of her face. Soft, warm . . . lovely. What he wanted but would not ever have. Sighing, he stood and lingered a moment, loath to leave her.

His mother ducked inside and straightened, groped and found his arm. "She'll be fine." She patted him on the shoulder. "Leave Kalen to us now."

He could stay no longer, but he looked at the medicine woman, who stared back at him . . . silent. Her lips curved in a near smile and she nodded.

Fortunately for him, his mother spoke little Comanche, so she couldn't converse much with the medicine woman, and she couldn't see the longing in his face that Pieces Of Sky Eyes had. When he left the tipi, he'd school his features and suppress his feelings for Kalen. No one else would know.

Hearing close breathing, Kalen fluttered her eyes, but seemed unable to open them. Teeth clenched, she forced her lids wide.

Lovely turquoise eyes hovered above hers.

Brow furrowed, Kalen tipped her head, then realized she lay on robes and her shoulder hurt like the dickens. "Wh . . . What happened? Who are you?"

"Rest easy, Kalen."

She shifted her gaze just past the woman. Miz Savage smiled.

"Where am I?"

Lael laid her hand on the woman's shoulder. "This is Pieces Of Sky Eyes, the tribe's medicine woman."

That was equivalent to a doctor in the white world. *But, blue eyes? How could that be?* Kalen trembled inside, afraid to try moving, but anxious at a perfect stranger touching her. "I'm . . . I'm all right, aren't I?"

"As near as we can tell."

Miz Savage knelt, her smile still in place. Kalen wished she'd stop doing that. It reminded her of someone trying to ease a body's fears. If she were truly all right, why should she need calmin'?

"You took a hard fall. You have a bruised shoulder, but we don't think anything is broken. Now that you're awake, move your legs, your arms. Tell us where it hurts."

In nothing flat, Kalen discovered not only her shoulder ached, but her left leg felt afire at the knee.

Miz Savage assured her it was only a sprain. "But that might take longer to heal than a break."

That didn't comfort Kalen one bit; in fact, it only added to a sudden headache she didn't need, either. Then she remembered. . . .

"Blair's okay, isn't she?" Holy smokes, had she caused Blair to sustain an injury?

"She's fine. Worried about you, as we all have been."

Kalen tried to sit up, but she couldn't put enough pressure on the elbow attached to the sore shoulder.

Without a word, the Indian woman slipped an arm beneath Kalen and lifted her. Miz Savage slid a robe-covered backrest behind her.

"Thank you." Kalen nodded at the Indian. "Does she speak English?"

"Not that I know of," Lael replied. "Pieces Of Sky Eyes is mute by choice. She speaks Comanche only when she has something to say." Lael sighed. "I grant you, not often, but she knows how to treat many types of injuries and illnesses."

Dressed like One Bear's wives, Pieces Of Sky Eyes set herself apart by wearing a turquoise-studded bone choker.

Her blond hair looked greasy as the dickens. Kalen stopped just short of wrinkling her nose at the peculiar odor in the close air. Bear grease? She'd heard Indians coated their hair with the stuff. Why? she wondered.

Pieces Of Sky Eyes brought a cup of something to Kalen's lips. The idea of drinking from a bone cup made her squeamish. What part of the animal was it? And only God knew what the brown liquid was.

"Drink it, Kalen. It will ease your aches."

Kalen inhaled the liquid's faint, though not offensive, odor. What choice did she have? Meeting the Indian's grave eyes, Kalen managed a slight smile, opened her mouth and drank . . . all of it.

She ran her tongue over her lips. "What was that?"

Lael settled near Kalen's shoulder. "Haven't a clue. Pieces Of Sky Eyes keeps her decoctions in her head. Neither of us is fluent in the other's language." She shrugged. "I doubt that she would share her knowledge with a white woman, anyway."

Kalen studied Pieces Of Sky Eyes. "But, Miz Savage, she's white."

"Only by birth. She remembers nothing of her infancy, Kalen, and doesn't even think of herself that way. One Bear said she was adopted by a powerful warrior as his child the day she entered his village."

Kalen had to admit that whatever the decoction was, it worked well. The ache in her shoulder and knee subsided, and by supper time she felt well enough to join the others.

After supper, the Indians built a fire, and they and their guests gathered in a circle before the long lodge. Kalen came to rapt attention when several men began a mesmerizing drum beat.

Soon several Indian girls rose and stepped into the circle. Facing out, they began a shuffling step, traveling sideways.

Kalen didn't want to appear rude, but she laughed softly. "That's dancin'?"

Graceful Bird passed in front of her, matching the beat of the music with her feet. A few people farther down in the circle began to clap in time to the beat. Then, Graceful Bird stopped before Taylor Savage.

He looked up, shook his head. His brother punched him on the shoulder. Reluctantly, it seemed to Kalen, Taylor climbed to his feet and joined Graceful Bird.

Drawing her in front of him, he began a forward shuffle while Graceful Bird mimicked his steps backward.

"That's the Indians' form of dancing, Kalen." Blair rose to her feet. "Excuse me while I join the fun."

Kalen grinned. "Show me how it's done."

Blair chose Uncle Jed. Kalen chuckled when his face turned beet red, but she had to give him credit. He joined Blair and didn't embarrass himself. While Aunt Livvie had never been able to get him to dance a reel, he could shuffle with the best of 'em.

Against her will, Kalen's gaze followed Taylor Savage and Graceful Bird around the circle. In the dim firelight, she couldn't see their faces very well, but Graceful Bird never took her eyes off his face.

On the far side of the circle, a couple suddenly stepped out of the line of dancers and disappeared into the darkness. Kalen sucked in a breath when Graceful Bird clasped Taylor's hand and he followed her out of the circle . . . toward her tipi.

Irrational as it was, Kalen couldn't stop the tears that pricked her eyes. She had seen the longing in Graceful Bird's expression at lunch. Now, Taylor seemed to return the Indian maid's affection.

And that makes not one bit of difference to you, Kalen Barrett, so mind your manners.

She leaned close to Miz Savage's ear and spoke above the drumming. "I think I should find my bedroll. Would you 'scuse me, ma'am?"

"I believe I'll join you. This dancing will go on into the night. Perhaps I can persuade you to walk me to Pieces Of Sky Eyes's tipi."

"Sure." Kalen waited while Lael gathered her skirts and stood, then extended her hand for Kalen to clasp.

"Ma'am, if you don't mind, I think I'll sleep in the wagon bed tonight."

Her employer tilted her head back and breathed in the cool air. "It's a lovely night, and I doubt it will get very cold. You should be comfortable under the stars."

"Yes, ma'am." *If I can block thoughts of Taylor.*

Chapter Eleven

What seemed like hours later, the drums stilled, and the village quieted, yet Kalen had not closed her eyes. She lay staring up at the stars, unable to get the image of Taylor and Graceful Bird out of her mind.

It didn't take a genius to figure out they were enjoying each other's . . . company. The hair rose on her arms. What would it be like to have Taylor Savage give her such attention?

"I need to get away from here. Far away."

Eyes long adjusted to the darkness, she peered around the village. The rustle of small nocturnal animals barely disturbed the silence. The bonfire had long ago died out.

Cautiously, she slid out of her bedroll and dragged the blankets after her as she climbed down from the wagon. Breathing shallowly for fear she'd wake someone, she rolled the blankets, tiptoed to the tipi to retrieve her gear, and picked her way to where she had last seen the horses.

Would miracles never cease? Her mount grazed near the edge of the herd. She would ride to the ranch, could surely find her way back easily enough. It had been a fairly straight shot north to the village. They'd only crossed two streams, the one near the house and another about halfway where they'd stopped for lunch.

Fortunately, the gelding didn't bolt or sidle away while she bridled him. Her shoulder screamed when she threw the saddle atop his back. Kalen bit back a moan. Lord love a duck, she hurt like the dickens, but figured she couldn't have done all she'd done in the past few minutes if anything were broken. So, ignoring her aches, she mounted and walked the horse from the village. No hurry, really. She'd mosey back, but she was *not* staying in that village another minute.

"Running Wolf lady."

Lael came awake to Pieces Of Sky Eyes's soft voice and a shake of her shoulder. "Yes?" she said, trying to get her bearings.

"Girl. No village."

Though it took a moment for her to understand the woman's meaning, Lael couldn't believe her daughter would be so foolish as to ride in the dark. And why? "Blair?" Then Lael realized her hostess had spoken halting but understandable English.

"Girl." Pieces Of Sky Eyes touched Lael's throat and cleared her own a couple times.

Lael blinked away sleep, understanding the medicine woman's pantomime. "You mean Kalen? Good heavens, why?" What a silly question. Pieces Of Sky Eyes wouldn't know the answer any better than she.

"Do you know where my son is? He needs to be told."

Pieces Of Sky Eyes touched Lael's shoulder, then left the tipi. Lael sat listening to her almost inaudible retreat. With no way to tell time, she waited far longer than she cared to for the woman's return.

When she finally ducked back into the tipi, Lael asked, "Did you find him? What did he say? Will he go after her?"

She said, "Sound Of Wind."

Lael couldn't fault the woman for not answering her in English. After all, *she* had never learned Comanche. She'd have to comfort herself with the knowledge that Pieces Of Sky Eyes had spoken with Taylor. Surely he would find Kalen.

Taylor searched for a good fifteen minutes before he found Cameron. He had no right to caution his brother about bedding an Indian maid. After all, everyone assumed that's what he'd done. And they were right, except for this evening.

He'd read the hurt in Grace's eyes when he left her without entering her tipi. Though he had never said anything outright, it was obvious his previous visits had led her to believe he would speak for her. He never would, so it was time to stop visiting in her tipi. Thunderation, he shouldn't have left the dance with her. Misguided, perhaps, he wanted to leave her with pride.

"Cameron."

His brother sat up so quickly, his forehead just missed hitting Taylor in the face. "Cripes, Taylor, what are you doing in White Doe's lodge?" He flipped the blanket over his bedmate's nude torso.

"Looking for you. I'm riding out and wanted you to know. You'll lead the group home tomorrow."

"Me? Why? Where are you going?"

Taylor shook his head. "Keep your voice down. Kalen has left the village—"

"Left . . . Cripes, it's the middle of the night!"

"You noticed." Taylor touched Cameron's shoulder. "Don't say anything to Barrett until you have to. And then say I took her to see Doc Summers just to be on the safe side."

"Will you?"

"No. That fool woman doesn't need a doctor, she needs some sense knocked into her head."

"And you think you can do it?"

Taylor heard the smile in his brother's voice even if he couldn't see him clearly. He ignored the barb. "I'll see you back at the ranch."

Taylor found his stallion and saddled up. He was unsure what kind of head start Kalen had on him, but traveling in the dark didn't bode well for her. One Bear had assured him not more than a month ago that hostiles were far to the north and not a problem. But bears and coyotes aplenty roamed the area. And snakes lay in wait for small game.

His chest tightened at the thought of Kalen accidentally stumbling upon a rattler in the dark. Well, he consoled himself as he left the village, at least she was on horseback.

* * *

Horsefeathers. Not more than a half hour after Kalen left the village, clouds had blanketed the sky, intermittently hiding the stars. She searched the heavens again, but the stars peeking between the clouds weren't bright enough for the North Star.

The only thing she knew for sure was she had crossed a stream hours ago. Now, she faced another one, and the ranch was nowhere in sight. Which meant she had traveled in a circle.

Sighing, she studied the stream and surrounding terrain. With few trees on this side of the river to block her view, she could bed down until daylight and be fairly sure she'd see an animal or person approach.

Her shoulder ached like a son of a gun, and her right leg felt stiffer by the minute. Maybe she should fashion a sling out of her extra shirtwaist. Easing her leg over the cantle, she stepped down . . . and turned her ankle on an unseen rock.

Sucking in a breath, she leaned her forehead on the horse's shoulder. "Damn, damn, damn! Now my shoulder, knee *and* ankle hurt!"

"Maybe I should warm your bottom for you, too."

Kalen jumped away from her horse. "Ouch!" She'd landed on her foot, further aggravating the ankle. "Taylor! You scared me witless!"

He dismounted and walked toward her, his eyes dark shadows in his face, his mouth a thin line. He stopped an arm's length away. "I doubt you had wits to begin with, brat. You don't wander off in this part of the world without an escort. You should know that!"

"Escort? Escort?" she questioned louder. "I can take care of myself, Mr. Savage."

He looked pointedly at the booted foot she rested gingerly on the ground, carrying most of her weight on the other foot. "Could have fooled me."

"No need to trouble yourself. I plan to bed down until daylight, then ride back to the ranch." She flicked her hand above her shoulder, indicating where she intended to go. With any luck it was the right direction.

"Fine." He strode back to his horse and pulled off the tack. "I'll get some shut-eye, too. I'm tired to the bone from searching for you the past three hours."

"No one asked you!" She yelled to hide her relief that he'd found her.

Kalen watched as he efficiently flung his bedroll on the ground and stretched out. Tipping his hat over his face, he propped his head on the saddle's seat. Just like that, he was comfortably bedded down and she hadn't even started!

Tsking, she turned to reach for the cinch. Her painful shoulder reminded her to move slowly. Because she could only pull the saddle with one hand, unable to handle the weight, it fell heavily to the ground. She stepped back to avoid bruising her other foot.

Setting her teeth to stop an oath of pain, she leaned her head on the horse for support, looping her hand over his neck. "Be still, fella," she whispered.

In the next instant, she was off her feet and cradled against Taylor's broad chest. Before she could catch her breath, he was lowering her to his bedroll.

"Don't you move, woman, or I swear I will whale your backside!"

Taylor finished untacking Kalen's horse, all the while casting quick glances in her direction. Thank the Spirits she stayed where he had put her. The woman was determined to cause him grief.

As he untied her bedroll from her saddle, he realized she probably hadn't given him a thought. It mattered not to her that he was ultimately responsible for every soul on his ranch. That while he might not show it, he cared about every injury, even one to ornery Jed Barrett if it came to it.

On one knee, he spread one of Kalen's blankets next to his. "Scoot over here."

For a second she narrowed her eyes. Only God knew why she would take offense at his order. She had to be tired. He certainly was, and he wasn't nursing an injured shoulder and right leg.

Finally, she levered herself onto her own blanket, closer to where he knelt. Her scent swirled into his nose. God of her people, she certainly didn't mean to tempt him, but she did.

"Lie down," he snapped.

"And if I don't?" she challenged.

All right, he was being an ass, but not for the reason she might think. He despaired at her reaction if she discovered he would gladly be her lover as well.

And how had that happened? What little contact they'd had between them had been confrontational at every turn. He gritted his teeth rather than further antagonize her.

"Cover with this other blanket if you like. It's warm enough now, but just before dawn will be cooler."

"Thank you." She snatched the blanket from his hands and spread one end haphazardly over her lower legs. Lying back, she closed her eyes tightly. "Good night."

Though he tried not to, he chuckled. She reminded him of a much younger Blair or Cameron squeezing their eyes closed pretending to sleep, hoping to escape imminent punishment.

Kalen opened her eyes and looked up at him.

He was lost. With not a thought in his head, he leaned over and captured her lips. Ambrosia. He felt her startle, but she didn't push him away, didn't turn her head. She lay there as if too stunned to move. And maybe she was.

Unable to stop himself, his lips moved over hers, claiming, exploring, tasting, wanting more. Her lips parted. He took that as an invitation to plunge his tongue into the warm recess, territory he claimed as his own.

Feeling himself begin to shake from the desire that flashed through his body like quicksilver, he drew back. Eyes still closed, Kalen sighed before looking up at him again. This time her golden eyes were rounded with . . . wonder, he thought, prayed.

"Why did you do that?"

Not what he expected, and he didn't know how to answer. He should not say what sprang to mind. *Because I want you.* That did *not* make sense, and Kalen wouldn't believe him. Their face-to-face interactions had been anything but easy.

With nothing better to say, he finally said, "I have no idea."

Hurt? He could not be sure that was what he read in her eyes.

"Don't worry. It won't happen again." He pushed to his feet and walked around to her other side.

As he settled on his own blanket and again rested his head on the saddle seat, he felt her rigid body next to his, so tense she would never get any sleep. He blamed himself for that. Stupid, stupid, stupid.

Some time later, Taylor hadn't been able to sleep himself, but Kalen had dropped off. Exhausted, no doubt. He examined his actions six ways to Sunday, but could not—no, make that would not—explain why he had kissed her.

She sighed in her sleep, sending more sparks through him. Serve him right if he burned up with want. He had no right to kiss this woman. None.

At that moment, with her uninjured shoulder next to him, Kalen mumbled something in her sleep and turned on her side, her arm flopping across his chest. She moved closer, nestling more comfortably, which brought her length flush against his.

Maybe *she* was more comfortable, but his body roared to life with a vengeance. He groaned in his throat. What could he do but lie there and not move? If he tried to push her away, it meant putting his hands on her warm body. *Not* a good idea. Not even for a second.

"Taylor." Her lips brushed his ear.

"What?" he snapped, sure his voice rose an octave as a portion of his body stood to attention at her sensual touch.

Silence.

Taylor moved his head over just enough to turn it. Kalen's peaceful face rested inches from his, her long lashes pillowed on her cheeks. Asleep.

The woman was asleep, dreaming, he guessed. He wondered if he figured in her dream. *She did say my name.* No mistake.

"Umm." She murmured and smiled, licking her luscious lips as if tasting something.

"Lightning strike me," Taylor implored the heavens. Of course, it didn't. Not even the Spirits would accommodate him this night.

Chapter Twelve

Eyes closed, Kalen sniffed and frowned. She could smell Taylor Savage. Loco! And what was she lying on that was so hard?

Opening her eyes a slit, she saw buckskin beneath her cheek. Her pillow didn't have a buckskin cover. What the . . . ? Ever so slowly, she lifted her head. And stared into Taylor Savage's intense, crystal blue eyes.

Startled, she reared back, wrenching her shoulder. "Ow!" Incensed, she cupped her injury and yelled, "What are you doin' in my bedroll?"

"Not sleeping," he retorted dryly. "For your information, I am lying on *my* blanket. *You* were sprawled all over *me*."

Bracing herself with her good arm, Kalen scrambled onto her knees. Another twinge reminded her that her knee and ankle were not in great shape, either. "I was *not* sprawled on you. I . . ." Well, she was, but she wouldn't have been if he hadn't insisted she lie so close when they bedded down.

Kalen knew she was a cuddler. She had cuddled a dog once. Unconsciously, she cuddled her pillow. Dadburnit, that's how she slept! And his big, warm body was there, so . . .

"You could have moved," she finally said, hearing the defensiveness in her own voice.

"I did. Twice. You followed me."

Kalen glanced down and had to agree. He told the truth. His soft sable hair no longer trailed over his saddle. She knew his hair was soft because she vaguely recalled her fingers sinking into it . . . sometime during the night. His whole body lay on the ground next to his blanket. The blanket she knelt upon.

Though discomfited, she managed to rise to her feet. "I'm sorry I disturbed your sleep, Mr. Savage. It won't happen again." She remembered too late he had said those same words to her.

"Mr. Savage," he repeated and smiled. Not necessarily a pleasant smile. "It was 'Taylor' in your sleep."

She couldn't stop the heat that flooded her cheeks. Though usually tan, her skin reddened at the least provocation, blossoming when anger or embarrassment washed through her.

She stared into his unwavering eyes and wondered if she had dreamed the kiss. She had dreamed other things, she knew, but the kiss? Without thinking, she touched her lips with trembling fingers.

A sudden darkening in his eyes told her that, no, she had not dreamed that kiss, and he knew she was reliving it. Taking a shuddering breath, she turned and limped toward the stream. Lord love a duck, she was in trouble here. Big trouble. Though certainly old enough, she had no clue how to respond sexually to a man.

Glancing over her shoulder, she found Taylor still on the ground, though he now watched her as surely as a predator stalks its prey.

No, she didn't know how to respond to him. More to the point, did she want to? And what should she do about it? Scooping water, splashing it over her hot cheeks, she settled that question quickly enough. If she believed for one second that love could build between them, she would learn how to respond to Taylor Savage.

But who said he shared her interest? What was the word? Fantasizing. Yep, that's what she was doing. How could she even *think* Taylor Savage might fall in love with her?

Yanking up the tail of her shirtwaist, she smeared most of the water off her face. What a pathetic woman she was. Love her? Uh-uh. Hadn't she seen him courting Graceful Bird? Just last night? She snorted. *He certainly didn't go to her tipi to talk about the weather!*

She glanced over her shoulder when she heard activity. As efficiently as he had last night, Taylor rolled both their beddings and tied them to the saddles. He tacked up her mount first, then his, all in less time than it would have taken her to do her own. But she was injured, she consoled herself. Only sprains and bruises. Still . . .

Coming to the riverbank, he knelt a few feet from her, cupped water and drank, then splashed some over his face as she had. His lashes spiked wetly.

"We should go. We don't have any grub, so we'll have to wait until we get home to eat."

Kalen looked toward the horses. Though only feet away, in the few steps from the bedroll to the water, she'd found out how painful walking could be. Gritting her teeth she rose and took one step.

"Wait." Taylor caught up her reins and led the horse to her. Without a word, he circled her waist with his calloused hands and tossed her up as if she were a mite.

"Th . . . thank you."

Ignoring her, he leaped on his mount and leaned in the direction he expected the horse to go. Vexed, Kalen watched Creation head in the opposite direction she had planned to travel.

Though she protested, Taylor carried her to the back door, then rode on to the barn to care for the animals.

Doreen fixed her an early lunch. Then, having flown through her chores, she made Kalen comfortable. The cook wanted her to rest in bed, but Kalen insisted she remain in the kitchen. She wasn't sure she could climb the stairs just yet.

Taylor had already carried her around enough. She feared her confusing feelings for him might show if Doreen called him back to the house to carry her upstairs.

By nightfall, she had managed to walk up, one painful step at a time until, with a grateful sigh, she reached the top. Though she longed for a bath, she donned her nightrail instead. As she climbed into the feather bed, a knock sounded on her door.

"Who is it?"

"Blair."

"Come in." Exhausted from the long day, Kalen nonetheless managed a smile for her friend. "You made good time."

"One Bear escorted us most of the way." Blair's gaze flicked over Kalen's quilt-covered form. "How are you?"

"I'll live. Not sure I'll be able to do my chores for a few days, though." She patted the mattress, inviting Blair to sit.

"Not to worry." Blair hiked her bottom onto the mattress at the foot of the bed, and settled back against the footboard.

Easy for Blair to say. She didn't need to worry about a roof over her head or where her next meal would come from. And laid up like this, Kalen couldn't keep an eye on Uncle Jed. He'd stayed sober for weeks now, but there was no guarantee he wouldn't ride into Burnett Station and buy a bottle this very day.

The subject of her fretting walked in the door. "What'd the doctor have to say?"

"Doctor? I don't—"

"Doctor Summers." Impatience laced Jed's voice. "He didn't check you like Savage said he would?"

Horsefeathers! What, exactly, had Taylor told her uncle? "Umm . . . No. I . . . uh . . . I didn't think seein' a doctor was necessary."

"You're better'n the rest of us folks at figurin' what ails you?"

Kalen knew his worry about her prompted that sharp tone. She was sorry she'd caused him undue anxiety. But, dadburnit, Taylor Savage could bear some of the blame. "No. I figured if I could move everythin', nothin' was broken. No call to go to that expense, Uncle Jed."

He harrumphed. "Well, I coulda brung you back."

"Yes. I'm sorry I didn't ask you. Mr. Savage was concerned, so . . ." She shrugged, thinking it better to shut her mouth before she put a foot in it.

He glanced at Blair, his face as red as Kalen's when embarrassed. "Well, next time you get someone to find me. You hear?"

"Yes, Uncle Jed. Hopefully, there won't be a next time."

He harrumphed again and left.

Blair cleared her throat. "Uh . . . that's not the way I heard it, Kalen. Cameron said you struck for home and Taylor followed you." When she didn't answer, Blair persisted. "Why did you do that? You could have gotten lost or worse."

"I could have found my way back."

"Really? That's not what I heard, either."

"I don't care what you heard," Kalen snapped, then clamped her mouth shut. *Say no more. Let it go.*

But, bless her, Blair wouldn't. "Taylor was really worried."

Her pulse quickened. *He was?* "His attentions were elsewhere. I . . ." *Shut your mouth, Kalen Barrett!*

Blair tilted her head. "You mean Graceful Bird?"

Her stomach dropped.

"He isn't interested in her," Blair said.

"Oh, come on. He went to her tipi. You think I don't know what goes on when a man and woman are alone?"

Blair smiled, a bit more knowing than Kalen liked. It didn't take much wit for Blair to see into Kalen's head, into her heart, to see her feelings.

"Mother says men have needs. That's why some are willing to care for more than one wife."

"Your father had more than one wife? Miz Savage sat still for that?"

Blair chuckled. "Well, no. She would have pitched a hissy fit if Running Wolf even suggested such an arrangement." She raised a finger when Kalen started to interrupt. "But Taylor isn't married yet. Cameron avails himself of women, too. It's . . . their way. They don't mean anything by it."

"I wouldn't stand for it! If a man was interested in me, he would be interested in *me* and no one else."

"That's the way it is for Clay and Springflower. He has spoken for her, and they plan to mate before the fall festival."

"Fall festival?"

"One Bear offers prayers and dances of thanksgiving to the Spirits. It's like . . ." Her brow knitted. "Like he's bribing the gods to provide for his people during the coming winter."

Kalen's eyes widened, her gaze flying to the window where night had fallen. The nights *were* beginning to cool, heralding the end of summer. "That works?"

"Maybe. My father's people thrive while other Comanche have not. One Bear is a wise chief."

"With three wives," Kalen said dryly.

Blair laughed. "You know, Kalen, if Nathan asked me, I would sleep with him. He's . . . well"—her cheeks pinkened—"all man."

"Of course he is!"

Blair shook her head as if dealing with one not quite bright. "Just look at him, Kalen. Don't tell me you aren't curious about a man's, uh, anatomy."

Kalen gasped when she understood. "Absolutely not. That's . . . unseemly."

Blair broke into a belly laugh. "You protest too much!"

"I do not!"

"The kid needs her sleep, Blair."

Startled, Kalen looked toward the doorway where Taylor stood, Cameron at his shoulder. Though her nightrail was cotton and buttoned to the throat, she drew the cover up to her chin. And when she found her gaze settled on Taylor's *attributes*, she glanced away. Heat suffused her cheeks. Lord love a duck, had he heard their conversation? She would kill Blair for puttin' the thought in her mind.

"I was just leaving." Blair patted Kalen's hand. "See you in the morning." Her eyes sparkled with humor.

Drat! Blair had seen her discomfort and knew what caused it. *Oh yes*, Kalen vowed. *I'll kill her the next time we're alone.*

From the hallway, Lael said in a no-nonsense tone, "To bed, all of you. We've all had a long day." She peeked her head around the doorjamb. "Will you need something to help you sleep?"

Kalen's brow creased. Had Miz Savage brought home some of Pieces Of Sky Eyes's decoction? "No, ma'am, I'll sleep fine in this soft bed."

Cameron saluted her with a cocky grin. Taylor's dazzling eyes remained on her for an uncomfortable moment longer. Then he clasped his mother's arm and led her out of sight toward her bedroom.

It was some time before the quiver of awareness in Kalen's stomach settled and she fell into fitful sleep.

Warm hands cupped her face. Eyes the color of a twilight sky smiled at her as he leaned closer, closer. Soft lips touched hers.

She moaned and lifted her arms to circle his neck.

He was no longer there.

She looked around the dark space. Where am I? she wondered, frustrated that she had been unable to deepen the kiss.

"*Taylor,*" she murmured.

Restless, eyes barely opened, Kalen's voice echoed in the room. A dream, only a dream.

Having left the door ajar, Blair peeked into the room. "Kalen, did you call?"

"No, I dreamed . . . Go back to bed."

"I can get you something to sleep."

"I'm fine, Blair, really."

In his room, Taylor laid an arm across his wide-awake eyes. Restless, he turned on his side. A moment later, he again flopped onto his back.

He shouldn't have kissed her. Now, his thoughts centered on her soft lips, that supple body, its total awareness when he touched her. She was ripe for the taking, but he would not be the one. No, he would not repeat his father's mistake.

Long ago, One Bear had observed the way white people shunned Lael Savage, and he discussed the situation with him. "Running Wolf's mate will suffer more in my village. Son of Running Wolf take care of her in the white world, where she will be more content."

But no white man would look at his lovely, gentle mother since she had been *soiled* by a red man. Not that she longed for another mate. But if a man, a white man, stirred her heart, she should have the choice.

Her own kin had made it abundantly clear she was not welcome near them until after Running Wolf died. But then it was too late. Suspecting her father or brother had shot her husband, she no longer wanted her family. Their approval no longer mattered.

Taylor turned on his stomach and pulled the pillow over his head. He refused to make Kalen Barrett a pariah like his mother.

Chapter Thirteen

"You need not worry about chores for a few days, Kalen," Lael Savage said.

The woman's even temper fascinated Kalen. Didn't she ever raise her voice? Didn't she ever lose her temper? And what would her son say, Kalen wondered, if she lay around doin' nothin'?

"I'll go find my uncle, ma'am."

Seated in her usual spot by the fireplace, Miz Savage tipped her head. "Are you sure you can walk that far, my dear? If you don't get plenty of rest, those sprains will take much longer to heal."

That might be, but she wasn't about to sit still. "I'll be careful, ma'am."

A few minutes later, Kalen paused beside a corral and looped her arm over a cross slat. Lifting her heel to take pressure off her injured leg, she panted, glaring at the appendage. The walk from the house hadn't been more than a couple hundred feet, yet the infernal knee and ankle throbbed like a son of a gun. Like she'd run a footrace.

She gazed up at the arch of endless blue sky, felt the almost indefinable change in the air signaling the imminent arrival of fall. This was possibly her favorite time of year, the change of leaves, a bite in the evening air.

She glanced over her shoulder at the house, her gaze trailing from the chimney to the peak of the pitched roof and beyond. No doubt the Savages would fire up the hearth and that would send out a wood smoke fragrance that bespoke pumpkin pie, holly and maybe a dusting of snow by Christmas.

While Uncle Jed had grumbled and cussed the few times she could remember snowfall on the farm, she had welcomed it. Never stayed long enough to fuss about, and it was beautiful.

She smiled at the memory of take-your-breath-away crisp air and scooping up a handful of snow too dry to form a snowball. Cupping her hands, she'd buried her face in the fluff and licked up the coldness.

Off in the distance, in the pasture-sized corrals, two hands worked horses on long lines. Someone, likely Jasper or Morris, whistled in the barn. Taking a deep breath, she lowered her heel and tested the leg again. Bearable, but it was going to hurt for a spell. She might as well get used to it.

Hanging on to the fence, Kalen inched to the far side of the barn and peered into the woods. If she took her time, maybe she could get as far as the river. Soaking her ankle in the cold water would be good.

Taking slow, gimpy steps, after a time she made it into the trees and braced her hands on trunks to support her weight. She pulled up short at a clearing's edge. Creation grazed near the tree line on the far side of the small meadow.

Her brow creased. He was loose, and there seemed to be no one around. That horse was a smart one. Maybe he had learned to mouth the latch loose on his corral.

Well, however he had come to be free, she couldn't catch him. Not with her bum leg.

Prepared to go back and find someone, she caught movement out of the corner of her eye. Taylor sat on the ground, a blade of grass stuck in his mouth, his attention on Creation.

Curiosity piqued, she braced against a tree to watch. What was Taylor doin' lollin' away the mornin'? More important, why did he allow his stallion to roam free? Granted, the horse was well trained, but he would surely wander off if left unattended.

Gradually, Creation munched his way toward Taylor. When he got within ten feet, he raised his head and looked at his master, nickered and nodded. Taylor remained perfectly still. Staring down his horse, he pulled up another blade of grass and stuck it in his mouth. Creation again lowered his head to nibble on the grass, as well.

More baffled by the minute, Kalen almost spoke but clamped her mouth shut when Creation meandered until he stood directly in front of Taylor.

Lord love a duck, he'd just missed stepping on Taylor's outstretched legs, yet her boss hadn't moved a muscle. The big animal lowered his head and nuzzled Taylor's hat, then nipped it off and tossed it aside.

"Why did you do that, my friend?" Taylor asked as though speaking to a person.

Creation lowered his head very close to Taylor. The big man reached out with both hands and cupped each side of the horse's broad jowls. "Ah, I know you like me, Creation." Brushing the hair in a rhythmic motion, he smiled, "I like you, too, boy."

Taylor patted the jowls, then pushed his palm against Creation's nose. The horse backed up as Taylor gained his feet.

Kalen could no longer contain herself. "What are you doin', Mr. Savage?"

Taylor whipped his head around to stare at her. Then he raised a brow and shrugged. The horse turned his head toward her and blew.

"I didn't realize we had an audience." Taylor combed long fingers through Creation's mane. "We commune with each other like this at least once a week."

Commune. As in talk to each other? That didn't make a lick of sense. "Uh—"

"It's how we train our horses, kid."

She opened her mouth, then snapped it closed. The man was daft.

When she didn't say anything, he picked up his hat and walked toward her. Creation dogged his heels.

Taylor paused before her, his gaze darting to the foot she favored. "You should not have walked this far from the house. I left orders you were to rest."

Kalen inhaled deeply, smelling the unique fragrance that was Taylor Savage. Her stomach contracted. Then, what he'd said hit her. Her eyes narrowed. "You left *orders*? When I spoke to your mother this mornin', she didn't pass on any orders."

"Mother probably thought she didn't need to caution you. She is perfectly capable of managing when I'm not around."

Kalen wondered about that. Though Miz Savage was a marvel, how she got around and all, she sure as shootin' couldn't see what was goin' on or spy what had to be done. It wasn't Kalen's place to argue with her boss. Best just to head over to her original destination. She took a halting step.

"Where do you think you're going?"

Kalen scowled over her shoulder. "If it's any of your business, I'm walkin' down to the river to soak my ankle. The cold water'll do it good."

"I won't argue that, but you can soak it in a bucket at the house."

"I prefer the river, thank you."

Taylor watched Kalen limp a few steps and sighed. He knew that leg must hurt like the devil, but she'd never give in to it. He hiked his chin at Creation. The horse stared at him a moment, then nodded his magnificent head and ambled away, snatching up grass now and then as he headed for the barns.

Taylor fell in step with Kalen, until she glanced at him and stopped. She looked back the way she'd come. "What are you doin'? Your horse is roamin' loose."

"He'll find his way home. I'll accompany you to the river."

"Why?" She edged back, her golden eyes searching his.

No matter how often he told himself this woman was not for him, there was something about her that drew him. But no woman would share his blankets for a lifetime.

"The first reason," he said, "is because before long you will be in a lot of pain. You'll need my help getting back to the house."

"I don't think so."

He ignored her protest. "The second reason is that I'm going for a swim. There are few days left before the river will be too cold."

"You're crazy. It's frigid now!"

"I'll find out, won't I?"

With a very unladylike snort, she started off again. He itched to pick her up and carry her, but decided he would let her hang herself. By the time she reached the river, she would be sore enough that he banked on her not putting up too much fuss when he insisted on carrying her home. The mere thought tightened his groin.

Once more he told himself, *not a good idea*.

Kalen paused at a spot where the river was shallow. Against his better judgment, he clasped her upper arm to help her sit. He let go the instant she settled. When she started unlacing her boot, he picked up stones and tossed them in the river.

"You don't need to stick around, Mr. Savage."

"I will head upstream to swim, but I must make sure the river is clear."

Kalen looked down at the crystal water. "Clear? How could it be any clearer?"

"Water moccasins, kid. If any lurk under rocks or in deeper water, the stones will scare them away."

"Oh, I knew that," she said in a small voice, eyeing the water with new respect.

"Undoubtedly," he said dryly.

When Kalen eased her foot out of the boot, then peeled off her sock, Taylor had the strangest urge to stroke her white, delicate foot. Loco! Instead, he pivoted on his heel and stalked away. Best to distance himself from temptation. He hoped the river was indeed cold. His blood needed cooling.

Kalen watched him walk upstream. At last he paused, threw down his hat and removed his shirt. She sucked in a breath when his muscled back flexed as he pulled loose the drawstring on his buckskins. When he slid the pants down over his taut flanks, she stopped breathing altogether.

Mesmerized, she watched him shed his small clothes and stand gloriously naked, apparently not the least embarrassed. Darn that Blair for puttin' the burnin' curiosity into her mind!

Fortunately, or unfortunately, however one looked at it, Taylor turned just enough to hide his . . . *interestin' parts* from her avid stare. With no hesitation he walked right into the water and stroked upstream, away from her.

Just as well, she thought, gulping. She lowered her foot into the water and sucked in a shocked breath. The water was like a block of ice, which would certainly help the swelling in her ankle. Her gaze darted back to Taylor. How had he managed to plunge right in without hesitation?

Kalen didn't know how long she sat there, her foot dangling in the water. After a while it didn't matter. Her foot was numb. Taylor had swum out of sight around a bend. She glanced idly around, taking in the quiet, tranquil setting.

One would never know a thriving ranch operated just a few hundred yards away. She smiled at two squirrels snatching up acorns and popping them in their mouths.

Cheeks bulging, they scampered up a tree and disappeared into a hole just above the first branch notch. Moments later, whiskers twitching, both scrambled back to the ground and began the process over again. Busy as the dickens, those two, preparing for scant rations in the cold months. Nature sensed far sooner than man that winter was on the way.

Some yards downstream from where she sat, a deer ambled to the water's edge and lowered her delicate head to drink. Enthralled, Kalen barely breathed for fear the beautiful animal would spot her and dart away.

Much to Kalen's delight, a buck strode majestically out of the forest to the doe's side, and drank. Prob'ly mates, she thought, and smiled.

"It is time to go back to the house, kid."

Kalen jumped as if poked in the back. Jerking her head around, she stared up at Taylor Savage no more than three feet away. "Quit sneakin' up on me!"

She swung her gaze back to the lovely scene of moments ago. Both deer had disappeared as if never there. She pointed. "Two deer were drinkin', and you scared 'em away."

"I saw them." He shook his head. "But your voice is what scared them, kid."

She pouted and pulled her foot from the water. He was prob'ly right. But dadburnit . . . Childish, but she ignored his assessment. "I'll go back to the house when I'm ready."

She shook her foot, belatedly realizing she hadn't brought a towel. But Taylor hadn't, either. His wet hair trailed on his shoulders, his shirt soaked where it clung to his muscled chest. And his wet trousers outlined . . . *Don't think about it, Kalen!*

Taylor scooped up her boot and stuffed the sock inside. He thrust it into her hands. Unprepared, she grabbed the leather without thinking. And the next thing she knew, Taylor Savage had scooped her up as easily as he had her boot.

"Wh . . . Put me down!"

He paid her no mind, simply strode up the slight incline and wove through the trees.

"I know you're not deaf. Put me down!" Her stomach muscles jumped with awareness. His scent surrounded her; his heat seeped into her body everywhere they touched. And the arm supporting her back left his hand inches from her breast. *Horsefeathers.*

"Taylor . . ." She hoped she'd managed a put-me-down-right-this-minute-or-else tone in her voice. Apparently not. He sauntered on as if out for a leisurely stroll.

"Dammit!" She bit her lip on the oath. "I can walk."

"Yes. But pressure on your ankle will undo the good you did by soaking it in the water."

She peered at her dangling feet. He was right, darn it. The swelling was barely discernible. But, dadburnit, her insides shook with . . . need? Not good. Having never experienced a man's . . . attentions, she was flummoxed.

Glancing up, unable to see anything but his stubborn chin, she looked back down at her body and inwardly groaned. All he need do was look at her and see her nipples beaded beneath her shirt. No, not good at all. He would probably laugh at her if he realized what galloped through her mind, what brought her body to sexual awareness for the first time. He called her kid at every opportunity. A grown woman in his eyes she was not!

Despair seeped into her heart. She wanted to scream. *How can my body react to him, betray me this way? Not fair. Not fair at all. I don't even like the man.*

It was a lie. She sneaked another peek at his face, or tried to. Taylor Savage was admirable in many ways. He treated his mother with infinite care. His bantering with Blair and Cameron was endearing. And how he handled the horses revealed the inner man. He might look formidable, but he had a soft heart. She knew that right down to her soul.

Four-legged animals told the tale about a person far quicker than anyone with two legs. Just thinking how Taylor had interacted with Creation warmed her inside. She'd never seen anything like it.

If nothing else came of her employment here, she wanted to learn how he did it. It was as if he and Creation spoke the same language. *And what else would you expect to gain, Kalen Barrett?*

He glanced down at her, his step faltering, his

brow creased. He'd apparently felt her relax and wondered what she was up to. She smiled inwardly. *Keep him guessin'*.

As Taylor swung through the door into the kitchen, Doreen paused in chopping vegetables at the cutting board. "Och, you be hurtin' your wee ankle again, Kalen?"

"No, she did not. And she won't if I have anything to say about it," Taylor announced. He sailed past Doreen on his way to the stairs.

Kalen looked over his shoulder at Doreen's startled expression and couldn't stifle a giggle. The motherly woman would do anything for this family, but Kalen was sure the younger Savages often tried her patience. It wasn't that any of them were rude or treated her badly. On the contrary, they treated her as part of the family, and as such she had to take their ribbing or abrupt behavior in stride.

Before Taylor could bound up the stairs, Miz Savage stopped them in the parlor.

"Taylor? Kalen left the house some time ago—"

"I've got her."

At the same time, Kalen said, "I'm here, Miz Savage."

Lael's unseeing eyes searched out their direction. "Are you all right, Kalen?"

"She is fine, Moth—"

Kalen elbowed him. "I can answer for myself." She waited a beat. "Would you please put me down?"

"I'll take you to your room."

"I don't want to go to my room!" Lord love a duck, the man was overbearin'.

Before he could retort, Lael said, "I could use the company."

"Fine," he snapped, and deposited Kalen in his usual chair. He straightened, speaking directly to his mother. "I have chores left to do before supper. I will see you later, Mother."

Lael nodded in the general direction of her first-born. Kalen watched Taylor's impressive form through the front door until he was out of sight.

Such a good-lookin' devil.

She sighed and prepared to make small talk with the good-lookin' devil's mother—from whom she must also guard her blossoming feelings. Because Miz Savage had married an Indian, she'd probably prefer to welcome Graceful Bird into her family as her son's wife. She certainly wouldn't want Kalen Barrett for her son.

Never.

Though Kalen tried to rise above it by doing good work—and darn it, she did do good work—nevertheless, she was no more to the Savages than an itinerant worker.

Kalen looked over at the elegant woman she had come to love. She shook her head, glad Miz Savage couldn't see her expression. *Though gracious, how could this lady want me in her family?*

A drunk's niece.

Chapter Fourteen

A week later, Kalen strode out of the house, confident her leg had healed. She'd been up and down the stairs since yesterday with not a single ache or stiffness. Her shoulder was still tender, but she could work that out.

The air had taken on a distinct nip, and she breathed in with a smile. Fall was here.

"Kalen." Her uncle hailed her as he walked a gelding between fences. He stopped and waited for her to catch up.

Jed looked down at her leg. "No gimp."

"Thank goodness! I'm ready to work, Uncle Jed. Bein' cooped up in the house ain't for me."

Nolan Woodruff stepped out of the barn, leading a young colt that pranced and dodged from side to side. Full of vinegar, that one, Kalen thought, but the foreman kept a steady hand on the frisky animal.

"Several saddles need oilin', missy," Nolan said. "Morris will show you which ones."

Though disappointed Woodruff hadn't assigned

her to exercise horses, she understood his reluctance to trust her with the Savages' stock. Few women handled horses, though she had been doin' just that for the past six years. But . . . she'd been injured.

Patience, she cautioned. She'd helped with the birthing, yet that guaranteed her nothing. She would have to prove herself in every chore required on a ranch this size. And tack needed care almost as often as the infrequently ridden horses.

Kalen had no more than entered the barn when she heard pounding feet. Blair skidded around the wide door and stopped when she saw Kalen.

"You need to come," the girl said breathlessly. "It's Mother."

Panic flared in her friend's eyes, and Kalen fought back sudden concern. "What about your mother?"

"She has a high temperature."

Catching Kalen's hand, Blair turned back toward the house, dragging Kalen after her.

"Do you know how high it is?"

"Taylor said it must have been over one hundred during the night. I don't know now. Mother mumbles deliriously."

The two leaped onto the porch and ran into the house, the door banging shut behind them. "Your ma was just fine last night. Surely it ain't too serious," Kalen said.

Her observation did nothing to calm Blair or slow her pace. The girl bounded up the stairs, Kalen dogging her heels.

For the life of her, she didn't know what Blair expected her to do, but she'd be there for support if nothing else.

Seated on Miz Savage's bed, Taylor cradled his mother on his lap, her long hair cascading down his leg almost to the floor. He loosened the nightgown's ribbon at her throat.

Silly of her, she supposed, but Kalen's cheeks flamed in embarrassment for Miz Savage at her son's familiarity with her clothing.

Unable to help herself, Kalen paused and studied Taylor's broad, bare chest. He wore nothing but trousers. His mother's head lolled to one side, her face flushed.

"Do you know of a quick way to lower a fever?"

It took Kalen a second to realize he'd asked the question of her. "I . . . Tepid water should work."

Cameron hurried off and a short time later reentered the room from the adjacent bathroom. "Water's ready."

Taylor pressed his mother's head against his muscled chest and rose to his feet. Miz Savage's arms and legs dangled limp and lifeless. He strode into the adjacent room and with no hesitation, stepped into the tub and sank. Some of his mother's long tresses trailed to the floor; the rest floated in the water. Her white cotton gown billowed, then settled, a nearly, transparent film, over her body.

Water sloshed over the lip of the claw-foot tub, but Taylor paid no mind. Instead, he pulled a washcloth from a hook just over his head, dunked it in the water and began bathing his mother's flushed cheeks. He swiped the cloth over her throat, then splashed the tepid water in a little wave over her chest, her arms riding just above the water's surface.

Blair ran out of the bathroom and returned in a

few moments, mop in one hand and a bucket in the other. She began wiping up the water pooled around the tub.

"Kalen," Taylor said, capturing her attention. "I'm too wet. Check Mother's forehead; see if the temperature has lowered at all."

She wasn't sure her assessment would be of any use. After all, she had not touched Miz Savage's burning skin before.

As she knelt next to the tub, Taylor snapped more orders. "Cameron, strip Mother's bed. If Doreen is back from the general store ask her to make it up with clean sheets. If not, you do it."

Like his sister and Kalen herself, Cameron responded to his brother's command with alacrity.

"Well?" Taylor questioned.

When Kalen looked into his eyes, she realized he awaited her opinion, and not too patiently. She understood. Miz Savage was precious to her children.

Kalen laid her hand on the lady's forehead. Warm, not burning. Sitting back on her heels, Kalen cupped her own forehead.

Not much difference, she thought. Unsure, she leaned over and put her cheek against Lael's. And without thinking, she pressed her cheek against Taylor's.

Realizing her action was far too intimate, she jerked back, nearly landing on her bottom before catching herself by clasping the wet porcelain. Feeling her own cheeks flame from the gesture, she lowered her eyes. "She is only a little hotter than you."

She knew the discomfort was purely her own

when Taylor spoke again. "Out of the way, kid." He rose, carrying a dripping Lael with him. "Towel."

Blair dutifully complied, drying her mother's limbs and then Taylor, though not too effectively. He tracked water and wet footprints into his mother's room and across the rag rug.

Not having found Doreen, Cameron was just finishing changing the bed linen. He turned back the quilt as Taylor seated himself in a bedside chair.

Blair fetched more towels, and wrapped up her mother's dripping hair.

Not once had the lady opened her eyes. She appeared totally unaware of her children's ministrations as Blair helped Taylor peel away the wet nightgown and coax her lifeless arms into a dry one. Miz Savage spoke incoherently when Taylor laid her on the bed, then quite clearly murmured, "Wolf."

"Would that he were here," Blair said, her dark eyes bleak.

Leaning over his mother, Taylor caressed her check, then rested his big hand on her forehead.

Kalen stepped closer to the foot of the bed. "Does she feel cooler to you?" When he didn't answer right away, anxiety crept up Kalen's spine. "Mr. Savage?"

He finally shook his head and stood. "Maybe a little. We should keep her warm."

Without being told, Blair scurried from the room and back in a moment with a quilt. Taylor plucked the quilt from her and spread it over his mother.

In the quiet, all four stared at the unconscious woman. And Kalen knew from their expressions that each worried, each wondered what caused the fever, and each prayed they had done enough to relieve the ailment.

"She seems quieter, resting." Hope quivered in Blair's voice.

"Maybe I should go for the doctor," Cameron offered.

Taylor shook his head. "He wouldn't do anything more than we have." He again laid a palm on his mother's brow. "She is cooler." He smiled reassuringly at his sister. "Mother is strong. Whatever ails her, she will fight it off."

Her gaze lingering on her mother, Blair put on a brave little smile. "It's just that I can't ever remember seeing her sick before."

"Cameron, you and I need to get to work," Taylor said.

"I'll stay with her," Blair offered.

Kalen wondered if it would be an intrusion to remain, until Blair erased the indecision. "You'll stay, won't you?"

"Of course. If you think I can be of help."

Out of the corner of her eye, she saw Taylor's speculative regard. Rather than argue the point, though, he motioned his brother to follow him.

Over his shoulder he said, "Come for me if she worsens again."

Taylor's leaving settled Kalen's heart about worry over Miz Savage's condition. She didn't think, as protective as he was, that Taylor would leave if he truly thought she might be in danger.

As the day wore on, Doreen looked in on the two girls and offered to spell them, but neither Blair nor Kalen was of a mind to leave Lael.

Toward supper time, Miz Savage opened her eyes. Her head turned toward Kalen. "Taylor?" she murmured.

Kalen brushed her hand, lying limp on the quilt. "He's workin', ma'am."

A glimmer of a smile flitted over the lady's dry lips; then, she sank back into slumber.

From the other side of the bed, Blair leaned forward and put a hand to her mother's brow. She glanced at Kalen, a smile in her eyes. "She feels normal."

"I know." Searching her employer's peaceful face, Kalen blinked, then looked closer. Carefully, she pulled the lace collar of Lacl's nightrail away from her throat.

"What?" Blair questioned.

"Measles. Your mama has the measles."

Blair's mouth fell open, then clamped shut. Eyes wide, she asked, "Who would have guessed? Cameron and I had measles about the same time when I was, oh, eight, I think. If she escaped them as a child, you would think Mother would have contracted them then."

Within the hour, supper smells wafted upstairs. Kalen sent Blair ahead of her to eat. She'd wait until the Savages finished. Easier not to have to cover up her confused emotions when near Taylor Savage.

"Measles?"

Taylor laid aside his fork, astonished by Blair's announcement. "It's a wonder I didn't kill her, trying to lower her temperature the way I did. Could have driven the eruptions back inside." He sobered.

"Cameron, tomorrow, ride to One Bear's village and alert him. It has been awhile, but perhaps the sickness was germinating in Mother for several weeks."

Cameron and Blair had long since called it a day by the time Taylor climbed the stairs at ten. All were tired, partly due to the scare their mother had given them before sunrise this morning.

"Measles," he murmured, still astonished, yet thankful he had not compounded his mother's illness.

His thoughts turned to Kalen, whom he had not seen since morning. His sister had made Kalen's excuses at dinner; she preferred to sit with their mother while Blair joined her brothers.

He paused at his mother's door. Giving it a light push, the door, already ajar, swung open noiselessly. His eyes widened in surprise.

The kerosene lamp turned low on the night table illuminated Kalen. She slept curled on the floor, propped against his mother's bed. One of Kalen's hands touched his mother's fingers; the other lay in her lap.

The sight warmed his heart; his mouth curved in a smile. Kalen Barrett never failed to be prickly in his company, but he doubted not that she liked his mother and sister. Cameron, too.

He drank in the peaceful picture. Well, he couldn't leave Kalen there all night. Better wake her and send her to bed.

As he approached, his mother's eyes opened. Taylor bent over her, unsure if she was really awake, if she knew he was there.

"Taylor?" she whispered.

He squeezed her hand and leaned close so he could keep his voice low. "You gave us quite a scare, Mother." His gaze traveled over her face, now spotted, leaving no doubt that Lael Savage had a violent case of red measles. He would see if there was any calamine in the house. Before long, she would itch beyond bearing. "Can I get you some water?"

She shook her head. "She is still here, is she not?"

"Yes," he whispered.

"Such a dear," Lael said.

His gaze roamed over Kalen. He didn't know if she was a "dear," but for a change she was clean. She wore her usual work attire, a pair of jeans and a shirtwaist. While practical, the trousers and her tousled mop only enhanced her ability to pass for a boy or young man. He wondered if she even owned a dress.

He started to shake Kalen's shoulder, then thought better of it. Knowing how she reacted to him, he feared if she woke, she would insist upon keeping her vigil by his mother. She had put in enough time at the side of a sickbed. She needed rest.

In his bed.

Where had *that* come from? Thunderation, if he got Kalen into his bed, rest would be the furthest thing from his mind. His loins tightened.

He banished those thoughts as quickly as they had slithered into his mind and eyed her speculatively. Perhaps he could carry her to bed and not wake her. Worth a try. He gave his mother's hand another squeeze and whispered, "I will take her to her room."

Going down on one knee next to Kalen's sleeping form, he paused, savoring her scent. He slipped an arm beneath her knees and the other behind her back. She mumbled and turned toward him. Taking quick advantage, he lifted her as he rose. Her head lolled on his arm. She nestled her face against his chest and flung an arm over his shoulder.

He sucked in a breath and looked down at her peaceful face. She made a funny little sound in her throat that reminded him of a cat's purr.

Shaking off the wanting that never seemed to leave him, he carried Kalen into her room and laid her atop the covers. He unlaced her boots and set them next to the bed, then pulled a comforter from the bureau's bottom drawer and covered her.

Frozen for a moment, he watched her sleep, finally forcing himself to back away. If he stayed, he would succumb to the need roaring through him.

He shook his head in an effort to dispel his father's voice speaking Comanche in his mind. *"Po?sa."*

Crazy.

Chapter Fifteen

Kalen opened her eyes to faint light and frowned at the ceiling. *Mornin'? What is that noise?*

She angled her head and saw that she wore her clothes . . . in bed. That didn't make sense. Feeling drugged, she struggled up and looked dumbly at the window. "Rain."

Surprised, she threw off the comforter and moved to the window. Pushing aside the curtain, she watched water drizzle down the windowpanes.

The crops could certainly use the rain. She had seen wagons lumbering into the barnyard loaded with fresh-mown hay, no doubt raised somewhere on this ranch.

"Oh, bother," she heard Blair say out in the hall. "We do *not* need another sick one."

Who? Kalen wondered. Another measles patient? After lacing up her boots, she opened her door and peered into the dim hallway. "Who's ill?"

Blair turned to her. "Doreen. She sounds like she's going to cough up her insides."

"Bad cold?"

"Beats me. She has a fever, though, and says her body aches like she rode from here to Waco on top of a coach."

"Influenza?"

"Maybe," Cameron said.

"Where's your brother?"

"On his way to Harmon's place down river, maybe fifteen miles. He's delivering two horses."

"Blair," Lael Savage called from her room.

"I'm out of here," Cameron said. "I have work to do."

"And I don't?" Blair snapped before disappearing into her mother's room.

Indecisive, Kalen waited a moment, then followed Blair.

"Mother, I have no idea how to take care of Doreen. Says she feels awful. Looks like it, too!"

"Well," Miz Savage said, "for starters, she must stay abed."

Kalen glanced at Blair and bit back a chuckle at the girl's woebegone expression.

"And who cooks? You know I can barely boil water."

Lying against stacked pillows, Miz Savage looked like someone had splattered red paint on her face and forearms, the only portions of her skin not covered by the nightgown. Unconsciously, she started to scratch the back of one hand, then curled her fingers and dropped the hand to the bed.

"Do you have any calamine in the house, Blair?" Kalen asked.

Blair blinked as though she'd forgotten Kalen was there. "Maybe," she said.

"Your ma needs some for the bumps. I think she's beginnin' to itch."

"So I am," Lael agreed, an apologetic smile on her face. "You will find a bottle in the bathroom safe, Blair."

Moments later, Blair slathered the smelly goop on her mother's arms and face and throat.

"I will try not to scratch elsewhere. That is the only bottle we have. You will have to ration use." Miz Savage turned her head toward the door. "Kalen, are you still here?"

"Yes, ma'am."

"Do you know how to cook?"

"Um. Yes. Not so good as Doreen, but I cooked and kept Uncle Jed's house for a spell after Aunt Livvie passed."

Blair rolled her eyes to the ceiling. "Thank the Spirits! Will you cook while Doreen is down? Honest, I have failed every time she has tried to teach me anything in the kitchen."

Tarnation, she hadn't signed on for kitchen duty, but she couldn't very well abandon the Savages at this juncture. "Uh, I guess so."

"Oh, thank you!" Blair exclaimed. "I would never hear the end of it from Cameron and Taylor if I tried to cook."

"That settles that, then," Miz Savage said. "Blair, before you go to the barns, give Doreen a dose of Pieces Of Sky Eyes's decoction for fever she sent home with me. It's in the safe next to the tub. And make sure Doreen has plenty of water."

"You have something to relieve fever?"

"Yes."

Blair looked at Kalen, then back at her mother, exasperation evident in her expression. "We certainly could have used it for you if we had known it was here, Mother."

"Very likely, Blair. But I was not aware that I needed it until I woke early this morning with Kalen holding my hand."

Kalen felt the flush on her cheeks. She had fallen down on her duty, unable to stay awake the entire night.

"I thought perhaps she was in my room because I had been sicker than I realized when I fell asleep the other night."

"It's a good thing Taylor checks on you every morning before he leaves the house. You could have . . . Well, I shan't speculate, but you had all of us worried, Mother." Even now, Blair's eyes reflected the fear she had endured.

Two hours later, Kalen had cooked and served the upstairs patients breakfast and cleaned up the kitchen. She was a famously messy cook, dirtyin' every pot in the kitchen, Aunt Livvie used to say.

Miz Savage and Doreen now napped, which would help their recovery quicker than anything she might do.

Kalen walked into the parlor and planted her hands on her hips. Now what? She so seldom had idle time, she was at a loss what to do with it. Her glance traveled over all the books, but she didn't think reading was the proper pastime. She should work.

Though the tables didn't look neglected, she swiped a finger over a wooden surface. A bit of dusting might be just the thing to get her mind off what she'd rather do: exercise horses. Shoot, she'd rather clean stalls than do housework.

Glancing out the window, she grimaced. Maybe not today. The rain, though no longer a downpour, still came steadily.

Gathering a broom, a feather duster, a rag and a tin of beeswax, she set to work. Midafternoon, she stopped to make lemonade and carried a glassful to each of her patients. Miz Savage felt much better than Doreen, but the cook was grateful when Kalen assured her the kitchen chores would be done. Maybe not as well as Doreen would do them, but they'd get done.

Returning to the parlor, Kalen surveyed her handiwork, pleased with the few changes she'd made. She closed her eyes and took a deep breath, savoring the smell of freshly waxed furniture.

The chimes began to toll four o'clock. What to fix for supper?

A quick check with Doreen, and she rolled up her sleeves, ready to work.

At five-thirty, Kalen heard the back door open and close as she pulled a skillet of cornbread from the stove. "I'm almost finished, Blair. Still haven't set the table, though. Maybe you could do that."

"Where is Doreen?"

Startled by Taylor's deep voice, Kalen whipped

around, still holding the hot skillet. "Ow!" The cast iron pan banged on the stove top.

She stuck a burned thumb into her mouth. "Now look what you made me do." Scooping a finger through the lard, she slathered it on the burning thumb. The greasy glob melted immediately upon contact.

Taylor's crystal eyes danced for a second, but he didn't argue. Instead, he again asked, "Where is Doreen?"

"Abed. We think she has influenza."

"Why isn't Blair upstairs tending Mother and Doreen?"

"We drew straws and I lost," she said, even though it hadn't happened that way.

"So you are tending and cooking . . . what?"

She heard the skepticism in his voice, and even though she wasn't the best cook, his attitude riled her. "I can cook!"

He didn't need to know that Doreen had chopped all the vegetables the night before, that she'd set the stew beef simmering on the stove all night. All Kalen had done was dump in the vegetables and add salt and a little water to replenish what had boiled down overnight. But darn it, she had made fresh cornbread—that had come within a whisker of crumbling all over the floor a moment ago.

"You need not get your back up, Kalen. Did you hear me say you couldn't cook?"

"You thought it!"

"Now you are a sorceress? You can read my thoughts?"

He was obviously laughing at her. She fumed but kept her mouth shut this time. Better to see laughter in his eyes than censure. *You haven't seen that. Not really.*

When she didn't answer, he asked, "Do you know if my mother is awake?"

"Maybe. I took up lemonade and then water to her and Doreen about an hour ago."

"I'll check on her." He turned to leave the kitchen.

Kalen hastened after him. Surely he would notice the hard work she had done in the parlor.

Distracted by her idiotic hope to receive even a snippet of praise from the man, Kalen plowed into him when he abruptly stopped. She glanced past him, waiting for the compliment.

Instead, he rounded on her, his features darkened to raging anger. "What in thunderation have you done? Are you trying to kill my mother?"

Startled, not to mention miffed, she glared right back. "I broke my back cleanin' and rearrangin' furniture for a little bit of change and you yell at me? You are the most ungrateful, pigheaded—"

"Mother can't find her way now."

"—son of a gun I've ever had the displeasure of . . ." She closed her mouth with a snap. "What?"

"We haven't moved furniture since my mother went blind." Though his face was still suffused with anger, he managed a more reasonable tone. "She has learned the placement of everything and can get around alone if need be."

Kalen clapped a hand over her mouth "Lord love a duck. I never thought. I just . . ." She looked up with beseeching eyes. "I'm so sorry." Rushing past him, she picked up a footstool. "I'll put everythin' back right away."

"Kid."

"It may take a few minutes, but I'll . . ."

When she grabbed at the back of the couch to drag it back to the center of the room, he realized she hadn't heard him. "Kalen!"

Anguished amber eyes looked up at him, her hands trembling on the couch. How in hell had she moved the heavy furniture alone, anyway? "Leave it for now. Mother won't be down tonight. Cameron and I will move it back after supper."

She wagged her head, curls bobbing around her face. "No. I moved it. It's my responsibility to put it back like it was."

She put her slight weight into pulling the couch again, which moved all of a few inches. Her claim that she broke her back wasn't an exaggeration.

"Stop!"

She paid him no mind. *Stubborn little* . . . He strode over and clamped his hands over hers. "I said, stop."

Fire sliced through him, from his hands to his groin. Spirits of the gods, the mere touch of her skin set him ablaze. He snatched his hands away and stepped back from her small body, from her scent.

"Oh, my."

He glanced up at his sister's quiet exclamation. Both she and Cameron stood in the doorway, astonishment written on their faces.

Taylor shook his head sharply. He had already said enough. In fact, belatedly remembering Kalen's expectant expression when he flew off the handle, he should apologize. Later, he told himself. He wanted to avoid causing further chagrin for her in front of his brother and sister. She could not know the routines his family had developed over the years since his father's death.

He sent Blair and Kalen to the kitchen to finish supper preparation. Fortunately, both women complied. That freed him to run upstairs to check on his mother and briefly look in on Doreen. When he came back down a few minutes later, Cameron had already pushed the furniture back to a semblance of the original placement. Later, after all were abed, he would finish the job.

Chapter Sixteen

Long before daylight, the house quiet around her, Kalen crept from her bed, gathered her few belongings and stole outside. A drizzle remained from yesterday's steady rain.

She marched across the clearing into the little room originally assigned to her. No way could she fit into the Savages' household. She shouldn't dream of winning Taylor's love.

And who said she *wanted* his love? One day he would marry someone who knew him, someone whom his family liked and respected. Prob'ly Graceful Bird.

It would be better if she and Uncle Jed left. Well, maybe not better for him. Not since Aunt Livvie died had he worked so industriously, smiled more, yammered with the other hands. Most of all, though, he had struck up a good friendship with Mr. Woodruff.

After dumping her belongings in the room, promising herself to return after noon vittles and make up the bed for tonight, she hotfooted it to the barn.

"How's Miz Savage doin?" Nolan asked as he led a lanky gelding from a stall.

"Better." Even though Kalen hadn't seen her since the day before, surely she was. "Doreen is down now."

Nolan paused as he came abreast of her. "Doreen O'Donovan has measles?"

"Oh, no. Influenza. Croupin' somethin' awful yesterday. Quieter today, though." Another fabrication. For all she knew, Doreen hadn't improved one bit.

"Here." Nolan thrust the lead rope at her. "Take this fella down to the pasture next to the Turner's horse. He needs some grazin' rather than eatin' us out of house and home here in the barn."

Surprised, Kalen clasped the rope. Would miracles never cease? While it wasn't ridin' to exercise the horse, nevertheless, Mr. Woodruff was trustin' her with one of the Savages' paints.

When she got back to the barn for further orders, Blair was waiting for her.

"Mother will be upset when she finds out you've moved back to the bunkhouse room."

"I'm more comfortable there." She had messed up so badly, she was embarrassed to face Taylor again. He had every right to be angry with her.

Where did she get off thinkin' she could rearrange furniture that didn't belong to her, and in her boss's house, to boot?

Shoot, she'd never once considered her actions

would confuse Miz Savage. She'd never lived with a blind person before. Never even met one until that fine lady showed how efficiently she could function. That is, she could if Miss Nosey-Rosie remembered her place.

"Blair, if your ma asks for me, just tell her I prefer sleepin' here. The men don't bother me at all. Actually, most of 'em treat me like kin."

Kalen crossed her fingers behind her back. Maybe God would forgive her these little lies. Well, they weren't outright lies. A few of the men completely ignored her. Others did treat her, if not like kin, at least cordially.

As the days passed and Miz Savage didn't send for her, Kalen relaxed and again pitched into the daily routine. She became a bit vexed that the Savages seemed to ignore her, then admonished herself. Horsefeathers, she couldn't have it both ways!

It grew cooler, and one afternoon, as she returned to her room, she thought about the cold river. Maybe she could persuade the men to let her use the inside tub if she promised not to take long.

As she opened the door to her room, a shaft of light fell across her bed. A brown-paper-wrapped parcel lay atop the quilt. She frowned and glanced back outside. Who had been in her room? She stepped in and closed the door.

Though she had washed the window the same time she mopped the floor, the room was gloomy. She lit a lamp and turned the wick fairly low, then eyed the package. What was it and who had left it?

"You won't know if you don't open it, dummy," she muttered to herself.

Happy Birthday, Kalen was scrawled across the paper.

"It isn't my birthday."

Her uncle would know that. It wasn't his handwriting, anyway. Bewildered, she pulled the string and unwrapped the soft parcel. Her eyes widened as she lifted a sheepskin coat.

"There must be some mistake." She glanced around as if someone else had spoken.

She brushed her hand over the rawhide, then fingered the soft inner lining. Boy-howdy, this would be warm this winter. Still, she rewrapped the coat, tucked the parcel under her arm and exited her room. She needed to find the person who'd made the mistake.

Finding no one in the cook shack and getting no answer to her knock on the bunkhouse door, she entered the stallions' barn. Taylor, a lead rope coiled over his shoulder, stepped out of a stall leading a young stud by the halter.

"Can I have a word with you?"

He glanced up, unconsciously scratching the horse between the ears. "I'm on my way to the bull pen to give this guy a first lesson in obedience."

Intrigued, she momentarily forgot her mission. "Can I watch?"

He thought for a moment. "These young ones are easily distracted. If you can be totally quiet, and above all, still, I suppose you may." He brushed the colt's forelock and scratched his jowl.

She fell in step with him, then remembered the parcel. "Someone left this in my room by mistake. It's a beautiful coat, but it's not—"

"No mistake. It's yours." He strode on, the colt frisking at his side.

She paused, her mouth gaping, then skipped to catch up with his long strides.

"But it's not my birthday!"

Never hesitating, he shrugged. "Have you had one this year?"

"No. It's in December."

"There you go. An early present."

"Oh, come on! Do you expect me to believe that? And who bought it, anyway?"

"Blair. It's from the family."

She halted again, staring after him. When he kept right on toward the pen, she hastened after him. "Wait!"

He stopped and turned the yearling around. "Kalen, I told you not to distract this stud. He will be far more skittish than he already is if you don't quit yelling."

The stud's little hooves fairly danced in place, giving credence to Taylor's argument.

"I'm sorry; I don't mean to yell. But you aren't listenin' to me."

He cocked his head. "I heard every word. I also said the coat is yours. A little early, perhaps, but nonetheless a present—from my family. What do you not understand about that?"

He waited. Behind and above him, a red-tailed hawk lifted off a tree branch and soared up on a wind current. She blinked, distracted by the pretty sight. The horse's ears twitched; he tried to turn his head, but Taylor held him in place with his firm grip on the halter under the colt's throat latch.

"It's too early for my birthday," she finally said. "And employers don't give expensive presents to ranch hands."

He arched a brow. "Is that right? I don't know of a law to prevent us." A half smile twitched the corner of his mouth. He turned the colt around again. "Besides, it wasn't that expensive."

Easy for you to say.

Before she could retort, he said, "Kalen, if you want to watch, you better stop arguing and let me get this boy into the pen. Your palavering is making him more nervous."

Biting her lip, she followed, keeping well back from the horse's hindquarters. Taylor was right. The colt's tail arched prettily, his feet danced over the dirt, as nervous as a skunk protecting her young.

Kalen followed Taylor into the bull pen and closed the high, solid gate behind her. She stopped at a short fence built like a barrier bullfighters might scoot behind for safety in a bullring.

Taylor led the animal to the center of the small enclosure. She bit her tongue rather than ask why he clipped both ends of the lead rope to the halter at each side of the head.

Taylor's demeanor bespoke calm. Odd how he could do that without opening his mouth. And somehow she knew he had put her presence completely out of his mind, his total attention on the yearling.

He backed away, both hands on the lead as though plow-reining; then she realized that's exactly what he was doin'. Equal pressure on each side of the horse's head left no question that he simply wanted the horse to follow in a straight line.

Slowly backing away, Taylor pulled on the rein. The colt tossed his head, hesitantly taking one step, then two. Kalen's glance swung between Taylor and the colt, noticing man and animal never lost eye contact. Strange.

Patient as a cat crouched before a mouse hole, Taylor walked backward in an ever-widening circle. The colt gained confidence as time passed: five minutes, ten. When Taylor stopped, the colt kept walking until his soft muzzle pressed into Taylor's cupped hand.

They stood quietly looking at each other. Kalen fought to keep from fidgeting. If she drew attention to herself, Taylor would undoubtedly send her out of the pen.

After a moment, he trailed the rope through his hands as he walked away. When it tightened, he paused for a second, then stepped forward, leading the colt with the two-rein method. Ears tipped forward, the horse followed without hesitation. Taylor again traveled 'round and 'round for several minutes. Only this time, his route took him over a couple of tree branches. He made a big production of lifting his feet high to step over them.

Behind him, the horse balked at the first branch and shook his head, his tongue licking nervously. Taylor halted when he felt the resistance on the rope. Without turning, he waited. Kalen noticed a slight tug on the rein; then the tension relaxed.

After several gentle urgings, the stubborn horse stepped over the branch, then over the second one without a problem. Taylor led him around the ring, repeating the steps over branches.

He finally turned around and wound in the colt, scratched his jowl and patted his neck. "Good boy. Good boy." He released the clips, coiled the rope and slung it over his shoulder.

Clasping the halter, he walked toward Kalen and paused in front of her. "That's the beginning stage of how we train our horses. You did well, kid, staying quiet."

Except for the kid part, she basked in his praise. *Pathetic, Kalen.* "It's not much different than using a longe line."

"Snapping a whip to send a horse into a mindless circle is a useless exercise." He went through the gate. "I ask the horse to do what I'm doing. I show him he can put his confidence in my leadership. Similar to the way a stallion gains power in a wild herd."

Kalen frowned. "I've seen stallions fighin' tooth and nail."

"True enough, but once a stallion has established his dominance in a herd, he leads by example. That is how we train our horses."

When Kalen followed Taylor into the barn, she realized she trotted beside him as obediently as any animal. She stopped in her tracks and watched him put the horse away. He spent a moment rubbing the animal's back and flank, talking quietly.

Kalen found her gaze following his hands. Gentle hands. She shivered, fantasizing how those hands would feel brushing her skin, then watched his tight butt as he backed into the corridor and closed the gate.

"Pay attention to a horse's needs, take time to calm him, and he will do your bidding."

What about my needs?

"Kalen, are you listening?"

"What? Oh. Yes. Take time to calm a horse."

"Good." He strode past her. "I need to check on my mother."

Dreamily, Kalen admired his loose-gaited progress out of the barn. Not until he was out of sight did she shift the package and remember she wanted to give it back to him.

"Mr. Savage! Wait!" She sped after him. Too late. The back door closed as he entered the house.

"Horsefeathers." She'd rustle up Blair or Cameron and return the coat. While she did need a heavy winter coat, she would not accept such an expensive garment from her employer. Nope. Not Taylor Savage. Shoot, he wasn't handin' out gifts like that to Uncle Jed and Mr. Woodruff. Well, she didn't know about the foreman, but she did know if her uncle received such a gift, he sure as the Lord reigns on high would have told her about it.

Face flushed, she relived what she'd thought as she trudged back to her room. What was she supposed to do with the flock of butterflies that had taken up residence in her stomach? Shoot them?

She snorted. "My needs. Ha!"

Chapter Seventeen

"Taylor!"

He heard the exasperation in Blair's voice before she rounded the door into the parlor. Seeing the parcel in her hand, he groaned and closed the book in which he'd read all of one paragraph.

"What's going on? Kalen handed me this package. She said I shouldn't have bought such an expensive gift." She tossed the package at him. "What is it?"

"You bought Kalen a gift?" Lael asked.

Figuring it safer to ignore his mother's question, he spoke to his sister. "Have you noticed that excuse for a coat Kalen wears? It's threadbare. Wouldn't keep a chill off a polar bear."

Blair's brows knit. "Polar bears don't get chilled."

"Exactly."

She shook her head at his cryptic remark. "Well, why did you tell her I bought it?"

"You would have if you'd thought of it."

"Taylor! That doesn't make sense."

"I agree," Lael said.

Taylor tunneled fingers through his hair. Thunderation. Fire danced and crackled in the hearth; he inhaled the pleasant wood fragrance. Increasingly, he heard Kalen's voice, even when she wasn't there, saw her lithe frame riding a horse or walking from one place to another, noticed how she filled out a shirtwaist and jeans. When she'd covered most of those tantalizing curves, he'd noticed the coat. Or what passed for one. He sighed and looked at his mother's serene but expectant expression.

Blair still frowned. "She said you told her it was a birthday gift. And to beat all, she said her birthday isn't until December. Twentieth, I think. Way too soon for a gift."

That answered that question. "Look, Blair, you know Kalen doesn't like me. I noticed her poor excuse for a coat. Thunderation, the other morning she shivered so hard, her teeth chattered. I rode into Burnett Station that day, saw the coat and bought it. But had I offered it to her, she would have thrown it back in my face."

"Okaay," Blair halfheartedly agreed. "But you could have told me. Let me give it to her. Instead, she threw it in *my* face, and now she's riled."

"Riled? Hmm," Lael said. "Pride is a fragile thing. I sense Kalen is not used to many of the conveniences we have. Things we take for granted are luxuries to her."

"Luxuries? We live on a ranch. We work in the muck. We—"

"Have running water and a porcelain bathtub. A cook who caters to each of us. More than one set of linens. Blair, many consider these luxuries."

"Okay," Blair agreed more readily this time. "But my stars, Mother, we don't lord it over her. Or anyone else, for that matter. Taylor treats all the hands the same." She darted a glance at her brother. "Well, maybe he feels more for Nolan, but Kalen *is* a woman."

"What did you say to her, Blair? Exactly," Taylor asked.

"Nothing. I didn't have time. She shoved the package at me. Stated in no uncertain terms, 'Employers don't give expensive gifts to ranch hands, Blair,' then marched off."

"Fine. I'll take it to her, and this time she'll keep it."

"Taylor . . ." The door slammed on Blair's warning.

Lael chuckled. "Don't waste your breath, dear. Taylor will have it out with Kalen."

"You think? Perhaps it's the other way around, Mother."

Lael smiled and said nothing. Instead, she quietly hummed a ditty, picking up her cross-stitch embroidery. Feeling along stitches to where she had left off, she poked the needle into the fabric.

Coming out of the gloaming, Cameron paused. "Where you headed?"

"To have a word with the prickly miss in the shed."

"Kalen?"

"Is there another prickly miss I don't know about?" He sounded disgruntled, but he couldn't help it. The woman was more trouble than a pack of coyotes.

"I think she's on her way to the river."

"Surely not to bathe."

Cameron shrugged. "She had a pair of jeans and a shirt draped on her shoulder. Think I saw a towel in her hand, too."

"And you didn't stop her?"

"Uh, have you tried to persuade Kalen to change her mind if she's set on something?" He shook his head. "Won't happen."

Taylor started for the river at a lope, wondering what dealings had transpired between Cameron and Kalen to make him so sure of her reactions. "I'll take care of it."

"Sure you will," Cameron called.

His laughter followed Taylor.

As Taylor neared the river, he heard a high-pitched yelp and knew he was too late. Just as he cleared the trees, Kalen splashed out of the icy water as fast as her shaking legs would carry her.

"Lord . . . love . . . a . . . duck!" She chattered as she darted toward a pile of clothes. The temperature had noticeably dropped at sunset, and now, wet as an otter, Kalen must be chilled to the marrow.

Snatching up a towel, she swung it around her shoulders, but not before Taylor got an eyeful of luscious curves, nipples beaded from the cold, and a patch of dark hair at the apex of her thighs. His member jumped to attention so quickly, he sucked in a pained breath. Gathering his wits, he walked toward her, unwrapping the coat he'd bought for her.

She heard the crackling paper; her eyes grew big as saucers when she spotted him. "Get out of here!"

"I don't think so." He opened the coat and flung

it around her shoulders, pinning her bent arms to her body. He folded the front closed and pulled her next to his warm, buckskin-clad body. She shook so hard, her efforts to push away were futile.

"Be still, Kalen. Bathing in that cold river this time of year is addlepated."

"Huh. I had to. Eau de Manure is not my perfume of choice."

He barked a laugh. That sounded exactly like something his mother might say. "Be that as it may, you should have used a proper tub and *hot* water."

She reared back, her eyes narrowed. "Where do you get off tellin' me where to bathe?"

"I have more sense than you do." Outrage flared in her eyes. He spoke again before she could let loose. "It is dark. Coyotes, bears and who knows what else roam this time of day. You will *not* tempt fate on this ranch. On *my* ranch."

"Hogwash! Besides, surely your property doesn't extend this far." Though her mouth was set, she looked uncertain. And well she should.

"The ranch's boundary is over a mile north."

Petulant, she didn't dispute him, though he was not fooled to think she would concede. He bit back a grin when she further argued.

"It's a free country, Mr. Savage. I can bathe here if I want to. Now, go away."

Thunderation, they argued like two children. Inspecting her expression, he figured she felt the same. Well, he would not leave her here to catch her death, and it appeared she wouldn't listen to him anytime soon, so . . .

Silent, he scooped her up.

"Put me down!"

"Seems to me I've heard that before, Kalen. Now, close your mouth, or I'll sling you over my shoulder." He envisioned his hand riding on her rounded derriere and swallowed hard. *Let it go, Sound Of Wind.*

"It is likely to be uncomfortable." Besides, he preferred to have her body nestled against his chest, one hand pressed deliciously close to her breast.

She wiggled an arm free and pounded his chest. He let her legs drop, flattened her against him and captured the back of her head in a firm grip. "Kalen, I swear by all the Spirits . . ."

The scent that was uniquely hers lured him, lassoed him. He melted into amber eyes. He assured himself that he had followed her with the best of intentions, but when she was near a mischievous spirit seized him, shattered his wits. Unable to stop himself, he took her lips.

She opened her mouth and sucked in a startled breath. Though still trembling from the cold, she stopped pounding his chest and moaned ever so softly when his tongue darted inside her mouth.

Though separated by his buckskins and the coat, Kalen couldn't help but feel his pulsing member press against her belly. Instead of the protest he expected, she pressed closer. Her free hand slid over his shoulder. Considering her work, the fingers she tunneled through his thick hair felt surprisingly delicate.

He tore his eager mouth from hers to look into her flushed face. She seemed to linger on a precipice for a moment; then, her golden eyes opened. Staring up at him as if in a trance, her perusal traveled over his hair, his face, dropped to his lips, then went back up to his eyes. His body hummed as if her hands caressed him everywhere her gaze lingered.

"You said that wouldn't happen again," she quietly admonished.

"I know, but I . . ." He wanted her. That was certain. But from all accounts, she detested him. Except when she was in his arms—like now, this moment. Something in her eyes drew him.

He tiptoed along his own precipice, telling himself he was nothing if not honest. He took the plunge. "I want you."

Fragile butterflies seemed to explode, consumed by the flame that erupted in Kalen's stomach. Though she hadn't realized how much she'd wanted to hear him say that, now it seemed wrong. Maybe untruthful.

Her voice shook. "Graceful Bird."

He laid a finger over her lips. "Do not speak of her. It's you I want."

How could that be true? She had seen him with the Indian woman. And no one could miss Graceful Bird's worship of him. "Suddenly, you want *me*?"

His chest expanded on an inhaled breath. "Not so sudden, Kalen."

Before she could retort, he lowered his head and again kissed her. Even she, as inexperienced as she was, could not miss the passion in his embrace. Nor could she deny that she wanted him, too.

Savoring her own budding desire, she felt sparks flash through her as his warm lips traveled over her cheek to her jaw. His teeth nibbled her throat. "Oh, God," she murmured, and tried to get even closer to his strong body.

Still, sanity niggled against the rapture flying straight to her heart. "Taylor, we can't—"

"Yes, we can. And we will." Again, he swung her into his arms and recaptured her trembling lips.

She knew where his long-legged strides would lead, but could no more deny that she wanted Taylor to make love to her than she could halt her next breath. It made no sense.

Warm lips devoured her mouth, kindling a yearning to feel his hands on her body. Time meant nothing as reality dimmed. When he lowered her to the ground, she didn't know how far he had walked or where they were.

She opened her eyes and gazed up at his face, only inches from hers. Behind him it was dark, and it looked like . . . a cave? She drew her arms from around his neck, then pulled the coat's tail over her naked thighs and curled her fingers into the soft fur on which she sat. "Where are we?"

"A private place to commune with the Spirits. I come here often."

As her eyes adjusted to the darkness, she peered around. This cave had been dug into the side of an arroyo. Five steep steps carved into the hillside elevated the floor of the cave several feet above the bed of the rocky ravine.

No more than seven feet from entrance to back wall, she looked out on the world in relative safety. A gully washer surging through the arroyo would flow by, leaving the cave fairly dry. She could stand straight, but Taylor had to stoop.

She twisted around, inspecting the cave's perimeter. The entire floor was covered with skins, probably bear. Close to the entrance but protected by the overhang, a shield hung from a lance braced by crossed sticks.

Following her wide-eyed inspection, Taylor said, "My war shield."

"Wa . . . war shield?"

"Though the Comanche of my family no longer war with the white man, I still honor my heritage, Kalen."

"Does anyone else come here?"

"I found it one day after my father rode into the Spirit World. I claimed it for myself, though my father's spirit lingered here for a long time."

She suppressed a shiver, but couldn't prevent another quick glance around. Was his ghost still here? *Stop it, Kalen. You don't believe in ghosts.*

"One Bear knows of my private place, but he knows not where. Nor do I know where he communes with the Spirits."

Kneeling on one knee beside her, he brushed a tendril of hair from her cheek. "You are the only one I have ever brought here."

Warmed by that revelation, she inhaled quick breaths to still her madly beating heart. "Do. . . . do Cameron and Blair have—?"

"No. Cameron never sought a vision quest to find his totem. Few Comanche women ever warred. Certainly not Blair."

As he spoke, Taylor moved to settle behind Kalen, facing the dark night. He clasped her shoulders and pulled her against his chest. His breath tickled her cheek, sending shivers through her.

"Night brings out the nocturnal creatures, Kalen. Watch and remain quiet."

His arms circled around just below her breasts; his chin rested atop her head. Though her bare legs were chilled, she sank against his warmth, laying her hands on his forearms.

The only sound was the occasional owl hoot. Aware, so aware of Taylor's hard body protecting her, she sucked in a shaky breath and wondered if he had changed his mind. Maybe he was giving her time to think about what they planned to do.

God would prob'ly get her for it, but for danged sure she hadn't changed *her* mind. Was it so wrong to make love with a man while unwed? Shoot, humans weren't much different from four-legged animals. To her mind, the only difference was critters didn't have worry and sorry buttons in their brains like humans. A body worried if something was a sin, then was sorry if he went ahead and did it, most times still unsure whether he'd sinned.

She searched the heavens studded with faraway stars, perhaps other worlds. If the Good Book were true, maybe heaven was tucked behind one of those brilliant sparklers. Or maybe one of them was actually heaven.

"Look!" Taylor spoke softly in her ear.

Lost in thought, she blinked to focus. "What?" she whispered.

"Behind that cedar break. Wait." He pointed. "There!"

A large bear ambled from behind the cedars, followed by not one, but two cubs. Fretful-like, one cub whined. His mama stopped, swung her head around and looked at her babies. The larger cub rose up on its hindquarters and pushed the complaining one over. At that, the little guy really set up a ruckus.

At the same time Kalen clamped a hand over her mouth to stop a laugh, a low rumble erupted from mother bear. She cuffed the aggressive cub on the head, sending him head-over-teakettle. Then, she sat down and waited for both cubs to mosey to her side.

While she didn't appear to hurt him, she put a paw atop the bigger cub so that he couldn't move, and with the other paw scooped up the smaller cub and cuddled him.

Kalen craned her head to look up at Taylor. "Isn't that sweet?" she whispered.

Taylor drew his attention from the tableau and looked at her. Smile slowly fading, his eyes roamed over her face, finally settling on her lips. "Very sweet," he murmured, then kissed her.

Chapter Eighteen

Kalen opened to Taylor's exploring tongue and moaned softly when his fingers trailed between her breasts all the way to her waist. He flattened his calloused hand on her belly. A belly that quivered so badly, she shook from the sparks of need erupting inside.

Taylor turned her in his arms and laid her back atop the warm fur. Braced on his side, he separated the coat, baring her naked flesh to cool air. Her nipples beaded. His big hand brushed over her shoulder and cupped her throat. She knew he would feel the fast flutter of her pulse, as though the butterflies sought to escape.

Taylor's warm lips moved across her cheek. She shivered when his tongue laved her ear, then nipped the lobe. He pulled back.

"Have you ever been with a man, Kalen?"

What if she said no? Would he stop? She didn't want him to stop. But she couldn't lie, so she shook her head.

* * *

A virgin. At her age. Amazed, though oddly blessed, Taylor tucked one wayward curl behind her ear, giving himself time. Time to . . . what? He wanted nothing more than to take Kalen to the edge of the stars. But should he be the one to take her maidenhead? She would likely wish to marry someday.

Unlike Indian maidens who often bedded warriors before mating, white women did not. Those who did were called whores. He masked a grimace. Kalen might be labeled whore if he . . .

"Taylor?"

He blinked away his troubling reverie and met her searching eyes. "You are untouched."

She placed her hand over his fondling her breast. "Not entirely." A small smile played on her lips.

He rolled her nipple between his thumb and forefinger, and she sucked in a breath.

"This is pleasuring before passion, Kalen." His calloused fingers brushed down to her belly and circled her belly button. He leaned down and licked her skin. "This pleasures both of us," he said as his warm breath lowered, and then he pressed an open-mouthed kiss just above her mons.

Her belly contracted as she inhaled shakily. "H . . . how does it pleasure you?"

He smiled into the kisses as he traveled across her stomach to her hip and nuzzled the top of her thigh. "Your soft skin, your scent arouse me." He licked her skin as if savoring hand-churned ice cream from a spoon. "You taste womanly, uniquely you, Kalen."

"Can I taste you?"

He groaned, his member pulsing so strongly he

wondered if he'd spill his seed without coming close to her heaven. Sitting back, he pulled his buckskin shirt over his head.

Kalen's gaze traveled across his broad chest. She reached up and brushed fingers over a flat nipple. Taylor drew in a quick breath as his nipple pebbled just as hers had.

She did it again and followed with a kiss on that responsive flesh. He trembled.

"We should not take this further, Kalen. Should I take you, it would be—"

"Heavenly." She blinked rapidly; a hesitant, questioning expression etched her face.

"There is more to consider. If I take you, you will be branded as my mother was, forever considered unfit to marry a white man."

Her eyes widened. "What?"

He tucked a shiny curl behind her ear. "Someday a white man will wish to claim you. If you are unchaste, he will think you are a loose woman."

Eyes narrowed, she jabbed a finger into his chest. "Wait just a minute! I don't cotton to that kind of thinkin'. Your mother is a wonderful person. She—"

His expression turned to stone. "Her father and brother do not agree."

Blair's words rang in Kalen's head. *Mother believes her father or her brother Ben shot my father.*

Kalen laid her hand on Taylor's bare, warm chest. He shuddered, but eager to make her point, she ignored his response to her touch. "That kind of thinkin' is what keeps Indians and whites at each other's throats. I lost my family to Indians, Taylor, but I can't hate every single Indian I see. It's just not ... neighborly," she finished lamely, wishing she had the words to express her feelings. "Maybe her family didn't have anythin' to do with your father's death."

Taylor gathered her close and stroked her cheek. "My mother banished her family from her heart. Running Wolf is dead. There is no going back. It is today that I speak of, and I am sure of white men's perceptions if I lie with you."

She started to protest, but he laid a finger on her lips and shook his head. "I will pleasure you."

"No. You ..." The protest stuck in her throat when his hand settled against her nether parts and began to stroke. "Don't." She sounded weak. Unconvincing, even to herself.

"Shh." He pressed her into the fur. "You will like it. I will take you to the edge of the stars. I promise."

Her breath hitching, she already savored how he made her feel. But, somehow, she didn't think what he had planned would be as fulfilling as coupling.

But he had magical fingers and lips. Her senses took flight when he suckled first one nipple, then the other. His busy fingers stroked and coaxed until she was wet with wanting.

When his mouth took the place of his fingers, her eyes shot open. She half rose from the shock and startling pleasure that seized her. "Taylor!"

He didn't answer. Instead, his mouth continued its exquisite torture while his fingers played her nipples. She moaned, dug her fingers into the fur beneath her. Unable to remain still, she arched up against his tongue.

He responded with a soft chuckle as he suckled and licked. Her eyes glazed over as she indeed soared to the edge of the stars as he'd promised.

Kalen continued to gasp and moan softly, her legs shaking with the aftershocks. Taylor didn't want to leave her like this. She had experienced pleasure, but there could be more to come if he entered her. Far more.

His member strained painfully against his buckskins. Rising over her on hands and knees, he smiled at the flush of satiation on her cheeks.

She opened eyes still dark with desire. "Taylor," she whispered.

Before he realized her intent, she had pulled the drawstring on his buckskins. Her fingers tightened around his penis, his bare penis. He strangled, gasping for breath. "No. We cannot."

"Finish it, Taylor. Make love to me."

He was a fool to think he could offer her less than penetration. She worked on a farm around all kinds of stock. She saw animals mindlessly humping anything that walked by. Though he had introduced her to his way of pleasuring before taking a woman, she wanted all of it. So did he, even though the Spirits in his mind chanted, *"No, no."*

Staring into her beautiful eyes, he slowly lowered his body until his cock nudged her wet entrance. With his resolve shattered, he pleaded for her help. "Kalen, it's wrong for me to do this, for us to do this."

She nibbled his lips, then shook her head. "I won't argue that point, Taylor. But I want to experience lovemaking . . . with you." She grasped his shoulders and pulled him closer.

As his penis penetrated her passage, she curled her legs around his hips. Sweating, holding back with the last of his dwindling willpower, he murmured, "It will hurt."

She nodded, a smile on her face. He pushed forward and felt the thin barrier give way.

"Ah." She grimaced and exhaled a breath, then roughly pulled him down and claimed his lips.

Taylor lay still while Kalen ravaged his mouth. Her way of handling the quick pain, he supposed. He waited a moment, allowing her to adjust to his size; then, he took over the intense kiss, easing the pressure, lingering on her lips. Savoring her taste.

He began to move, slowly at first. Kalen instinctively lifted her hips, meeting his thrusts. Together they set the age-old rhythm that built and built as they climbed right back to the edge of the stars— this time, together.

Moments later, he lay heavily atop her, his face nestled against her neck, unable to muster the strength to lift his weight. It didn't seem to matter to her that he crushed her slighter body. Her arms circled his torso, squeezing him close. Her breathing rasped, matching his.

Spent, he nevertheless managed to lift his chest enough to look into her face. Her eyes were closed, and a smile played on her lips. Her lashes fluttered. The smile widened as she met his eyes.

"You keep your promises."

* * *

The next morning, a knock on her door roused Kalen. Sleepily, she glanced around, unable to get her bearings. When had she come back to her room? The last she remembered, she lay in Taylor's arms.

The knock sounded again. "Kalen?"

Uncle Jed. Bright as the dickens, light flooded through the window. *What time is it?*

She clambered out of bed, calling, "Just a minute," then realized she was stark naked. A blush warmed her cheeks as she yanked on trousers and a shirt, buttoning up as she strode to the door.

Silhouetted against the brilliant sunshine, she couldn't see her uncle's face, but she heard his curiosity and underlying concern. "You feelin' poorly this mornin', Kalen? You're lookin' a mite feverish."

Uh-oh, the blush shows. "I'm fine, Uncle Jed." She squinted against the glare. "What time is it?"

"Eight o'clock. Ain't like you to sleep so late, 'lessen you're sick."

"Well, I'm not. I'll be right there, soon as I get my socks and boots on."

"See that you do, girl. Nolan's put you with me today to exercise one of the young studs."

"Me? I get to ride? Hallelujah!"

"Yeah. Miss Blair's busy, and Savage don't want no man's weight on the little feller's back just yet."

Kalen spun around, rummaged beneath her cot, and came up with her last clean pair of socks. She'd have to wash tonight, but right now . . . A smile split her face as she rushed out to follow her uncle.

Though the paint stood no more than fourteen hands, Kalen still had to ask for a knee up.

The young stud had allowed the hackamore with no balking, but Kalen chose to take a page out of Taylor's book and school the young horse slowly to a rider. No saddle for a day or two while he got used to minimum weight on his back.

Sitting as carefully as possible, Kalen felt soreness between her legs. She hoped her uncle hadn't seen her grimace as she took up the reins and waited for the horse to settle. Wrapping her legs around his belly, her thigh muscles screamed, reminding her of the previous night's activities. The swaying motion sent little shocks of awareness to parts Taylor had awakened so vividly.

She swallowed, determined to concentrate on the colt as he tossed his head, sidestepped, then backed a few paces. Fortunately, he didn't buck.

"He ain't too balky."

Focusing on the horse's twitching ears, Kalen murmured, "He's a good boy."

Sure enough, his ears flicked back, and he nodded as if he agreed. She chuckled and brushed her hand on his withers. "Good boy," she praised again as the horse stopped fidgeting.

It really worked, this gentle approach. Though uneasy, he didn't fear humans. That meant Taylor, or someone, had spent a lot of time touching, brushing, draping a pad on his back . . . and probably leading him around like Kalen had seen Taylor do with the other horse.

"How's it goin'?" Mr. Woodruff asked.

Kalen let her uncle answer rather than split her attention as she set the horse to a slow lope.

"Surprisin' how easy that horse is to work," Jed said. "I'd a bet the best bottle o' whiskey in Texas that he'd buck, but he ain't raised a hoof."

Kalen flicked a quick glance at Mr. Woodruff. He lifted his hat and scratched his gray head. "Savage stock don't usually buck, Jed. One of the Savage kids takes 'im from his mama and starts handlin' 'im before he's weaned. Thataway, he ain't never spooked by two-legged folks." Woodruff resettled his sweat-stained, faded brown Stetson. "In all the years I've been here, I never did see a horse buck. Instead of runnin' away, they follow folks like pups."

Leaning back, Kalen said, "Whoa," gratified when the young horse slowed. True, this horse had been handled by a master trainer. Though her sole purpose was to exercise, not to teach, she hoped to follow around after Taylor, Cameron or Blair and learn their tricks.

Near dusk, as she led another horse back to a paddock for the night, she saw Taylor riding toward her down the corridor. Simply looking at him, she felt her cheeks warm, and she vividly remembered last night. She felt a rush of wetness between her legs. Admonishing herself for the wanton reaction, she breathed deeply and closed the gate's latch.

She didn't know what Taylor would think of last night's doin's. Actually, she had been the one to seduce him, but the man's mouth and hands had been amazin'. She'd experienced feelin's that would sing in her heart for a long time. And they'd have to, she thought soberly. One day he would take Graceful Bird to wife, not her. He'd take Graceful Bird to bed each night.

* * *

Taylor dismounted and palmed the reins. Today he'd ridden Comanche Moon. Both of his favorite stallions willingly trotted after him. They were spirited rides, yet each had a definite personality. Comanche Moon loved to jump, while Creation relished a run toward the horizon.

Kalen wore the coat he'd given her, which pleased him. The sun was near to setting, the air chilly. His breath fogged before his face as he eyed her warily. What he had allowed to happen the night before was wrong. A white woman married the man she slept with. That was the way of their world. But he would not take Kalen to wife. Her uncle might disown her, as the Taylors had his mother so long ago.

His gaze swept her slight form. "Are you all right?"

Kalen ducked her head and scuffed the dirt with a boot heel. "Yes," she murmured just above a whisper.

Taylor sighed, thankful he had some news that would keep them both occupied for a couple days. By then he vowed to have his carnal urges under control.

"One Bear and a few of his people will be here by nightfall."

She blinked. "Really? I didn't know they ventured from their village."

Kalen fell into step. He fought against sudden desire when her scent enveloped him. It was best they part company. And they would as soon as they reached the barn. Thank the Spirits.

"You will have to move back to the house. The

women One Bear brings stay in the spare room you have occupied."

She glanced up, eyes narrowed. "Women? Who? Which ones?"

What difference did that make? He wondered at the sudden tightening of her jaw, though his concern centered on his own dilemma. It was so difficult to have Kalen across the hall, but in his mother's house he could—would—must—curb his desire. "I know not. My uncle may come with a few warriors, or he may bring a dozen people. We never know until he arrives."

"Uh, how long will they be here?"

He cast a sidelong glance her way. She appeared to ignore him, but her cheeks were unnaturally red, and he doubted it was from windburn. Perhaps she was as uncomfortable as he about sleeping near his bed, but it could not be helped.

"One Bear is welcome here for as long as he wishes to stay."

"Why doesn't *he* stay in your house?"

Taylor laughed, picturing One Bear's consternation if offered such confinement. One Bear might tolerate wooden structures in his village, even see the advantages of a large lodge house for meetings, but he preferred a tipi for his personal quarters.

"Only the women will stay in the room. He and his men will pitch tents."

Kalen paused, forcing him to stop, too. "I don't mean to be nosey, Mr. Sav—uh, Taylor—but if your father lived in the house, why can't his brother?"

Taylor thought back to the only argument he had

ever heard between his mother and father. It had been over building the house, and then how large it would be.

Running Wolf could see no reason for a wooden structure in which to raise his family. For generations his people had lived in tipis, pulling up and moving with the seasons or the need to find better pasture for the tribe's hundreds of horses.

But his mother had been adamant. "You have settled this land. We will build a house like the one in which I was raised, Wolf, only larger. I intend to have ten children!"

Taylor had been only five or six at the time, but he still remembered his father's chest filling as if he'd burst with pride. His mother surely believed Running Wolf's medicine was powerful if she thought he would sire so many offspring.

The house had been built as it stood today. Then, after Blair's birth, his mother had decided three, rather than ten, was enough. She had gone to the tribe's shaman for assistance. Whatever the Indian had given her worked, for she had not conceived again.

Taylor was not fool enough to believe his father had refrained from making love to his mate. Running Wolf had been a powerful, resourceful warrior and virile as a stallion.

Perhaps I am as virile as my father. I must not tempt fate and make love to Kalen again. It would not do for her to become pregnant from his seed.

A pang of regret plucked at his heart. He would never see any woman grow round with his babe.

Forcing himself from that melancholy thought, Taylor glanced at Kalen's earnest-faced attention. Apparently, she really was curious.

"I suspect One Bear is uncomfortable living as white men do, just as my father was. For many centuries, the tipi has functioned well for Indians. There is little reason to change."

Just as there is no justification for me to tempt fate and again take Kalen Barrett.

Chapter Nineteen

"Kalen? Is that you?"

"Yes, ma'am. Horsefeathers," she muttered. Miz Savage could probably hear a fly land on the table. But how did she know *who* had entered the house?

A gunnysack full of dirty laundry in one hand, a satchel in the other, Kalen paused at the parlor's threshold, thankful her flushed cheeks would go unseen by this elegant woman. Lordy, she had slept with her son!

Miz Savage sat in her usual place beside the hearth. Fire crackled, chasing away the day's chill. A book lay open on her lap, a finger poised on the page.

A book? What was she doin' with a book? Kalen took a few steps into the room and saw nothing but blank pages. Now that didn't make a lick of sense.

"I thought that was you." Miz Savage closed the book. "I was passing the time reading."

"Reading? How . . . ?" Kalen clamped her mouth shut.

Lael smiled. "I have found a few books published

in Braille." She beckoned. "Those of us who cannot see use these raised bumps to read." She opened the book. "Here. Run a finger over the page."

Kalen dropped the gunnysack beside her feet. Her finger skimmed a series of little bumps readily felt but not easily seen.

"Each of those sets of bumps is a letter, Kalen. Each word is spelled out one letter at a time."

"Tarnation. That's somethin'!" She squinted at the faint markings. "You can read a whole book thataway?"

"Yes. Quicker than you might imagine." Closing the book again, she turned to Kalen. "Your room is ready for you."

My room? Not likely. But she didn't argue the point with Miz Savage. "Thanks."

"Inform Doreen that you'll be joining us for supper this evening."

"I don't—"

"Perhaps your uncle might wish to join us, also?"

"Uncle Jed—"

"One Bear will be at the table, as may others from his party."

"Uh . . ." Bad enough when Uncle Jed found out Indians would be campin' on the ranch. He'd likely have a conniption if he found 'em inside the house at the supper table. Didn't look as like she'd wiggle *her* way out of eatin' with the family, though.

"I'll ask 'im," she lied, "but don't count on 'im, ma'am."

As was his due as chief of his band, One Bear sat at the head of the formal dining table. Taylor took his mother's usual place at the foot. The women and Cameron sat on either side.

Kalen was amazed at how at ease One Bear seemed. While he didn't crack a single smile, his speech was cordial, even flowery when he commanded the conversation . . . which was often.

She was glad the women's voices were still. It was bad enough to sit beside Miz Savage, who might think Kalen had betrayed her trust. And every time she glanced Taylor's way, Kalen's cheeks got so warm she felt feverish.

Four small tents had been pitched behind the stud barn. Besides Nathan and Clay, Kalen had seen two other men from the tribe. But what really intruded upon her comfort was Graceful Bird, one of three women cooking for the visiting men who had not joined the Savage family in the house for supper. Did they need three women?

One Bear leveled his dark eyes at Taylor down the table's length. "Sound Of Wind, no usual make trade while eat." He shrugged one pelt-covered shoulder. "Maiden need *cíen*—one—gelding, carry belongings. I trade," he paused and counted his fingers, "*cíen, uah, pieste.*" Then he backed up and extended two fingers. "*Uah* bear pelts." He nodded. "Okay, *cíen* horse."

"Sound Of Wind?"

Kalen didn't realize she'd spoken aloud until Blair turned to her and whispered, "That's Taylor's Indian name."

"Odd," she murmured, and hoped no one heard the exchange.

Kalen sure as shootin' didn't understand why

Blair fluttered her fingers in front of her mouth. "Huh?"

"Tell you later," Blair whispered.

Doreen carried a bowl in from the kitchen. Taylor never missed a beat as he took the delicious smelling chicken and dumplings heaped above the rim and set it close to his mother.

Speaking as gravely as One Bear had, Taylor countered, "One Savage gelding is worth three bear and three beaver pelts."

One Bear spoke as Miz Savage began serving the plates stacked in front of her. "No so many. Two bear, maybe one beaver."

Kalen noticed he quickly picked up the English words for numbers.

Blair took a plate and hiked her chin, indicating that Kalen should pass it on. She set the plate before Mr. One Bear. He paid her no attention.

Not surprised, Kalen suspected thanks from an Indian man to a lowly woman would not happen in her lifetime.

"My uncle, I will settle for two bear and two beaver pelts. No less."

Choosing not to respond, the older Indian took up a spoon—a spoon! Kalen marveled—and began eating. At the village, most of the Indians had used their fingers or poured directly from a bowl into their mouths. She remembered seeing a few men using dangerously sharp blades as eating utensils.

Nothing was said for several minutes as all followed One Bear's lead. Having missed the noon meal, Kalen didn't need to be prompted twice.

Oh, my. She closed her eyes and swirled a tasty,

tender dumpling in her mouth. Doreen could cook like nobody's business! Opening her eyes, she found Taylor watching her, his eyes dark, a smile barely lifting his lips. Kalen ducked her head to hide her heated blush.

Fortunately, Mr. One Bear chose that moment to speak again. "You bargain Running Wolf way."

Taylor inclined his head. "Thank you."

Kalen looked at the staid Indian's face and saw a measure of pride there. She suspected it was for his nephew.

No matter how white folks tried to paint Indians as vile savages, she knew better. Yep, they had dark skin and warred on the white man, but usually to protect what they considered their homeland. In the village, Kalen had witnessed for herself that they laughed and they cried. And they possessed an inordinate amount of pride.

Following supper, Kalen waited only long enough for the Savages to bid Mr. One Bear good night; then, she scooted up the stairs before being corralled into small talk in the parlor. Tired from the long day, she preferred peace and solitude. Besides, the room she occupied was exceptionally comfortable. There was space for a chair and a tall bureau in addition to the soft bed.

She'd no more than changed into her nightgown when a light tap sounded. "Kalen? You still awake?" Blair's soft query came though the panel.

Sighing, Kalen crawled between the crisp sheets before answering. "Come in."

Blair had also changed into a flannel nightgown, and for the first time, Kalen saw the young woman's abundant hair unbound and hanging almost long enough to sit upon. Thick and shiny, the tresses framed her delicate features.

As she settled on the foot of Kalen's bed, Blair brushed her hair back over one shoulder. "Taylor held his own against Uncle One Bear tonight." She chuckled. "That's unusual."

"Held his own?"

"Mother has accused Taylor of practically giving away horses to some folks, our Indian relatives in particular."

"Depends on what value she puts on things, Blair. Uncle Jed would say your brother'd done just that if he didn't get hard cash for his stock."

Blair shook her head. "Uncle One Bear has no money like the white man. He knows only one way to gain goods, whatever they may be, and that's bartering."

"What will your brother do with animal skins?"

"Various things. Find a good seamstress who works with hide to fashion a coat or vest, maybe a pair of chaps. From two bear pelts he could have two pairs of chaps, and maybe a coat from the beaver pelts."

A good horse would bring about one hundred dollars, and it would probably cost near that for apparel such as Blair described. If you could even find it at the general store. There was no arguing Blair's point.

Still fretting about who the women might be that traveled with One Bear, Kalen hesitantly asked, "The women didn't pay their respects to your ma."

Blair's giggle warmed her heart. Oh, to be so content and happy with your life.

"Did you notice how Mother and I joined in the conversation?"

Kalen frowned. "You didn't say a thing until after supper when Mr. One Bear was takin' his leave."

"Exactly." Blair chuckled again. "In this house we women may sit at the same table with my uncle, but we aren't supposed to speak unless spoken to."

"That's just plain—"

"Loco? Not the way Uncle One Bear views women and their opinions. Did you notice how so many of the Indians sat separately at the village?"

Kalen nodded.

"That's because Indian men think they're smarter than women . . . most of them, anyway. I think my uncle listens to his wives' opinions, especially Pieces Of Sky Eyes because she is a proven shaman. But he certainly doesn't discuss things with his women in front of men."

Kalen flinched, thinking of how often she flew off the handle with her uncle. Mr. One Bear would prob'ly backhand her from here to the Staked Plains.

"If Mother has anything to say to my uncle, she usually speaks with him privately. You might say their relationship is formal rather than familiar. And I can count on one hand the times I have spoken directly to him. He's very uncomfortable speaking to women. But, Kalen, you asked me about Sound Of Wind."

"That sounded so strange. And you said it's your brother's Indian name?"

Blair absently pulled her hair to one side and began to braid it loosely. "Do you know how Indian men get their names?"

"Uh . . . no. Can't say that I do."

"Boys as young as eight will go off on what is called a vision quest."

"Go off?"

"Leave their village. One day they just pick up and walk away. Comanches take a robe with them because they cover themselves all night while communing with the Spirits."

"Blair, I don't believe in that stuff. I mean, I believe in God, but spirits . . ." She shook her head.

"You don't have to believe as we do, Kalen." She grinned as she pulled out a short strip of hide from a pocket and began tying it around the end of the braid. Finished, she looked up. "The important thing is, we believe in the Earth, the sun, the moon. Many things, like bears or coyotes, have a spirit."

"Surely not like folks!"

Blair shrugged and stuck the end of her braid in her mouth. Thoughtful, she sucked on her hair a moment. "No, not like you and me, but I think all creatures on Earth are important for one reason or another."

"Well, yes, I'll agree with that."

"Anyway, according to Mother, one day she couldn't find Taylor, and when she went to my father with concern, he told her not to interfere. His son was becoming a man on his personal vision quest."

Still fiddling with her hair, Blair stared off as if picturing another time. "My father had given Taylor a flute. He had taken that, a knife, and a robe when he left." She shook her head and looked at Kalen. "He didn't know how to play the flute when he left, but he did when he returned. I don't know what he said to our father, but from then on all our Indian brethren have called him Sound Of Wind."

Kalen shook her head, her brow creased. "What does it mean?"

"Taylor learned to play by copying the sound of the wind wafting across the hill where he communed with the Spirits."

Kalen blinked, intrigued. "How interestin'! What's Cameron's Indian name? And yours?"

"Cameron never went on a vision quest, and no one has ever bestowed a name on me." She grimaced. "If my mother has one, I don't know it. When she's addressed, it's usually as 'Running Wolf's woman.'"

Kalen pondered that. "Seems to me your ma should be called "Sees With Her Heart."

Blair's eyes widened. "My stars! That's poetic, Kalen."

Feeling her cheeks warm, Kalen ducked her head. "Don't know 'bout that, but your ma sure loves the pants off y'all, and she can't see, so . . ."

Blair patted Kalen's fidgeting fingers. "Don't fret. I won't tell anyone you're a budding poet."

Kalen scooped up the pillow propped against the wall and threw it at Blair. "Go on with you. I'm just . . ." She grinned at her friend. "Plain old Kalen Barrett from West Texas."

"I don't know. I think some in this family don't think you're plain at all."

"What?"

Blair pushed up from the bed, a crafty smile on her face. "I best get to my room."

"Blair!"

The girl gave her a little wave as she slipped out the door. It did no good to call her back. Kalen heard Blair's soft chuckling until her door closed across the hall.

Tarnation! Kalen framed her own face, cheeks warm against her palms. *Well, landsakes, Kalen Barrett.* She shook her head with disgust and slid deeper beneath the covers. No secrets in *this* house! But she had to stop dreamin' about a man she couldn't have.

Taylor Savage was spoken for.

Chapter Twenty

Kalen should have expected it. Still, the next morning when Graceful Bird stepped into her path as she neared the river, Kalen jumped back. "Oh!" She clutched the gunnysack full of dirty linen against her chest like a shield.

Though shorter than Kalen, the Indian woman managed to look down her nose at Kalen while eyeing her head to toe, disdainful.

She pounded her chest and declared, "Mine. Sound Of Wind." She nodded and repeated, "Mine, *nercomackpe . . . hoosban.*"

Another surprise. The woman spoke halting English. Kalen wondered how much Graceful Bird had understood of the conversation swirling around them while at the Indian village. Thinking back, she assured herself that she had not spoken out of line to anyone. Blair's enigmatic words of the night before not withstanding, no one really knew her feelings for Taylor Savage.

And dadburnit, what were her feelings, exactly?

Apparently, Graceful Bird wasn't finished. Pointing a finger at Kalen, she stepped closer. "Go. No stay." Her round body quivered with indignation. The garish yellow-red-and-green-print dress she wore danced before Kalen's eyes. "*Hoosban . . . nercomackpe*, mine," the Indian repeated, thumping her own chest.

Kalen understood the woman's ranting. If not her husband in fact, he sure as shootin' would be very soon. And Graceful Bird wanted Kalen gone.

Persistent, the Indian waved her fingers as if shooing a flock of chickens. "*Ein meadro . . .* You go."

If she hadn't been so upset by Graceful Bird's claim, Kalen might have laughed at the woman. But she had a sneakin' hunch the Indian stood on far sturdier ground than she.

An older, dignified woman walked into view. Kalen didn't remember her, but the woman obviously recognized Kalen. And it was evident she feared for Graceful Bird. Her few words in Comanche sounded authoritative.

Graceful Bird gave Kalen one more assessing look, then lifted her chin and turned to follow her friend. Her carriage spoke confidence—she belonged here; Kalen did not.

Remaining still, Kalen clutched the dirty laundry. Her heart pressed painfully against her ribs, suddenly feeling too large for her chest.

It wasn't until a black bird swooped from a limb and came close to landing on her head that she ducked and started off at a trot. No matter what she decided to do, the day was rushing on, and she had yet to wash clothes. She angled away from her favored clearing, fearing that's where the Indians might be.

Two hours later, Kalen sat across from her uncle at the ranch hands' long table. Thankful Mr. One Bear and his people had gone back to their village, she took a bite of collard greens, and watched from beneath her lashes as her uncle animatedly conversed with Morris and Mr. Woodruff.

Jed Barrett had found his niche. He was happy as a pup suckin' his mama's teat. Chewing thoughtfully, she wondered what right she had to ask him to leave. What excuse could she give to get him to move on? To leave a job he'd finally settled into. Where, as far as she knew, not a drop of whiskey had wet his lips in months.

On the other hand, if she were completely honest with herself, and whether she willed it or not, her feelings for Taylor Savage ran deep. Far deeper than they should for an employer.

"Kalen, you listenin'?"

She snapped out of her reverie, glanced around and found a half-dozen pairs of eyes trained on her. Her cheeks warmed as she looked back at her uncle. "Sorry, I was thinkin'. . . . What did you say?"

Her uncle cocked a thumb at the foreman. "Nolan here says them Injuns can train horses a lot quicker and easier than us. You think he's right?"

Now, there was a dry-powder question. She hedged. "What difference does it make? Ever'body here does the job he was hired to do. That's all the Savages ask." She leveled a glance at the foreman. "Ain't that right, Mr. Woodruff?"

He shrugged. "Jed thinks we ought to have a contest of some sort. Could settle the question real quick-like."

Or end up in a brawl. Keeping the thought to herself, Kalen said, "Mr. One Bear and Mr. Savage don't strike me as the kind who need to prove themselves. In fact, none of the Indians we saw at the village looked like they needed to prove anythin'."

"Tarnation, Kalen, you don't hanker for any fun with that kinda talk."

"Have you watched Taylor Savage train a green colt, Uncle Jed?"

"No. But I can ride any buckin' bronco into the ground. Same as you, girl."

Kalen's heart warmed at the pride for her in her uncle's eyes. But she wanted to steer clear of possible hard feelin's when he saw how easily Taylor gentled a young horse. "Maybe," she said. "Point is, the Savages don't see any call to ride a buckin' horse in the first place."

Keeping his own counsel until now, Mr. Woodruff spoke up. "That's right, girl. It took a spell of watchin' and learnin' for me to figure the Comanche know a heap more about horses than I do." Nolan hiked his chin, acknowledging Nathan, the only Indian at the table.

"Who you joshin', Woodruff? I been 'round horse-flesh all my days, and they's only one sure way to make them jugheads know who's boss. That's climbin' on that hurricane deck and breakin' 'em to bridle and saddle. I'll go right out yonder in the bull-ring and show you."

Nolan shook his head. "Not with Savage stock you won't. All the young horses hereabouts belong to them, and they's mighty ornery if'n they think their horses are bein' mistreated."

Uncle Jed hooted. "Holy Jehoshaphat! Horses is born to work, and the work they do for me is hard. They better be tough."

"Be that as it may, Jed, you ain't ridin' a green horse on this ranch. Stick to your doctorin'. You do right well with that." Woodruff nodded sagely, a crooked grin on his lips. "Leave the trainin' to the young'ns. That's what I do, and my bones thank me when I lay my head on my bunk at night."

"My bones don't . . ." Jed clamped his mouth shut.

Elbow on the table, chin resting on her fist, Kalen curled her fingers over her mouth to hide a smile. While he could be irritatingly boastful, she'd never heard her uncle tell a lie, and he stopped before he did so now.

Later that afternoon, when Jasper handed off a foal for her to march 'round 'n 'round in the covered arena, she thought back on the noon conversation.

Mr. Woodruff had said, "You do right well with that." Meanin' Uncle Jed's doctorin' skill. From a laconic man like Nolan Woodruff, that was high praise indeed.

And that meant she would swallow her grief when Taylor Savage married up with Graceful Bird. Kalen would hide her feelin's for him if it killed her.

She would stay right here where Uncle Jed could work without drinkin' hisself to death.

A week later, Kalen had second thoughts as she again watched Taylor handling the young horse she'd watched him work in the bullring. Today he'd led the colt to the meadow.

It was much colder now, and the trees dropped leaves without argument. Taylor's and the colt's breaths fogged before them, and Kalen reckoned the next heavy rain might turn to sleet or snow. It had been a number of years since she'd seen snow this far south, but they wouldn't avoid it forever.

Even through the soles of her boots, she could feel the cold ground, so she chose to stand, leaning a shoulder against a tree. Like before, she kept quiet, didn't move.

Today, he'd bridled the horse and brought a blanket and saddle. Guess he thought the horse was seasoned enough to manage some weight on his back.

With a patience Kalen doubted she had, Taylor rubbed the horse's ears, jowls and neck. When he brushed the colt's back and flanks where the saddle would sit, a shiver shook Kalen as she tried to throw off the desire to feel Taylor's broad hands on her skin again.

All the while, he spoke quietly or whistled softly. The horse's ears swiveled to the side or back, tracking wherever Taylor moved.

She nearly jumped out of her skin when a hand brushed her arm. Whipping her head around, she stared into Uncle Jed's grinning face. He had a finger across his lips for quiet.

That was a new wrinkle. Her uncle seldom moved so quietly. He'd apparently spoken to Nolan, though, before comin' here and had been cautioned about disturbin' Taylor.

Jed's arrival didn't cause a break in Taylor's concentration or the colt's fidgety attention. Another fifteen minutes elapsed as Taylor led the horse over logs, weaved him between trees, even coaxed him over a small boulder. Not once did the animal hesitate, and Kalen found herself inordinately pleased that Taylor got such marvelous results.

But why shouldn't he? That's the way the Savages and their Indian relatives before them trained horses. Taylor allowed the lead to feed about four feet from his hand as he turned the horse in a half circle, then moved directly into his path.

When Taylor stopped no more than three feet from Kalen, the horse stopped, too. He didn't take one more step. She grinned, itchin' to clap, but knowin' she shouldn't. The colt would prob'ly hop two feet at such a sudden noise.

"Would you like to be his first rider, Kalen?"

Startled by the offer, her gaze jumped to Taylor's steady, blue-eyed regard. "You're joshin'."

"No. He is ready for a rider. You're lighter than I. Eventually, he will be sold to someone looking for a small horse." Taylor brushed a hand along the colt's neck. "He has good conformation, but he won't grow much more." Taylor gave the horse an affectionate pat. "An ideal mount for a young girl or a woman."

"Don't reckon that's a good idea, Kalen," Jed said. "He ain't big, but he'll prob'ly buck purty good."

"Ah," Taylor said, "forgive me. I was led to believe I need not consult you where Kalen's activities are concerned."

"Where'd you get such a loco idea, young fella? I'm her—"

"From me," Kalen snapped, her mouth set stubbornly. "I'll ride this horse if Taylor wants me to. You don't have a thing—"

"Just hold on now. Don't get your drawers in a twist."

Taylor bit back a laugh, his attention swinging from one to the other as Kalen stepped forward, reaching for the reins. The Barretts were as thorny with each other as he and his siblings sometimes were.

This argument would be funny if Kalen wasn't twenty years younger than her uncle, a man she had undoubtedly taken care of for quite a few years. Now, when he was sober and concerned for her, she couldn't see past the weak drunk he had been.

Even Taylor realized that Jed had taken fresh interest in life. And he was not going to be the source of enmity between the two. "Perhaps your uncle—"

Her eyes narrowed. "All of a sudden you don't think I'm capable of ridin' the horse?"

Not good. "No."

Kalen crossed her arms over her chest. "Then what's the problem?"

"Me!" Jed clasped her upper arm and gave it a little shake. "I got a say in what happens, what we do. And you ain't gonna break your fool neck ridin' this here green horse."

Kalen jerked away and glared at Taylor rather than Jed. "Is this horse gentle enough to ride?"

"Well—"

"Yes or no."

She wasn't making this easy. In fact, her attitude

was beginning to rile him. "I would trust a baby on this animal. But not a woman in a fit of temper."

Her eyes rounded at the realization of how she must have sounded. She turned to her uncle. "I'm sorry. You're perfectly right to question and be concerned, Uncle Jed. At the same time, you've worked here long enough to know that Mr. Savage won't let just anyone ride his stock, and certainly not until he's mighty sure the horse is ready."

"Well . . ." Jed flicked a glance at Taylor . . . and backed down. "Mebbe so. But, Kalen, I ain't no good at doctorin' folks, only horses. So you be mighty careful."

Kalen palmed the reins, flashing a grin at Taylor. As she stepped near the colt, he tossed his head and backed up. "None o' that," she soothed. But she stopped until the horse settled, ears pricked toward her, velvet brown eyes blinking.

Taylor stood with Barrett, his attention on Kalen, on her shapely legs. His mouth went dry as she leaned over to pick up the saddle blanket lying atop the saddle he'd brought along.

When she swung her leg over the saddle, heat welled within as he envisioned her straddling him. Thankfully, he wore his warm coat, which hung to midthigh. Otherwise, Kalen—or worse, Barrett—might notice his body's reaction.

Taylor had already broken his vow to not take Kalen. Better keep his member in his pants from now on. Torn, he hoped he hadn't put a babe in her belly. On the other hand, his chest swelled with the misbegotten wish to see Kalen round with his babe. *You cannot have it both ways.*

Barrett lingered for another few minutes, until he assured himself Kalen would not break anything. In a low voice, he said, "I best get back. Nolan prob'ly wonders where I got off to."

Unable to take his eyes off Kalen's grace in the saddle, Taylor nodded but said nothing. After Jed left, Taylor spoke quietly. "Walk him over the limbs on the far side of the meadow, Kalen."

Taylor put Kalen through the paces Blair usually performed on newly gentled stock: loping, backing, weaving in figure eights.

When Taylor finally called a halt to the training, Kalen was reluctant to dismount. The colt had an easy, comfortable gait. Far better than any horse she'd ridden in the past. Even those that her uncle had sold for a pretty penny didn't stack up to Savage stock.

She dismounted and patted the horse's neck. "You're a mighty fine fella."

The horse's ears swiveled to her voice; then he mouthed the snaffle. He blew, turning to nuzzle Kalen. While she had occasionally given some of the horses in the barn a treat, she didn't have any with her today, nor would she dare hand one out to the young colt in front of her boss.

"He's yours," Taylor said in a soft voice.

Her brow crinkled. "What?"

"You like this horse?"

"Well, sure. Who wouldn't?" She patted the neck again. "He's got a good gait and a steady disposition. I could ride the trail all day on him."

"He is yours."

She stared at him, dumbfounded. "I can't afford a

horse like this, Taylor. Why, even though he's young, you can get top dollar for him."

Expression intent, his gaze roamed over her face, down her body. "If you want him, he is yours, Kalen. I said nothing about payment."

Quelling the heat that suffused her from his naked perusal, she wagged her head. At the same time, her heart leaped at the thought of owning the beautiful animal. Nevertheless, she declined. "No. It ain't proper for me to take gifts from my employer."

Before she realized his intent, Taylor lifted his hand and caressed her cheek. "I give gifts to those who deserve them. You do. I see how you defer to your uncle. I see *why* you defer to him. And you deserve to ride a good horse." He stared into her eyes. "This horse is out of the same line from which my father's stallion was sired. I want you to have him, Kalen. With you, I know he will be well treated."

His touch sent a quiver of desire racing through her. A desire she must crush. That night in the cave, Taylor had satisfied his lust. Nothing more. And it could *not* happen again.

Though she spoke little English, Graceful Bird had made it perfectly clear that she and Taylor were destined for each other. Kalen was merely a passing fancy.

Now he offered her a gift far above her ability to pay, but she would accept it . . . for the moment. If, *when*, they were told to move on, the horse would stay behind.

Chapter Twenty-one

Kalen shrugged into her warm coat and headed for the door.

Miz Savage called, "Kalen."

Pausing to peer up the stairs, she answered, "Yes ma'am?"

Lael clasped the banister and started down, one slow step at a time. "Blair scooted out this morning before I arose. If you see her, please ask her to come back to the house. We must begin Thanksgiving preparations."

Kalen came to the base of the stairs and extended her hand to take her employer's delicate fingers.

"She's prob'ly in the arena this mornin'. I'll find her, ma'am."

"Every Thanksgiving, Doreen, Blair, Tom Dunigan and I put together a big meal for the entire ranch. We have a great deal of fun doing it. Doreen and Tom engage in a friendly rivalry to see who's named the best cook."

Kalen thought back to the pie bakes Aunt Livvie used to compete in with a few far-flung neighbors. Not always real friendly-like. "Don't that spark hard feelin's?"

"Heavens, no! As judges, Taylor and Cameron declare the race a draw, and everyone goes to bed happy." Lael patted her stomach and chuckled. "Full, too."

Kalen laughed. "I'll scare up Blair and tell her you're lookin' for her, ma'am."

As Kalen turned away, Lael again delayed her. "Why don't you come back with Blair and sit in on the planning?"

Kalen winced. "Uh . . . when I cooked, you was too sick to eat the vittles. I ain't great shakes in the kitchen."

"Go on with ye." Doreen entered the parlor, blue eyes atwinkle. "It's bibble-babble, mum. When I was abed, Miss Blair brought me a glass of sweet milk and a piece of Miss Kalen's cornbread. It was good."

Though heat rose on her cheeks, Kalen savored the praise. Pitiful, maybe, but kind words were few and far between since Aunt Livvie's death. And ever'body needed a kind word now and again.

"If Mr. Woodruff says it's all right, I'd be pleased to join y'all."

"Nope, ya ain't! I'm stuffin' and cookin' the bird this year, Miss Doreen," Tom argued. "I been stuck with pies for a long spell."

In the bunkhouse, seated at the plank table, Doreen perched beside Kalen, Miz Savage sat at the head. Across the table Tom frowned at Doreen. Next to him, Blair grinned, enjoying the battle.

Miz Savage thought this would be fun? Kalen was glad a table separated Doreen and Tom. They sounded like a pair of fightin' cocks.

Keeping her own counsel, Kalen hoped she wouldn't be called upon to do any of the cookin'. Servin' was fine, but that's as far as she wanted to go.

"We's gonna be eatin' at *my* table." Tom punctuated his words with knocks on the worn wood. Tin cups jumped and clattered. In the big house he would have rattled the china, but here no one objected, least of all Miz Savage.

"This here is the only table big enough for the whole outfit." Tom blathered on while Miz Savage and Blair lifted their cups and drank.

After one sip, Kalen realized the coffee was left from early breakfast. She set the cup aside. Tom didn't lace coffee with spirits, but his brew was strong enough to ream out a body like turpentine-peeled paint.

"He has you there, Doreen." Though Miz Savage couldn't see the cook's reddened cheeks, she knew Doreen well and cut her off before Doreen could disagree. "Besides, I like your mincemeat pie, and your pumpkin melts in the mouth."

Pour a little honey on anythin' and it was tasty, Kalen thought, ducking her head before anyone saw her smile. Though she was used to eatin' with the hands, she didn't much cotton to Thanksgiving dinner in here. Try as they might to keep the place passably clean, a bunkhouse didn't smell like prairie flowers.

Though still surly, Doreen backed down. "Well, if the missus says so, ye can be cookin' the turkey this year." She pointed a finger like a schoolmarm admonishing a student. "Next year, the kitchen and dinin' room tables together will be room enough for everyone, I'm thinkin'. And sure enough, we'll be eatin' in the house."

A week later, Mr. Woodruff stood directly across from Kalen, head bowed as he said the blessing. "Lord, bless all these folks here, keep the peace between us and renegade Indians, and thank You for all this bounty we are about to receive. Amen."

Sixteen people scraped chairs into place at the long, white-cloth-covered table. The men's hair was pomaded and slicked back, all buttons sewn on shirts. She had seen Morris and Jasper jawin' each other as they cleaned beneath their fingernails with sharp knives.

Kalen had helped Blair set candles along the length of the table, greenery spread at their bases. The biggest bird Kalen had ever seen steamed on a platter set before Taylor. Breathing in the wonderful smells of pork-seasoned green beans, sage dressin' and the browned turkey, her mouth watered in anticipation.

There was nothing to compare with a gathering of folks for a good meal and good talk. Traveling the past few years, she had missed this. She still marveled at how easy the Savages were with the hands, at the lack of formality.

Voices erupted around her, too many conversations to keep track of. Rather than try, she picked up a dish of whole cranberries and passed them to the right, followin' Mr. Woodruff's directive. Mashed potatoes, giblet gravy, and homemade sweet pickles made the circle. The fare was so bountiful, Kalen was sure even her plate groaned.

Midway through the meal, she found Taylor staring at her from halfway down the table. He smiled when he caught her eye, sending her stomach into a summersault. She ducked her head, cheeks heating with remembered pleasure.

Pitiful, she thought. A simple smile from the man put her in a dither. But then, there was nothin' simple about Taylor Savage.

Before Kalen knew it, Christmas was upon them. While Aunt Livvie used to create beautiful hand-made garments, doilies, or quilts to give to family and friends, Kalen had never been one to get caught up in the festivities.

Her folks had lived on the edge of what her ma referred to as "Wonder-where-the-next-meal-is-comin'-from." Kalen couldn't remember ever goin' hungry, but the threat was always there, accordin' to her ma, anyway.

On the other hand, the Savages were keen on holly and mistletoe, a tree that brushed the parlor ceiling, strung with popcorn and bright paper cutouts, and presents hidden away until Christmas Eve.

And, like Thanksgiving, they'd included all the hands in their giving spirit. Each showed up sometime during the day to receive a surprise wrapped in brown paper tied with a colorful yarn bow.

Unlike Thanksgiving dinner, Christmas vittles

would be celebrated separately, the men in the bunkhouse, the family in the house. Undoubtedly because of her, much to Kalen's chagrin, she and Uncle Jed were to dine with the Savages.

Only Uncle Jed was havin' none of it. He wanted to be near his jawin' friends. "Besides," he argued, "got a horse I'm keepin' a close eye on. He's doin' poorly, and I ain't figured out the what-for just yet."

Kalen wanted to argue that he could come and go from the house as easily as from the bunkhouse to check the horse, but decided not to waste her breath. It wasn't true, anyhow. Uncle Jed would up and amble off whenever he pleased from the men, but with Miz Savage present, it was another matter. He gave her the courteous regard he'd once given Aunt Livvie.

Christmas Eve night when Kalen descended the stairs, she felt a little better to see Mr. Woodruff spruced up in his best flannel shirt and polished black boots, seated in the parlor, a cup cradled between his rough hands. Even Doreen perched in a corner, the table beside her laden with two pots and extra cups.

Kalen had never seen Doreen so dressed up. She wore a lavender dress with white lace at the throat and cuffs. Her gray hair braided in the usual coronet, she had stuck in a sprig of greenery.

"The Turners will be here right after the New Year to settle the sale of that little mare for their daughter," Taylor was saying as Kalen eased into the room. She found a seat on a footstool Miz Savage wasn't using.

She thought she had gone unnoticed until the

lady leaned forward, her hand settling on Kalen's shoulder. "I thought that was you, dear."

Suddenly everyone's attention was on her, and Kalen felt her cheeks heat with embarrassment. She might have known Miz Savage would detect her presence. The lady, much like a savvy, instinctual animal, scented rather than saw others close by.

"Oh, good!" Blair slid to the floor near the base of the large tree.

Surprised to see Blair in a dress, Kalen noticed she wasn't the least bit hampered by the long skirt as she crawled around to the back, then scooted out with a wrapped box. "This is for you, Kalen."

Eyes wide with denial, Kalen stared at the gift as if it were a snake. "No, I . . . I don't have presents to give. It's not right that—"

"Who cares about that?" Blair shoved the box into Kalen's unwilling hands. "Open it. This one is from me. The family has others for you and your uncle."

She wondered if Blair thought it eased her discomfort to include Uncle Jed. It sure as shootin' didn't.

And more gifts? Horsefeathers! This was beyond embarrassin'. Even if she could afford to buy things, it never entered her mind that she needed to. Her thoughts always circled back to a truth that these folks seemed to ignore: she was a hired hand, nothin' more.

But, with Blair's eager smile urging her on and Taylor's hot eyes boring into her, she pulled the yarn loose and opened the lid on the box. A spankin' new Stetson nestled in the bottom.

Eyes wide, Kalen lifted it out to Blair's, "Try it on! I had to guess at the size."

Dumbfounded by the expensive gift, she didn't have time to comply before Blair ripped it from her hands and squared it atop Kalen's curls.

Blair sized her up. "It fits! And brown was definitely the best color, too." A smile of satisfaction curved her lips. "It will protect your face from the hot sun a lot better than that felt hat of yours."

Shoot, the brim on her old hat was so soft from years of wear, it offered no protection at all other than to keep rain off the very top of her head. She removed the hat and brushed her hand along the edge of the stiff brim. But this hat? Lord love a duck, it must have cost the earth! She glanced up.

Blair shook her head. "Don't dare say it, Kalen. That's a gift from me, and you're going to accept it."

"But I . . ." She scanned the circle again. Befuddled by Taylor's intent attention, she lost her train of thought. "I . . ." Shaking her head, knowing she would get nowhere refusing the gift, she could only accept as gracefully as possible. "Thank you, Blair. It's a mighty fine hat. I'll keep it for special occasions."

"That's the silliest thing I ever heard." Blair laughed. "A bonnet might be saved for special occasions but not a work hat like that one."

Tears threatened when Kalen opened a shirtwaist from Miz Savage. Cameron gave her a belt. Blair shoved a large parcel toward her. "This is for your uncle."

After a moment of silence, Miz Savage said, "I believe there's one more."

Blair turned to her brother. "You want to give it to her?"

Elbows resting on the chair arms, fingers tented before his mouth, Taylor wagged his head.

Reaching under a tree bough, Blair picked up a flat package and handed it to Kalen. "This is from . . ." She cast a quick glance at Taylor again. "All of us."

Kalen couldn't help but follow Blair's glance. Taylor looked at her through lowered lids as if he were half-asleep. Her gaze traveled the circle. All waited for her to open this last gift.

Inside the crackling paper, she found leather gloves, far more finely made than the hand-me-downs her uncle passed on to her. She brushed a finger over the soft leather and blinked hard to keep tears from flowing.

Through a clogged throat she whispered, "I've never seen such a fine pair." She braved looking around the room, her mouth trembling ever so slightly. When her glance settled on Taylor, she whispered, "Thank you . . . all."

Later, as she climbed the stairs, arms full of gifts, Kalen jumped at the sound of a tread behind her. Turning on the landing, she looked into Taylor's unsettling eyes.

He paused a step below her, their heights matched eye-to-eye. She swallowed when he said nothing, his gaze roaming her face.

"What makes you so tempting?"

She blinked, wondering momentarily if he really expected her to answer, but thought not. He raised his hand, slowly, as if giving her a chance to back away before his fingers caressed her cheek.

"You are, you know. Far more tempting than is good for either of us."

Her pulse sped up as her eyes closed. Savoring his touch, she nuzzled her cheek into his palm.

"Kalen, go to your room . . . now. And close the door. Lock it."

Feeling drugged, she opened her eyes to stare into his, brilliant, crystalline, blue as the spring sky. She shivered, wanting . . .

Then she heard Blair's voice and stepped back, turning toward the rear of the house just before her friend started up the stairs. It would not do to be seen with Taylor. Not with such stark desire on her face.

Chapter Twenty-two

In his room Taylor stood at the window, asking himself the same question again and again. What was so tempting about Kalen? She wasn't beautiful in the conventional sense, as, say, his mother. But he was drawn to her as surely as flame licked wood.

Flexing his fingers, he looked at the hand that had cupped her cheek. He still felt her rosy skin, now chaffed by the cold wind as winter was settled over the prairie.

He remembered Kalen's childlike joy at the gifts she had received this evening. Nothing special, just everyday items she could put to good use. Yet she had reacted as if they were gold. His lips curved in a smile.

Absently, he watched the trees whip in the wind and determined to put Kalen out of his thoughts.

"Good night," he heard Blair say, and a door closed.

As he turned from the window, he pulled his shirt over his head, folded it and laid it on a chair; his trousers and small clothes followed. He shivered as he slid between the cold sheets.

If the weather got any colder, he'd have to pull out a union suit to wear under his buckskins. Moments later, his body heated the sheets to toasty comfort.

And that heat sent his mind wandering to Kalen again. Lately, he found himself watching her when she didn't know he was around. She was a good hand at everything she tried.

He admired her devotion to her uncle, too. Surprisingly, Jed Barrett had remained sober for months now, and Taylor wondered how much longer it would last. For Kalen's sake, he hoped forever. She didn't need that heartache.

And you don't want them to move on.

A drunk would not be allowed to handle his stock. Not ever. He would be forced to send Jed packing if he started drinking again. Taylor wasn't fool enough to think Kalen would allow her uncle to leave alone.

He rubbed his chest to relieve a sudden ache, then stilled and blinked in astonishment. He sat straight up and rubbed his chest again. A revelation sweeping through him that scared the living hell out of him.

"Spirits of the people, I . . . love that woman," he whispered. Brow creased, he tried the words on his lips. "I love Kalen Barrett."

He fell back on the pillow, covering his eyes with his forearm. *Not good.* She would probably run for the hills if he asked for her hand. He would not do that, anyway.

The decision not to take a mate had been made long ago. His reasons had not changed.

Taylor lay for what seemed an hour rubbing his chest. The ache only grew worse.

The New Year arrived in a flurry of windblown rain. Head down against the battering deluge, Kalen trudged to the barn. She wore her old hat and hand-me-down gloves. Silly, maybe, but she couldn't bring herself to get the fine hat and new leather gloves wet. Not yet.

It was enough that she wore the warm coat. Entering the barn, she ripped off the hat, shook it and clamped it back on. She brushed as much water as she could from her shoulders and the front of the rawhide coat.

While it pained her to soil the garment, the Savages had given it to her to wear on days like this. Besides, her threadbare coat had disappeared. Doreen had probably collected it when she did the laundry, thinking it belonged in the rag bag. Which it did.

"Taylor, are you going to let Turner's daughter ride that horse here?" Blair's voice rose a notch over the rain pounding the barn's tin roof.

Kalen watched Taylor lead a frisky filly across the covered ring, then turn and take her back. All the while, the brown, white-spotted mare mouthed the snaffle in her mouth, shaking her head as if annoyed.

Taylor stopped next to the fence Blair leaned against and shook his head. "This girl isn't ready for a young one to ride. She's too full of spit."

Kalen paused behind Blair when Taylor gazed directly at her for just a second. Then he returned his attention to his sister. She couldn't figure what she'd said or done to make him mad, but recently he sure as shootin' ignored her every chance he got.

"Do you have another one ready?" Blair persisted.

He sighed and rubbed the mare's pole, which settled her a bit. She nudged her long face against his arm for more. "We have that two-year-old gelding, but Turner wants a mare."

Taylor seemed to study his feet, his face hidden by his hat brim. Lifting his head, he shrugged. Again, he spoke only to his sister. "Turner said he would come about the fifteenth of the month. Think I'll send word to hold off another couple of weeks." He looped his arm over the mare's neck and gave her a good scratch. "I'll work her. You can, too, if you have time."

Dadburnit. He was deliberately ignoring her. Not sure how she found the gumption, Kalen spoke up. "Maybe I could help."

Blair glanced over her shoulder. "Good idea. Taylor wants lightweights on her back, and you're lighter than I am."

Kalen held her breath, waiting for Taylor's refusal, but it didn't come. Instead, he shrugged and turned away, leading the horse to the gate. "That's fine," he said over his shoulder. "But she's worked long enough this morning. I'm putting her away. Perhaps one of you can exercise her this afternoon."

Tarnation, what had she done? Clearly, Taylor was mad about somethin', but she couldn't figure him out. Well, if he wanted to be jughead-stubborn, let him. Except . . . Maybe she should suggest the horse he'd given her to ride. She refused to think of the pinto as a gift.

"I have to groom Moonrise, Starduster and her baby this morning. Perhaps we can meet here after lunch," Blair offered.

Kalen sighed, putting her perplexity about Taylor out of her mind. "Sure. I don't know what Mr. Woodruff has planned for me, but—"

"The usual," the foreman broke in as he came up behind her. "The stalls in barn two are mighty pungent. And"—he shook his head—"we have a new boarder in the hayloft that needs movin'."

Blair and Kalen frowned, glancing at each other, then back at the foreman. "A boarder?" Blair asked.

"Yeah. The scrawniest cat I ever saw has nested up there, and she's got two kits nursin'."

"A cat? Good grief, we haven't had cats or dogs around here for years. Not since old Brownie died," Blair said.

"I'd say that cat ain't long for this world, neither. She barely has enough flesh to cover her bones. Nursin' will be the death of her if she don't get some food in her."

"She's probably wild." Blair said, exactly what Kalen was thinking. "We probably can't get near her."

"Prob'ly right. But tell ya what, get some milk and maybe a bit of meat from Tom and take it up to her. Don't get too close, mind. But I bet she'll gobble up that food right smart. Then, maybe by evenin' or tomorrow, you can take the kits down to the shed by the bunkhouse. That mama cat will prob'ly follow where you take her babies."

"You mean where Brownie used to bed down out of the weather?"

"Yep. That old crate is still there. Get some rags and make her a bed, and she'll be right cozy there."

"What about spiders? I'll bet that whole place is alive with them." Blair shivered. "I hate spiders!"

Mr. Woodruff looked at Kalen. She chuckled. "I don't like 'em neither, Blair. But we can sweep 'em out, just like I swept the little room."

The foreman backed away. "I'll leave you to it, girls. When you're done, go about your usual chores. And, Miss Kalen, before you do the stalls, your uncle's frettin' with a couple geldings. You might give him a hand. He's in the south end of the big barn."

"Grrr."

That was no purr. The cat might be scrawny and hungry, but her back arched. Kalen could see her claws extended against the floor.

Her coloring was brindle, with a lot of orange mixed in the midlength fur. Head down, yellow-green eyes glaring her displeasure, the cat was determined to keep Kalen from getting near her babies.

Blair stood a little behind Kalen, a piece of chicken in one hand, a bowl of water in the other. "I wonder if Nolan tried to move her and decided to leave the chore to us."

"Maybe, but we ain't goin' to move her by takin' her kittens. Not right now, anyway. Why don't you just leave the food and water right where you're standin'. We'll back off and see what she does."

"Grrr."

Kalen figured the cat didn't weigh five pounds, but she was mighty fierce and could do a passel of damage with her claws.

Blair knelt and slowly pushed the bowl and food as close as she dared. The cat growled. Both women backed a few steps, then sank onto a bale of hay to watch.

In moments, nose tipped up, the cat's nostrils quivered. She smelled the food, but still wary of humans, she crouched.

"Poor thing," Blair said. "She's hungry but scared."

Kalen knew the feeling. Fear so profound she hadn't been able to go near the house when she saw her ma lying in the doorway. She'd knelt in the scrub and watched for so long, her legs cramped.

The only sound had been the snap of sheets in the wind. She and Ma had washed that mornin'. Kalen had been allowed to go visit with Etta Sue for a short spell, but Ma had said to be back by three to take in the laundry and help start supper.

The mewl of one kitten sent shivers down Kalen's spine as the sound of Dillon's pitiful cry of long ago again echoed in her head. That was the only thing that spurred her to move from the meager protection the brush provided.

She'd run to see what she could do for her brother. Behind the house, near the well, blood had been everywhere. Dillon had apparently crawled to Pa's side. One arrow protruded from her father's throat, another from his chest. And he'd been scalped.

Dillon was arrow-shot in the back. Blood trickled from the corner of his mouth. Dropping to her knees, she'd gagged at the close view of Pa's mutilated head.

"*Look,*" Blair whispered.

Startled, Kalen blinked. Palms damp, she raised

her hands and brushed at her eyes, trying to erase that hideous scene of long ago. She focused on the cat. It had inched close enough to grab the meat. Though she never took her eyes off Kalen and Blair, she devoured the meat in a few bites. Again, she lifted her nose and tested the air.

"We'll have to bring more," Blair said. "That was barely a mouthful."

"Let her settle a few minutes. If she eats too fast, she'll be sick."

Blair backed away to the ladder and descended to the first floor. Kalen stayed where she was, watching and hoping the cat would drink water. After assessing Kalen for the longest time, she did. She'd quit growling, but Kalen figured if she moved one foot toward her, the mother cat would be all over her, claws bared and lethal.

Kalen didn't look around when she heard the rustle from the ladder. But when boots came into her peripheral vision, they weren't Blair's.

Her glance traveled up until she met Taylor's intense eyes. "What are you doin' here?"

"Nolan told me you and Blair are in the moving business this afternoon." He glanced at the wary cat. "Looks like you haven't convinced her."

"She's really scared. I don't know if we can move her." Kalen shook her head. "Why can't she stay here in the hayloft?"

"Wild as she is, she is apt to pounce on one of the horses." He crossed his ankles and sank next to Kalen. Picking up a spear of straw, he stuck it in his mouth and eyed the cat. "If you want me to, I can distract her while you grab her kits."

His body heat radiated around Kalen. She gulped nervously. "She's apt to claw a layer of skin off your hands."

"Maybe." He chewed thoughtfully on the straw.

"Blair's bringin' more food. If the cat's not worryin' about an empty belly, maybe she'll let us take her babies."

He glanced at Kalen, a half smile lifting his lips. "Lull her with kindness?"

Kalen ducked her head, hiding the flush that blossomed on her cheeks. He was much too close for comfort. "Somethin' like that."

With one finger Taylor lifted her chin. And natural as breathing, he leaned over and kissed her softly on the lips. He pulled back, his gaze roamed her face. He shook his head. "I don't know what comes over me. I should not kiss you. I should not touch you at all."

That was the Lord's truth, but she wanted him to. Also the Lord's truth, she wanted much more than that.

"I've got milk this time," Blair called from below.

Taylor rose and stepped to the edge of the loft. "Hold on. I'm going to capture the cat while Kalen gets the kittens."

"I didn't know you were up there."

Turning back, he found Kalen on her feet, too. The cat had retreated, spine humped.

Moving ever so slowly, he eyed the cat as intently as she did him. She hissed, tail swishing behind her.

"Taylor, she's gonna be all over you in a . . ."

He lunged, grabbed the loose skin on the cat's

nape and lifted her straight in the air. With his other hand, he clasped her tail.

"Yeowl!" The cat writhed, trying to get her back claws into his hand holding her at the nape. He chuckled. "She's none too happy. Get her babies while I maneuver down the ladder."

"How can you do that?" Kalen asked as she watched the spitting-mad feline.

"Wait," Blair called. "I'll bring up a gunnysack."

In seconds Blair clambered up the ladder and opened an empty sack beneath the hissing, yowling cat. Taylor dropped her inside, closing the top before she could claw her way free.

He glanced around at Kalen, who hadn't moved a muscle.

She grimaced. "It's a miracle both of you weren't scratched somethin' awful."

Blair grinned at her brother. "He, not me. Her claws were after him. But we work well together . . . sometimes."

Most of the time, Kalen thought, as she turned around and found the tiny kittens curled together in the corner beneath some hay. They squirmed in her hands. Inside the sack, their mama growled and carried on something fierce. She found a small hole and stuck a paw through, claws extending and contracting as, blindly, she tried to swat anything in reach.

"Oh, boy. How are you going to let her go, Taylor?" Blair asked.

"Very carefully." He grinned as he started down the ladder, Blair following.

Kalen watched them to the bottom, then started

down. It surprised her that Taylor would take the time to help them. As he carried the mother cat to the shed, he sent Blair for more chicken and a second bowl, so the cat would have food, water, and milk. He even got some rags out of the tack shed and lined a box.

After Kalen placed the tiny kittens in the new bed, Taylor hiked his chin at her and Blair. "Stand outside the pen. I'm going to put her close to the bed, then let her find her way out."

As he exited the shed, he closed the gate and turned around. Kalen stood on one side, Blair on the other. He draped his arms over their shoulders and watched the cat fight her way out of the sack.

He and Blair chuckled, but Kalen stood still, savoring the weight of Taylor's arm on her shoulder. She looked up at his chin, then across to Blair.

It was like . . . like she was part of the family.

The wish that it were really true made her stomach ache.

Chapter Twenty-three

The next morning, Kalen made a detour to the shed to check the cat family. The mama hadn't moved 'em. She looked up and blinked languidly. Her two babies suckled, their tiny paws kneading her belly. The bowls of milk and chicken were empty, but she still had plenty of water.

Just as Kalen turned away, Taylor rounded the end of the barn with food for the cat. She smiled at him, pleased that he would take enough interest to see a scruffy cat had food and shelter.

He shrugged, apparently reading her thoughts. "No one goes hungry on Savage land, not even four-legged critters."

It surprised Kalen when he brushed by her, opened the gate and went right in. The cat didn't twitch with fear. She stayed where she was as he knelt to leave her food.

"Tarnation. She sure don't seem vexed by folks this mornin'. I didn't think she'd ever let a body near without pitchin' a hissy fit."

"Animals sense if they are threatened. Most will respond to calm authority."

Kalen shoved cold hands into her jacket pockets and blew out a cloud-cold breath. She knew that, especially after watchin' the Savages work for so many months. Except . . . "She sure didn't like you yesterday."

He chuckled. "Yesterday she was hungry and protecting her babies. After she ate, she realized I wasn't a threat." He crossed his arms atop the fence, his eyes on the cat. "*You* can feed her this evening if you like."

"If she ain't goin' to scratch me bloody, I will."

"What chores has Nolan assigned you today?"

"Um. I haven't talked to 'im yet."

"We both better get to work," he said.

Walking away without a second glance, he dashed her hope that he might include her in whatever he planned today.

"Papa! I want that one. Can I have that one, Papa? Please! Please!"

The child's shrill voice felt like glass shards going through Lael. Privately, she thanked the Lord Blair had been blessed with a mellow timbre.

Long ago Lael's mother had admonished, "Never scream unless blood is imminent."

Blair had never needed that reminder. Having little contact with other girls, she had grown up with brothers—the older stoic and closemouthed beyond his years, the younger boisterous but mindful of never spooking horses.

"Minnie, keep your voice down," Miz Turner admonished.

"But I want that one!" the girl insisted.

Lael discovered "that one" was carrying her mistress when Blair said, "Sorry, this horse is not for sale."

"Papa, you said I could have whatever horse I want," the girl wailed.

From the sound of the child's whining, Lael didn't think she'd had much discipline. Lael fancied Mr. Turner was embarrassed when he spoke more forcefully than he probably intended.

"Hush, Minnie. I shall deal with Mr. Savage in short order. We have already settled on an excellent mount for you."

"But—"

"Not another word, young lady!"

Lael cleared her throat, pulling her shawl close around her shoulders. While the sun made a valiant effort to warm the air, it was chilly as the dickens on the porch.

Perhaps it was unneighborly of her, but she decided not to invite mother and daughter inside. From what she had ascertained, the little tart of a girl wouldn't stand for staying behind, anyway. She'd be all ears, and even more loudmouthed when Taylor led her father to have a look at the young mare chosen for her.

Blair apparently sensed her mother's rare discourtesy. "Excuse me, I'll find Taylor for you, Mr. Turner."

For the first time in her life, Lael stood as if

serenely unaware the Turners should be invited inside, out of the cold.

The little girl had no intention of keep her mouth shut. "I'm cold, Mama. I want some hot chocolate."

"Shh," the lady said.

"But, Mama—"

"You heard your mother," Mr. Turner snapped.

Lael was about to relent when she heard the clop of horses approaching at a trot. She sighed with relief.

"I didn't expect you until next week, Mr. Turner," Taylor said. "The mare is still in training."

"I'm sorry, Mr. Savage. I realize we may not be able to take the horse today. It's just that—"

"But, Papa, you said—"

"Shut up, Minnie!"

Lael covered her mouth, hiding a smile. At last the man showed he had a backbone. Though perhaps too late to teach the child the world didn't revolve around her.

After a protracted silence, Taylor finally said, "The mare is in a pasture some distance from the house, Mr. Turner. If you would follow me?"

"Happy to, Mr. Savage." Briskly he added, "Myra, Minnie, back in the carriage."

Lael listened to the three people climb into their seats, the slap of leather on a horse's rump, the wheels creaking as the carriage pulled away.

Several moments later, all was quiet until Blair said, "Mother, I don't blame you one bit."

Lael could hear the smile in Blair's voice. "I do believe, had I allowed that child into my parlor, I would have chastised her. And that would have been rude to the extreme."

"It's evident her mother doesn't know how to discipline the girl. You could have taught her a valuable lesson."

Lael picked up her skirts and headed back into the house. "That's very nice to hear, dear. Especially from one who was occasionally on the receiving end of a switch."

The door closing behind her cut off Blair's laughter.

In the stud barn tack room, Kalen oiled one of the dozen halters pegged on one wall. She had finished four spare bridles, and when she finished with this halter, she would tackle a couple saddles.

"Miss Kalen, you 'bout done with the tack?"

Kalen swiveled around on the low stool, eyeing Mr. Woodruff in the doorway.

"I haven't gotten to the saddles. Need me to do somethin'?"

Woodruff stepped into the shed out of the brisk wind. He cupped his hands before his mouth and blew to warm them.

"You forget your gloves this mornin'?" Kalen asked.

His face was chafed red from the bitter wind of the last few days. Nolan rubbed his stubbled chin. "I've looked myself silly for those gloves. I thought they was in my spare trunk, but . . ." He shrugged. "They'll turn up."

Kalen hung the halter on a peg.

"I come to tell you your uncle is doin' some eye medicatin'. You've learned right smart from Jed, and I wondered if you'd like to look on."

"Oh, yes, I would."

"He's doin' some other stuff on the way to pasture twenty-six. That's—"

"I know where it is, Mr. Woodruff."

"Fine, then. I'll let you get goin' "

Kalen washed her hands. Cold wind slapped her face as she exited the tack room. She tugged her hat brim down and dug in her coat pockets for the new gloves and drew them on. Jamming her hands into fleece-lined pockets, she sent up a prayer of thanks for the warm clothing provided by the Savages.

Her path took her through a second barn where the mare Taylor had given her was stabled. Several horses had their heads hanging over the gates. Kalen fancied them gossiping over fences. The filly saw Kalen coming and nickered.

She paused beside the stall and gave the mare a good scratch. "Think I'll hoof it on my own today, girl. You don't need to get cold."

As affectionate as an old dog, the horse nudged Kalen's shoulder for more scratching. Grasping the mare's head between her hands, Kalen let her gaze travel over the well-shaped head.

"I'm not givin' you a name, girl. Whether Taylor realizes it or not, he really meant you are for me to ride as long as I'm here. Sure as shootin', when Uncle Jed and I move on, you'll be left behind."

Again, the horse nudged her and blew as if disagreeing. Or maybe agreeing, Kalen thought and turned away. Her heart ached a bit thinking about Taylor's gesture. But mostly from the thought that one day she'd more than likely have to leave this place. Leave Taylor and his family.

The horses pastured alone had their rumps facing

the cold wind, heads down. Other than a mare with a foal, Kalen hadn't figured out how decisions were made to put two or more horses together in some pens. Those who were, huddled side by side, head to rump for warmth.

Walking the length of a large paddock, Kalen turned into a corridor that marched straight ahead of her for a quarter-mile or more. In the distance a carriage moved slowly, with Taylor riding Creation alongside.

Taylor and the strangers paused while he spoke with Uncle Jed, who was just about to enter a paddock where a lone horse stood, its rump to the gate.

Not close enough to make out the exact words, Kalen only heard Taylor's low voice, then Uncle Jed's in return. She picked up her pace when Taylor and the carriage moved on.

While Jed secured the gate, Taylor stopped at the next paddock and dismounted, tossing Creation's reins loosely over the fence.

The man driving the carriage stepped down, then handed a young girl and a woman Kalen presumed was his wife to the ground.

At the same time the man followed Taylor into the paddock, Jed caught Kalen's attention. He moseyed along with what looked like a bottle in his hand. Head down, he was apparently reading the label.

She watched him walk directly behind the only horse in the enclosure. In all the years she'd seen her uncle around stock, he'd never been careless. Until now.

Uncle Jed, watch where you're headed!

Before she could open her mouth to caution him

aloud, in the next paddock the little girl emitted a high-pitched squeal, followed by, "Papa, I want to ride her!"

Startled, the young mare took off for the other end of the corral, and the horse in Jed's paddock kicked out.

The kick caught Jed in the chest, lifting him off his feet. The impact sent him flying backward, arms flung wide. The bottle arced away and landed in ankle-deep grass just as Jed hit the ground on his back.

"Horsefeathers! You know better than to get in striking distance of a horse's hindquarters, Uncle Jed."

She started jogging to her uncle and heard the man say, "Minnie, you must learn to curb your mouth. You startled the horse."

Kalen scowled and mumbled, "Two of 'em."

Again, she paused when Jed lay unmoving. *Must have knocked the wind out of 'im.*

She waited.

He still didn't move.

Sudden tension zipped down Kalen's spine. She whispered, "Uncle Jed?"

Vaguely, she heard the other man speaking again, but his voice faded away as Kalen sucked in a painful breath. She felt as though she had dropped into a hole.

"Uncle Jed?" she called louder. "Get up."

Pulling her hands from her pockets, she bagan to run, a litany of "No, no, no," bursting from a tight throat. She tried to haul in another breath but couldn't.

"Uncle Jed!" she screamed.

* * *

Kalen's anquished cry pierced Taylor's back as if she had thrown a knife. He whipped around.

In an instant he saw Jed lying on the ground, a gelding placidly cropping grass no more than five feet away.

"Hear me, Spirits of my father. No!"

He sprinted to the fence and was through the slats in an instant.

"Uncle Jed!" Kalen left the pasture gate ajar as she ran.

Her breaths huffed loud enough for Taylor to hear. He knelt and felt for a pulse on Jed's neck.

Nothing.

"Uncle Jed!"

Taylor surged to his feet and met Kalen little more than a yard from Jed's prone body. She plowed into him, beating his chest as if she already knew.

Perhaps she did, he thought, and wrapped unyielding arms around her shaking body.

"He's gone, Kalen. He is gone."

"Noooo!" she wailed, pushing with all her might against Taylor's chest. "He's just winded!"

Taylor ignored her ineffectual pushes and held her tighter, tucking her head beneath his chin, pressing her cheek to his heart. "He's gone," he murmured into her curls. "I'm sorry, Kalen, he is."

Over her head he saw Nolan and Cameron running toward the paddock. They, too, had heard Kalen's heartbreaking cries.

"Mr. Savage?" Turner said behind him. "Is he all right?"

Taylor ignored the question. The man had eyes in his head, ears to hear Kalen's anguish.

She had stilled against his frame, now as quiet as death herself. Taylor held her far enough away to see her face.

Not a tremble of her lips, not a tear moistened her eyes. She stared into the distance as if in a trance.

"Kalen?"

Cameron knelt next to Jed, checked for a pulse the same way Taylor had, looked up at Nolan and shook his head.

Nolan walked toward the paddock where the Turner family stood. "Nothin' to see here, folks," he said. "You best go on home and come another day."

"Go home? But, Papa, I haven't rided the horse yet!"

And you will not, Taylor thought. *Not today.*

Nolan said as much to Turner. But his words faded to nothing as Taylor swept Kalen into his arms. "Take care of him," he ordered Cameron, and started for the house.

Chapter Twenty-four

Blair pulled on a coat as she stepped out on the porch. She couldn't stop shivering. These days were the coldest they had seen this winter, and she hoped they would soon pass. Though today was gloriously bright, winter was not her favorite time of year.

As was her habit, probably Taylor's and Cameron's as well, she glanced over the ranch, a measure of pride swelling her chest every time she looked upon what her father had built. What Taylor continued to build. She and Cameron had a hand in it, too, as did Nolan and the loyal hands, most of whom had been with them for five years or more.

She spied Taylor striding in the corridor between the north and mid paddocks. It looked like he carried something. Her brow creased. *Someone?*

Indeed, as he rounded the end of the last fence, she discovered Kalen in his arms.

"Oh, dear." The cold forgotten, Blair flew down the couple steps and ran toward her brother. "Is she hurt?"

"No. It's Barrett."

Blair fell in beside him. "Can I help?" It was then she saw that Kalen appeared catatonic. "Taylor?"

"He is beyond our help, Blair."

She paused, a hand against her chest. "No! It can't be," she argued to Taylor's back as he walked up the steps.

Blair ran to catch up, darted around him, and flung the door open, then slammed it shut. "Mother!"

"I'm right here, dear."

Lael descended the stairs, alarm rising at the distress in Blair's voice. "What is it?"

Along with her daughter's voice, Lael detected another pair of footsteps. Cocking her head, she was sure a second person had entered. "Taylor? Is that you?"

"Yes," he snapped, and brushed past her on the stairs.

Something was dreadfully amiss. Taylor was never short with her. She listened to his receding steps and ascertained he had entered Kalen's room. She turned back when Blair touched her hand resting on the banister.

"It's Mr. Barrett. He . . . Taylor says he is dead."

"Oh, my God in heaven!" Lael covered her mouth with her hand, unseeing eyes wide. "How? When?"

"I don't know . . . how. But just now, I think."

Lael heard the tears in Blair's hitched speech.

"And Kalen?" She had perceived the girl's unique fragrance mingled with Taylor's.

"I don't know. She's . . ." Blair seemed to be at a loss for words.

But Lael knew. Oh, yes. She knew how it felt for your world to shatter in an instant. Mr. Barrett had been Kalen's sole remaining relative. And no matter how difficult the man may have been, Kalen loved him.

Lael turned around and walked to Kalen's doorway. She paused and clasped the door frame. Not a sound emanated from within.

Though she had been as traumatized as Kalen undoubtedly was now, Lael could still remember the bleak, helpless words of remorse from Taylor upon his return from school in the East when Wolf died.

While he had not voiced it, Lael knew that somewhere in her son's grief-ridden heart, he irrationally blamed himself for his father's death. He had said enough for her to know he thought it should have been him rather than his father who was shot to death. And he believed as she still did to this day that her family had hated Running Wolf and his offspring enough to kill.

Approaching the bed, she felt Taylor's aura, his heat, and realized he sat on the side of the bed. Probably holding Kalen's hand, just as he had hers long ago.

She touched his shoulder. "Taylor, what happened?"

There was no way to ease Kalen's pain. She would have to work through that on her own. No matter how others, Taylor, in particular, wanted to unburden her sad heart, sudden death was a fact of life on the prairie. Accident or murder, the result was the same. It took time to come to grips with a shattered world.

"One of the horses kicked him in the chest. Stopped his heart, I guess," Taylor said in a rough voice.

"That's not usual from one of our horses. They are so—"

"The Turner girl squealed fit to send all of us running for cover. Startled the gelding. And Barrett was . . . I don't know why he put himself directly behind that horse."

She felt Taylor turn his head to look up at her.

"Kalen is as still as death herself. She has not cried. She has said nothing at all since I told her he was dead. You . . ."

Lael knew he compared Kalen's reaction to her own when Wolf died. And perhaps it was similar. Desperate denial, then anger, then despair. Followed by the ache of loss that never completely went away. Kalen would have to experience all of that.

"Let me sit with her, Taylor."

He rose and guided her to take his place. When his heat remained close, Lael looked up.

"I wish to speak privately with Kalen."

Perhaps it was presumptuous of her, but of all the people on the ranch, Lael thought perhaps she could best empathize with Kalen's heart-wrenching grief. And one way to help was simply to be here if Kalen wanted to talk.

Lael thought back to when she had gone to bed alone for the first time after eighteen years of Wolf's presence in every breath she took, every thought, every passionate touch.

Lael ducked her chin and let the tears fill her unseeing eyes as they had more times than she could count. While tears could not take away the pain, could not bring Wolf back, they eased her heart in some indefinable way.

She groped for and found Kalen's limp hand lying on the quilt. "It is all right to cry, Kalen," she whispered. "Your uncle is with the angels. You cannot appreciate that right now, but in time it may be a comfort to know that."

Lael squeezed Kalen's lifeless hand and subsided. She didn't expect a response, but she knew that somewhere behind that black curtain of pain and denial, Kalen heard what was said. In time she would remember.

"May the God of our white brethren comfort you."

After several moments of silence, Lael took a deep breath and brought up the subject that the girl must face now rather than later. "Kalen, I know you can hear me. You don't have to answer right now, but I do want you to know that we will bury Mr. Barrett on Savage land if you wish." She paused a moment and considered where she herself would like to be buried someday. "There is a pretty knoll to the west of the house where an old oak stands. Your uncle would have a lovely view of the valley and of the last ranch where he worked. I think he was happy here."

Oh, how well Lael knew the pain of making a decision such as this, but she had said all she could say. Now it was up to Kalen.

She patted the limp hand and rose. "Rest for now. We will talk again in a short while, dear."

Taylor met his mother at the base of the stairs. "How is she?"

"The same as you left her. She is thinking nothing at all right now. It may take awhile for her to think rationally, Taylor." She rested her hand on his forearm. "Give her a little time, just as you did with me after you returned to the ranch."

"Should she be left alone?"

Lael heard more than passing concern in her son's voice. She heard the ache to take Kalen's burden into his own heart.

"She is resting. Not sleeping, mind you, but likely running the scene over and over in her mind. She will do that for some time to come, trying to make sense of it."

Forty-five minutes later, just as the Savages finished an unusually quiet luncheon, Kalen walked into the dining room.

Surprised, Taylor rose. "Kalen?"

The rest of his family turned to her in the doorway. "Where is Uncle Jed?"

Taylor walked around the table to stand before her. Surely she realized he was dead. "Nolan has taken his body to the barn."

Kalen pivoted and headed back the way she had come.

"Wait!" Taylor strode after her and caught her by the arm at the front door. "You cannot go out like that."

She looked down at herself, then back at him, a frown on her face. "What do you mean?"

"A coat. It's bitter cold out there. Worse than this morning."

"No. I—"

"Yes," he snapped and clasped her arm. "You will wear a coat, or I will not allow you out that door."

"Here!" Blair handed Kalen's coat to her. "Taylor's right. You'll get sick if you don't take care of yourself."

Without further argument, Kalen shrugged into it, whipped around and fled through the door, Taylor on her heels.

Just as they both arrived at the stud barn, Blair huffed up with Taylor's coat and thrust it in his face. "Idiot. Put it on." She and then Cameron followed them into the cavernous barn.

Even out of the wind, it was bone-chilling cold, but Taylor didn't feel a thing. His attention was on Kalen and Kalen alone.

Moments later, midway up the corridor between stalls, Taylor spied Nolan's Stetson visible above the wooden slats as he moved around in one stall. Kalen spied him, too, and beat a quick path to the stall door, pausing when she got a look inside.

Taylor came up behind her, his siblings following.

Jed lay on a table brought in from the tack room. Tom was there as well, helping Nolan dress Jed in clean jeans and a flannel shirt.

Taylor looked down at Kalen's impassive face. *Spirits, she needs to cry.*

Looking down, she slowly walked over to Jed's

body. Taylor could not see her eyes, but he saw her reach, hesitate, clench her fingers, then open them and brush her uncle's wispy hair off his forehead.

"He has a good pair of go-to-meetin' boots, Mr. Woodruff. I'm sure he'd want to wear 'em through eternity."

While Kalen's usual voice sounded husky, Taylor winced at the added rasp today. Beside him, Blair bit back a sob and clamped her hand over her mouth.

Nolan glanced at him, then back at Kalen. "You know where he keeps 'em, Miss Kalen? I'll get 'em."

She remained where she was, saying nothing, her hand resting on Jed's cheek. It was as if she had forgotten anyone else stood nearby, that she had spoken.

Taylor walked up and laid a hand on her shoulder. "Where are your uncle's good boots, Kalen?"

She looked over her shoulder at him, her golden eyes dimmed to a dull hue. "Boots? Uh . . ." She rubbed her forehead. "Boots. Yes. In the room where I stayed." She started to turn. "I'll get 'em right away."

Taylor tightened his fingers on her shoulder. "No. Nolan will."

"But I have to tell Miz Savage . . ." She looked off in the distance. "Oh, yes. I remember. The knoll."

She turned around and leaned close to Jed's face. "Would you like that, Uncle Jed? It's a right pretty spot. Miz Savage said you can look over the ranch every day."

Kalen glanced up at Taylor, her eyes nearly as lifeless as Jed's were the last time he saw him. She nodded. "He would like that."

* * *

Down to the last man on the ranch, everyone stood on the knoll for Jed Barrett's short service. Although few were churchgoers, they nevertheless removed hats in respect for the dead.

While it was not their way, Nathan and Clay were as respectful of the white man's ceremony as they would have been had Jed been sent to the After World in the same manner as a Comanche.

Nolan cleared his throat and bowed his head. "Lord, we don't rightly know why You saw fit to come for our brother, Jedediah Barrett, but we sure can't argue the point. Keep him safe in Your house, Lord, until Judgment Day. Amen."

Kalen stood on Nolan's right, Taylor a step back so he could see her in profile, her head bowed. He wondered if she even heard the foreman.

The words might not be exactly what a preacher would say, but Taylor knew they were heartfelt.

Chapter Twenty-five

Lael wore a bonnet and wool shawl over her most sedate dress, her gloved hand tucked around Taylor's arm. She whispered, "We need to give Kalen a moment alone, dear."

He knew that, but he hated to leave her. She looked so lost, so small, so vulnerable. But his mother was right. Kalen would have to live with the loss of her uncle for the rest of her life. That meant she must start coming to terms with it.

He clasped Kalen's upper arm. "When you are ready, come back to the house."

She didn't acknowledge him at all. Her bleak eyes seemed to see nothing as she gazed into the endless bright sky.

Sighing, he turned with his mother and followed his brother and sister. The ranch hands had ranged themselves back a respectful distance, and one by one, each clapped on his hat and trailed the foreman. As the family neared the house, Taylor looked back.

Sunlight filtered through the oak tree's leaves. Kalen looked even smaller from this distance. She had dropped to her knees and now sat back on her feet, head still bowed.

Ahead of him, Cameron opened the front door and allowed Blair to precede him into the warmth of the house. Taylor ushered his mother up the steps, across the porch, but stopped at the door.

"Mother," he said as she passed before him over the threshold, "I cannot leave her there alone. She's . . . I don't know how to explain it. She appears . . . broken."

"All right, dear. But when she is finished at the grave site, be sure she comes back to the house with you. If left to her own devices, I fear Kalen will lock herself away in the shed room."

Taylor closed the door behind his mother and headed back toward the hill. He had no idea what he planned to do, but his heart . . . hurt.

Sitting on her feet folded beneath her, Kalen vaguely felt the chill from the cold ground through her jeans. Eyes narrowed against the breeze here on the knoll, she glared at the simple cross Mr. Woodruff had pounded into the ground that morning.

HERE LIES JEDEDIAH BARRETT
MAY HE REST IN PEACE
FEBRUARY 21, 1871

Mr. Woodruff had asked if she wanted birth and death dates on Uncle Jed's cross, but she didn't know the exact year of his birth. Ma had said he was two years older than her pa, but since she'd never known her pa's exact age . . . Ma also said they had a younger brother and sister, who'd barely made it into the world before the Lord saw fit to take the wee ones back to His house in the clouds. Or wherever the Lord lived.

She looked down at the freshly mounded earth and frowned. "I don't think the Lord had a hand in your passin', Uncle Jed. It was your all-fired carelessness. Horsefeathers," she muttered, and brushed fingers over gritty eyes.

Maybe it was wrongheaded to be angry with her uncle, but here she was, alone. No one to travel with. No one to look after.

"What am I supposed to do now, Uncle Jed? Folks hired us because they got a man and a woman for the price of one. I thought sure as shootin' that drink would take you. Not some stupid accident with a horse."

"I will destroy the horse if that is your wish."

Kalen glanced over her shoulder at Taylor, standing no more than three feet away. Even in boots, the man was incredibly light on his feet. His second-nature stealth could probably give a ghost a run for its money.

He'd probably heard her bitter musings, too. But dadburnit, that's how she felt. She shook her head when what Taylor said sank in. "No. That horse ain't mean. He just . . ." She shrugged and returned her gaze to the grave. "Killin' the horse won't bring back Uncle Jed."

When she stood, Taylor stepped close and

wrapped his arms around her from behind, pressing his length to hers.

"You are not alone. You're welcome here as long as you wish to stay."

She closed her eyes and savored his warmth. But her ever-practical mind wandered. While Taylor's invitation sounded sincere, he had not expressed love. Not even simple affection.

What do you expect, Kalen Barrett?

The Savages had lived here for a generation, needing no one, managing to thrive simultaneously in the white world and the Indian world.

Could you, Kalen? a little voice asked. *Would you have that kind of courage?*

Uncle Jed had been a drunk, but that wasn't as damnin' to the white man's way of thinkin' as marryin' an Indian. However, none of that held a candle to bein' born a breed.

Lingering in his embrace a moment longer, Kalen wished . . . But she was kiddin' herself. Taylor's feelin's for her would never go beyond courtesy. That one time with him was all she would have. She didn't know why he had put off askin' Graceful Bird to marry, but that was none of her business.

She straightened, and his protective arms dropped away. Turning, she forced a smile. "I appreciate that. Thank you. I will stay . . . for a spell."

Within a few days, life returned to normal, at least for the Savages and all the hands. For Kalen, the days remained off-kilter. Though she still slept in the big house, she managed to grab a biscuit in the morning and head out before the family came down for breakfast. She just couldn't bring herself to sit at the table and pretend she was one of the family.

Kalen couldn't fault any of the Savages, though. All were exceedingly accommodating and kind. Although Taylor was a bit short with her if she lingered of an evening after supper.

Lael laid aside her Braille reading and asked, "Taylor, what is wrong with you?"

He looked up from the chessboard at Cameron. His brother shrugged, indicating Taylor was on his own. He glanced over his shoulder. "Nothing that I know of, Mother. Why do you ask?"

Lael faced him, brow furrowed. "I was conversing quite easily with Kalen at the table this evening. When you joined in, she fled."

"And that means . . . ?"

"You snapped at her for no reason."

"I did not snap at her. I reminded her to exercise the horse I gave her. The gelding has not been out of the barn for over a week."

Blair leaned against the chair in which Taylor sat, and lightly batted the back of his head. "A bit more forcefully than was necessary, brother dear."

He ignored her.

"You gave her a horse?"

The surprise in his mother's voice told him he had made an error by not telling her. But, thunderation, Kalen had needed a good mount. Jed's raw-boned horses were only fit for harness.

Now he made another error. "I did not think I needed your permission to gift a horse to a hand."

"Of course you may gift horses to whomever you please. Now I hear a defensive tone in your voice. I am blind, not deaf, Taylor. I also heard a sharp tone when you spoke to Kalen earlier."

"I'm sorry. Must I watch the *tone* of everything I say?"

"Son . . ."

Every word he uttered dug him into a deeper hole, so he forestalled his mother with action. He pushed back the chair and rose. "I think I'll take a turn outside before I go to bed."

After favoring his mother with a perfunctory kiss on her hair, he started for the door. Shrugging into his sheepskin coat, he said, "Good night. See you all at breakfast."

Silence descended for a moment after Taylor left. Then Cameron asked, "What's wrong with him?"

"I believe he's trying to come to terms with his feelings," Lael replied.

"What does that mean?"

"When the dilemma attacks you, dear, you'll understand."

Blair laughed when Cameron rolled his eyes at her as if to say their mother talked in riddles. She slid into the chair Taylor had left.

"What?" Lael asked.

"Cameron is as mystified as Taylor, Mother."

Lael smiled. "One day, Cameron, the same bug will bite you."

"That doesn't tell me a thing!"

Blair said, "I'll finish Taylor's game of beating you, Cameron."

Lael rose and headed for the stairs. "Time for me to retire, children. Sleep with the angels."

"Blair?" Cameron said as his mother reached the upper floor.

"I do believe our dear brother has met his soul mate, Cameron."

"Here, kitty. I won't hurt you."

Passing the lean-to on the way to the stud barn, Taylor heard Kalen's coaxing.

He paused next to the fence and looked in. She sat cross-legged on the straw a few feet from the mother cat. Back arched, legs stiff, the scrawny animal hissed at Kalen's outstretched hand.

"Come on, now. I fed you some leavin's that you gobbled up. The least you can do is let me pet you."

For her efforts Kalen got another hiss from the cat as it backed away, keeping itself between Kalen and the kittens. Drawing on her glove, Kalen muttered, "Ungrateful ball of fluff."

At Taylor's chuckle, she glanced over her shoulder and rose to her feet. "I didn't hear you." She brushed dust from the seat of her pants. "Don't look like she's cottonin' to me like she did you. I better turn in."

Inhaling Kalen's unique scent as she started past him, he clasped her arm. "Wait. If I was short with you at the table this evening, I'm sorry. I do not mean to be."

Head down so he couldn't see her lovely eyes, she murmured, "Don't give it a thought, Taylor."

He didn't release her when she tugged slightly to break his hold. How he yearned to gather her in his arms again. To kiss her rose-tinted lips. Instead, he asked, "Are you faring well here?"

"Well enough."

Her eyes were still downcast, making it difficult to read her expression. "That doesn't say much. Has Nolan given you exercise duty?"

"A few times. Most of the horses are still in from-the-ground trainin'. Mr. Woodruff says I ain't real good at those skills yet."

Taylor curled a finger beneath her chin and tilted up her face. Gaze as bleak as dry grass, she stared up at him. No way could he stop his reaction to the lonely anguish burning in those dull eyes.

He lowered his head and covered her lips with his warm mouth, giving in to his desire to hold her close. He longed to be able to take away the grief of her loss, to comfort her.

Kalen trembled in his embrace but didn't resist his advances. Nor did she respond to his kiss.

Despite his intention to simply console her, desire whipped through him. Involuntarily, he tightened his arms, bringing her body flush against his arousal.

She pushed against his chest and twisted her head away. "No. I don't . . . Let me go."

While her plea wasn't desperate, it served to douse the fire raging in his body. But he didn't release her.

"I'm sorry," he murmured in her ear as he again tightened his arms around her. "I do not mean to frighten you, Kalen. When you are in my arms . . ."

Not good. Control yourself and release her.

Chapter Twenty-six

Several times during the following weeks, Taylor spied Kalen sitting, hunched over crossed arms, beside Jed's grave. He considered taking a bench up there for her, but thought better of it.

What she chose to do with her free time was really none of his business. But while he worked the horses, Kalen's bruised eyes were never far from his thoughts.

On an especially bright day that bore inklings of spring, Taylor saddled one of three horses he would deliver to a buyer in ten days. Nolan led another back to his stall from the bull ring. Taylor noticed the young animal responded well to the foreman's gentle but firm command to halt.

"He's doing fine at halter. Anyone been on his back?"

Nolan nodded. "Both Miss Blair and Miss Kalen. Figured Cameron could give him a workout tomorrow. He's ready to go when you say the word, Taylor."

"A week from Friday. The weather is warming by the day. Unless we have a late cold snap, our ride north to Murray's spread should be uneventful."

"Who's goin' with you?"

"Blair and Cameron." He shrugged. "Cameron and I can handle the three, but Blair pestered me until I agreed she could tag along."

"You think it's safe for her to go that far north?"

Taylor's brow furrowed in thought. "The Comanche are uncommonly quiet these days. Besides, if we encounter any we don't know, our mode of riding and speaking the language ought to give us passage."

"Well, I hope so. Don't rightly worry about you and your brother. But Miss Blair might attract a warrior intent on havin' her."

Taylor grinned. "He would throw her back quickly enough."

Nolan chuckled. "Better not let your sister hear you talkin' thataway."

Noticing the horse he had just thrown the saddle on had bloated, Taylor kneed him in the gut and yanked the cinch tight at the same time, then secured the buckle. He unhooked the stirrup from the saddle horn to let it dangle in place.

As he lowered the stirrup one notch, he casually asked, "You said Kalen exercised the horse. How is she doing?"

The one Nolan held mouthed the snaffle. He scratched the jowl to quiet the animal. "Miss Kalen's comin' along right smart. But her heart ain't in it yet. After noon vittles, she usually goes up to Jed's restin' place for 'bout an hour afore she settles in to afternoon chores. The girl's grievin' mighty hard, Taylor. 'Cept, I ain't seen a tear in her eye. Not one. Ain't natural that a woman don't cry."

Taylor had the same thought, but chose not to express it. "Help her move on to ground training, Nolan."

"Me? You'd be better at that, Taylor."

Yes, he would. But his mind and, more importantly, his body were never focused when Kalen was near. "Just do it. Please."

Nolan nodded and turned away, mumbling, "A body's got enough to do without . . ."

His voice faded away as he trudged on to the barn. Taylor mounted, and, with supreme effort, put Kalen out of his mind and began teaching the horse to respond to leg pressure alone. While the others were ready, this gelding needed several days' work before he would be fit to turn over to Murray.

Taylor had failed to appear for supper. When Kalen asked about waiting dinner for him, the family declined and didn't seem the least bit concerned.

Later, as Kalen and Blair mounted the stairs, Blair said in an offhanded manner, "He's probably off communing with his gods."

"What kind of gods?" Kalen asked.

Blair flopped across her bed and indicated the chair for Kalen. "Ever heard of father sun, mother earth? Then there's mighty wind, gentle snow." She shrugged. "All have significance in the Indians' spiritual life."

"Accordin' to my pa, *one* Almighty God made all of that."

Blair shrugged again. "I pray to one God, but if Taylor prays at all, he probably prays to the god he believes most influential in his life."

Half an hour later, Kalen retired to her own room. Elbows propped on the sill, chin cupped in her hands, she sat before the window, looking out on a moonlit landscape.

Blair's talk of a passel of gods made her wonder if that was one of the reasons white folks called Indians heathens. Along with the hellish things Indians did to captives or those they murdered.

She shivered, remembering something Aunt Livvie once said. *Kalen, I heard tell white men were the first to scalp.*

Then, as now, she didn't want to believe either side could commit such horrors. But Uncle Jed's abidin' hatred of the red man told her it was possible.

Unable to sleep, she rose, found her coat and gloves, and tiptoed down the stairs. Crisp air slapped her in the face when she stepped outside. No sound greeted her. No wind soughed through the leaves.

Stars glittered like ice crystals. Beautiful.

Once, an itinerant salesman who sold kitchenwares and dry goods had shown her a photograph of a saloon with men standing out front on the dirt road. She couldn't buy it, of course, but it sure was somethin'. Glancing around at the beauty of the night, she wondered if photographs could be taken in the dark. That would be somethin' to see, all right.

Jamming gloved hands into her pockets, she sauntered toward the river, cautioning herself to keep her eyes peeled for night hunters. She walked along the bank, enjoying the flicker of moonlight through the trees on the water. "One God or many," she murmured, "sure made a beautiful world."

Pausing, she raised her face and sniffed. Though faint, she detected smoke. Could be dangerous.

It hadn't rained for a spell. Despite the cold, fire would sweep through dry grass somethin' fierce.

She picked up her pace, and the smell grew stronger. Then she heard a sound that had captivated her once before.

A flute.

Paying no attention to where she was going, her boots crunching on dead leaves, she neared the sound. It stopped. So did she.

Listening to eerie silence, she held her breath. When a hand fell on her shoulder, she jumped a foot and whirled around.

"You should not be here," Taylor said.

Fascinated by his appearance, she barely heard his reproof.

A white cloth band circled his forehead. His broad chest was bare. Silky sable hair dusted his shoulders.

Her gaze shifted lower. He wore nothing but a loincloth and moccasins.

"You're gonna freeze," she blurted.

"Hardly. You should not be here," he repeated.

"I'm sorry. I didn't mean to horn in . . ."

From his sober expression, Taylor had come out in the woods for privacy. He wanted her gone. But she was too curious about what he had been doing besides playing his flute. Some sort of Indian ritual?

Her glance flicked toward the blanket spread beside a small fire. "I heard your flute." She looked into his shadowed eyes. "You play very well. Did your father teach you?"

"No," he replied shortly. Returning to the blanket, he crossed his ankles and sank down by the flute. His palms came to rest on his knees, spine straight.

Ignoring her, he looked toward the far side of the stream. Rather than disturb him further, Kalen found a stump and sat behind him.

While he remained as still as a fright-frozen deer, she fidgeted in the cold, blowing on her gloved hands, pulling the tail of her coat over her knees.

After several minutes elapsed, he sighed and picked up the flute. As he began to play, the haunting notes lulled her senses. She realized now why Taylor's Indian name fit so well. The plaintive notes reminded her of the sound of wind wailing through a canyon, while quick notes conjured tree leaves rustling in a breeze.

Beautiful music, she thought, wanting him to continue. But a final note whistled mournfully for a long breath, then faded away.

He laid the flute across his bare thighs and again sat unmoving. Kalen waited, wondering what he was doing. Prayin'? Finally, she murmured just loud enough for him to hear, "That was beautiful, Taylor. Did you make it up yourself?"

Glancing over his shoulder, he rose gracefully and turned to face her, the flute cradled on his bent arm. "I play what I hear."

" 'Scuse me?"

"I play what I hear in my head. I learned long ago when I first visited the cave."

He didn't have to elaborate about which cave. The memories, the feelings she'd experienced there washed over her in a rush. Her woman parts heated; her cheeks warmed. She ducked her head.

"Um . . . I heard you playin' in the house once."

"I do not read the white man's music. I listen to the notes played on the piano."

She looked up, startled that he spoke directly in front of her. Again, she had not heard him move. In the next instant, his fingers slid beneath her chin. His mesmerizing eyes, darkened with desire, roamed her face, settled on her lips.

She licked them in response. "I . . ."

He shook his head. "Do not speak. Only feel."

His warm fingers moved up her cheek to cup the side of her face in his palm. "You fail to listen to my warnings. You play with fire, Kalen."

Tongue-tied by his closeness, she gazed into his eyes . . . wishing.

"I want you, woman. I should not, but I do."

"Want me?" She scowled. "You may want me, but you don't like me."

He cocked his head. "I beg your pardon?"

She stepped back from his touch. The touch that sent butterflies aflutter in her stomach. "You've ignored me for days. You hardly speak."

"We are destined to part one day."

"Maybe, but couldn't we . . ."

Taylor moved close again. Her eyes drifted shut. His scent surrounded her; his heat befuddled her.

"I want you. You tempt me beyond control . . . again." He dipped his head.

He intended to kiss her. She wouldn't stop him. No, she wouldn't.

A guilty thought of Graceful Bird flew through her head, then snuffed like a star winking out in the morning sky. As Taylor's warm lips settled on hers, his arms circled around and drew her against his naked chest.

She was lost.

One moment Taylor had known someone approached; the next his senses knew it was Kalen. He had given her the opportunity to leave. Truly, he had.

She did not.

Desire, need, flashed through him, quick and hot. He fostered no thoughts of right or wrong. He could not think past the burning in his soul for this woman. The Spirits might damn him, but right now he had to have her.

He stepped backward, relentlessly drawing her to the blanket by the meager fire. She did not resist when he guided her down to sit.

He tasted each corner of her lips, then looked into her flushed face. Evidently, her needs already matched his own. Amber eyes clouded by desire, she looked up at him. So trusting.

She pulled off her gloves and tossed them away. "Take me there again. Please?" Her restless hands brushed his bare shoulders, trailed down his arms.

When they slid around his ribs, he groaned.

"Take me there." From plea to demand.

"Where?" Blood sang through him, roaring in his head like a waterfall.

"To the edge of the stars."

His member jumped. She remembered. Nuzzling her lips, he nibbled his way down her throat, over the swell of her firm breast and found a taught nipple beneath the cotton shirt.

She gasped when he licked one, then the other, wetting the material.

"My pleasure," he murmured, and lost himself in her giving body.

Chapter Twenty-seven

When Kalen joined the family in the kitchen for supper, her gaze immediately landed on Taylor, seated at the foot of the table. Doreen bustled from stove to table with heaping dishes of potatoes, steak, hominy—which Kalen detested—and bread-and-butter pickles. The hominy and pickles, she knew, were from Doreen's stock of canned goods from last summer's garden.

"Have a seat," Doreen and Miz Savage said simultaneously.

It never ceased to amaze Kalen how the lady of the house perceived people.

Without a word, Kalen slid into the seat between Miz Savage and Blair. Highly sensitive herself to Taylor's presence, she was glad not to have to sit close to him.

Would she ever be able to sit in the same room with him and not have her cheeks warm at thoughts of the intimacy they'd shared?

The Savages never said a word, but she couldn't

help thinking they all knew about those glorious en-
counters. All they had to do was look at her flushed
cheeks. And Kalen had learned both Blair and
Cameron weren't shy about speakin' their minds.

"I wonder if it's safe for you to travel with your
brothers, Blair."

Travel? Where? Kalen had arrived apparently in
the middle of a conversation.

"Mother, the Murray place is only twenty-five
miles or so north." Blair cast a quick glance at her
older brother, then finished her argument. "Taylor
wouldn't let me go if he thought it was unsafe."

"Thirty-five or forty," he corrected. "And don't
put me in the middle of this, Blair," he cautioned, although his lips curved in a faint smile. "I said you
could go if Mother had no objection."

Miz Savage located the knife and fork lying beside her plate and proceeded to cut up her steak. "I
don't know that it is an objection, per se, Taylor."

Per say? Kalen looked from one to the other. Tarnation, she wished she understood all Miz Savage's
fancy words.

Finished serving, Doreen took her usual seat at
Miz Savage's left. When the Savages chose to eat in
the kitchen, Doreen joined them. Her presence
made Kalen a bit more comfortable, though she'd
prob'ly never feel she belonged in this big house.
These folks were . . . rich, for one thing, and smarter
than her by a long shot.

In short order, Blair, who was really good at per-
suasion, shot down a possible objection from her
mother. The conversation continued without Kalen's
input, and that suited her just fine.

Right after Doreen served pie, Kalen discovered that the children, as Miz Savage never failed to refer to them, would be leaving in the morning for most of a week, delivering three horses to a Mr. Murray.

While she didn't expect it, Kalen wished she had been invited to go along. Maybe it was for the best. Her thoughts were too scattered when Taylor was around. With him gone, she could think, could decide what she should do.

What she wanted in her heart-of-hearts would never happen. The unsettling image of Graceful Bird intruded. Kalen's glance flew to Taylor.

She still didn't have the courage to come right out and ask him, but she thought Graceful Bird was howlin' into shiftin' wind. Looking soberly at herself and how she fell into his arms whenever he crooked a finger, reality sliced her heart with a blunt-edged knife. Shoot, she thought bleakly, if Taylor got what he wanted so easily, why would he ask a woman to marry?

He wouldn't. The words whispered in her head, then shouted, *He won't!*

The next morning, Taylor searched in vain for Kalen. He had hoped she would see them off. But she failed to appear at the breakfast table, and Nolan said she had saddled the gelding Taylor had given her and ridden off early.

"Said she was gonna check on a geldin' that might need doctorin'."

Nolan scratched his jaw thoughtfully and said no more, so Taylor let it go. He had to deliver the horses. Best not to dwell on Kalen's anguish right now. Time enough to talk to her upon his return.

And say what? he wondered, as he handed each sibling a lead rope. In truth, he did not know Kalen that well. Yes, he knew her body, reveled in making love to her. But he knew little about her thoughts. Her dreams. If she had them.

"You will keep an eye on your sister, boys?" his mother called, her hand resting on Doreen's arm.

"Must we?" Cameron asked.

"Son," Lael warned, mock threat in her voice.

"All right, all right!" Chuckling, he ducked when Blair batted his shoulder with her hat.

Taylor rolled his eyes as he mounted. "I will doubtless regret taking both of you along. It would probably be easier to lead all three horses than arbitrate between you two."

Blair batted her lashes. *"Moi? Ange que je suis?"*

He grinned at her innocent expression. "Angel?" He shook his head. "Hardly. You two better ride the straight and narrow, or I'll send you home in a heartbeat . . . together."

Both dramatically clapped hands to their chests. "Spare me," Cameron said. At the same time, Blair squealed as if pinched.

Wearily, he ordered, "Move them out before I smack both of you even sillier."

"Go with God," Lael called.

Kalen sat her mount at the paddock gate and looked at the gelding that had kicked her uncle. Several yards away, he stared back at her as if he knew who she was and why she was there. He snatched up some grass, then went back to staring at her, placidly chomping the greens.

She'd told Taylor she didn't want him destroyed, so Mr. Woodruff or one of the hands had undoubtedly doctored the horse. His eyes looked clear.

She had no trouble with that. She surely didn't. This horse was not a killer. It was an accident. Uncle Jed had been careless and paid the price.

A mighty high price.

She fought back the tears she'd managed not to shed thus far. Why that seemed important, she didn't know. Well, she did, because Miz Savage had said the sweetest thing.

He is with the angels.

Kalen wanted to believe that. If it were true, her tears would be for herself, not Uncle Jed. He was in a better place and no longer had to fight demon drink.

"That's a blessin'," she whispered, and sniffled.

She dismounted, loosely tied her horse and slipped between the slats. Taking deliberate steps, she walked toward the gelding, clicked her tongue and extended a hand. "Here, boy."

The horse, mostly black with a few splotches of white down on his flanks, blinked his long eyelashes. He blew, not taking his eyes off her as she moseyed toward him.

Kalen reached in her pocket for a carrot she had filched from the pantry. The horse stopped midway to grabbing up another mouthful of grass, whinnied and took a few steps nearer.

"I thought so," she said. "You like these, huh?"

He extended his neck and snuffled the carrot before daintily nibbling it from her hand. The carrot crunched a few times between his strong teeth; then, all was silent.

The horse nudged her shoulder, watching her from soleful eyes. Those big, sad-looking eyes were her undoing.

Kalen turned her face into the horse, looped one arm over and the other under his warm neck, and let the tears flow. "Oh, God, why? Now, I don't have anyone."

Her sobs wrenched hard, deep, and she couldn't stop. It didn't matter. There was no one to see. The gelding stood stone still, as if he commiserated with her sorrow.

Weak from the racking sobs, she tightened her hold on his neck. Yet he remained still, allowing her to bawl all over him. After what seemed like forever, she finally sniffled and wiped her drippy nose on the back of her hand.

Loosening her death grip on the pinto, she patted him, crooned her thanks, and rubbed his ear. "You won't tell anyone I cried like a baby, will you?"

He turned his head just enough to look at her, ears twitching. Kalen gave a watery chuckle and wiped tears from her hot eyes.

"I'm a mess. You won't have to tell; everyone will see."

The horse nudged her side. She patted her pockets to show him there were no more treats. "Sorry, that's all I have. Maybe tomorrow."

With one last pat, she turned away and stopped dead.

Across the corridor in another corral, Nathan watched her from atop a horse, his dark eyes troubled. A red-and-white bandanna circled his forehead, taming his midnight hair cut raggedly to below his shoulders. Like Taylor, he wore buckskins.

Oh, Lord, she had bawled and carried on so loudly, she hadn't known he was there. And he'd seen everythin'! She took a hitching breath and walked closer to him.

He waited until she had edged out through the fence before he nodded. Sober-faced, he touched a finger to his headband, reined the horse about, and rode toward three others stabled in the big-as-a-pasture corral.

As she considered his somber, respectful demeanor, it dawned on her what he'd been doin'. He'd watched over her until she cried herself out, assurin' himself she was able to take care of herself before he left her alone with grief.

She looked skyward. "See, Uncle Jed? Indians really are just like us."

When she returned to the barn, even though Mr. Woodruff and Jasper could see she had been crying, neither said anything. In fact, Mr. Woodruff looked relieved. Surprisingly, the foreman gave her a horse to school on a lead. Later, he put her atop another to exercise in the big, covered ring.

By late afternoon, Kalen had settled into the routine again and helped with the feeding before calling it a day. By the time she approached the back door, lamps glowed from the windows.

She stepped into the warm kitchen and shrugged

out of her beautiful coat. "Oh, my, it feels wonderful in here." Lifting her chin, she sniffed. "Smells good, too."

Pulling bread from the oven, Doreen glanced over her shoulder and grinned. "My bread is tasty, to be sure. If I do say so meself."

"Is that apple pie?"

" 'Tis the mum's favorite. With the bairns gone for a few days, I be cheerin' her as best I can."

Doreen gave Kalen the once-over. "You'll be wantin' to wash up before supper, I'm thinkin'."

Kalen grimaced at her stained work pants and shirt, then looked back at the steaming pots on the stove. "I need a bath, but since you're ready to eat, I'll wait until after supper."

She headed through the house and passed the parlor with only a quick glimpse at Miz Savage, one of those books on her lap. Kalen called, "I'll be right down, ma'am. Got to hang up my coat and wash my face and hands."

If the lady acknowledged her, Kalen didn't hear over the clatter of her boots on the stairs. After hanging her coat on the back of the door, she aimed for the pitcher of water Doreen replenished every day.

Kalen splashed a little into the bowl and scrubbed her face. Eyes closed, she groped for the towel draped on the hook at the side of the washstand. As she dried her face, she caught sight of herself in the oval mirror.

Horsefeathers. Her bloodshot eyes looked like Uncle Jed's after a night nursin' a bottle. Even a comb wouldn't tame her dusty, unruly hair. Doreen had been working in the house all day and looked cleaner and more ladylike than Kalen could ever hope for.

Well, Miz Savage couldn't see how she looked, so she would sit at the table and pretend she belonged there. Maybe her presence would ease the absence of the lady's children.

A sobering thought, that. One day she herself would have to eat alone.

Chapter Twenty-eight

Stretched out in his bedroll, hands beneath his head, Taylor watched a star streak across the ebony sky, leaving a phosphorescent trail. He sighed, glad to be communing with the quiet of the night.

Though he loved them both from their mischievous hearts to their sparkling laughter, Cameron and Blair had worn on his patience today. But it wasn't their fault he had to hie off forty miles for several days rather than stay near a grieving Kalen.

When the horses made faint noises, he inspected the tie-line. Only resettling, thank the Spirits. He expected to make this trip without incident. The last time he spoke with his uncle, One Bear had said Comanche bands to the north were quiet. For the moment, anyway.

Well he knew that Comanche could strike for sport, inflict death, and carry off captives as swiftly as a blue norther could deep-freeze the prairie. But he had heard no grumbling from the white world of late, so he hoped the Comanche would remain quiet, at least until warm weather.

Another star dove for the horizon. For no good reason, he tensed. *What?* he asked his inner spirit.

Sitting up, he peered into the darkness surrounding their small camp. The cook fire had long since died. He listened. No wind tonight, only the faint sounds of animals running from night hunters or hunting for themselves.

"Whooo," an owl hooted somewhere in the distance. A long way off, came the distinctive yip-bark of a pack of coyotes, undoubtedly running a meal to ground.

A chill slithered down his spine when a third star crossed the heavens to burn itself out. If those were signs of something amiss, he had no clue of what they warned. He lay back down and listened to . . . silence. Total, deafening silence.

Long into the night, his mind churned over what he knew so well . . . training horses, the pitfalls of existing in the white world. But his last waking thoughts were of Kalen, which led to fitful dreams.

The taste of her.

Soft skin beneath his fingertips.

Lael Savage sat primly eating supper, Kalen watching her every move. The lady's spine was as straight as could be. She didn't look stiff or anything, just elegant in her blue muslin dress trimmed in beautiful white lace. Today, she'd caught her abundant, silver-streaked dark hair in a crocheted snood at the back of her head.

Kalen suspected her glinting earbobs were diamonds, but she didn't think it proper to ask. Miz Savage always wore them. Once in a while she also wore a necklace of black jet or pearls, but nothing gaudy.

"Do you like to read?"

Her question caught Kalen off guard. "Some." It wasn't as if she'd had a library to choose from like the Savages did. They were lucky. Even when Aunt Livvie was alive, they'd only owned a half dozen books. The Bible, of course, and a few well-thumbed storybooks. Novels, Aunt Livvie had called them, and it was she who did the readin', not Kalen or Uncle Jed.

"Have you ever read Shakespeare or Lord Byron?"

Kalen shot a glance at Doreen, who was looking expectantly at her. "Uh, no, ma'am. I heard tell of that Shakespeare fella, but I don't know much about him. Who's Lord Byron?"

Lael finished chewing the last of her supper and laid the fork across her plate, just like she had the knife when she finished usin' it. Kalen had noticed all the Savages did that when they were done eatin'.

When she asked about it, Doreen said that was the mannerly way to end a meal. "When I was a wee one in Ireland, me mam served in the lord's house, where me pa was head groom. When the gentry finished a meal, a footman whisked away the dirty dishes."

Although Kalen didn't know what the dickens a footman was, she laid her knife and fork across her plate and leaned back against the chair. Miz Savage smiled, that sweet smile that cramped Kalen's heart every time. If only her own ma had lived.

"Lord Byron wrote poetry. I have a book of his poems that you are welcome to read, dear."

Ducking her head, she hid her expression from Doreen. Poems? Boy-howdy, she'd never read much of that flowery writin'. Only psalms, and precious few of them.

"Thank you kindly, ma'am," was all she said.

On the third night of eating without the children, Lael waited until Kalen retired upstairs before she sought Doreen in the kitchen. As she entered, she heard the usual clatter of washing and putting away of cutlery and pans.

"Are you about finished, Doreen?"

"Yes. Would you be wantin' a posset, mum? You seem off your feed these last two nights, I'm thinkin'."

"I've been listening."

Doreen hung up the wet towel and turned to her boss. "Listenin'?"

"To Kalen. Mostly her silences. She has something on her mind. Something about which she is dissatisfied. And I don't believe it has anything to do with her uncle's passing."

"Whatever could it be, mum? She's not a flibberti-gibbet, thank the saints. And she's certainly not as friendly and outgoin' as Miss Blair. I be thinkin' she's just a quiet miss."

"Something preys on her mind," Lael said with conviction, then sighed. "It's such a curse not to be able to see someone's expression."

"Ah. I see. However, I be thinkin', if you fancied yourself readin' Mr. Taylor's expressions, you'd be flummoxed."

Lael chuckled. "I beg to differ with you. Now, my Wolf, I could read him like the North Star."

"Ah, but he was your husband and your lover, mum!"

Lael laughed aloud this time and felt her face warm. It had been years since she had blushed.

Before she could speak, Doreen said, "Oh, to be sure, my mouth gets in the way of my thinkin' sometimes. That was forward of me. I be beggin' your pardon."

Still smiling, Lael said, "Think nothing of it, my dear. You are probably right, anyway. Mothers believe they know their children so well. And perhaps we do when they are tied to our apron strings. But once grown . . . perhaps not."

Seated at the window again, looking out on the star-lit heavens, Kalen came to a painful conclusion. She didn't fit here. The Savages were far and away more book learned than her. Always would be. Shoot, she knew how to read, write, and cipher, but when her ma died, Kalen's schooling died with her.

Kalen had not been raised to be a lady. She had been raised to be a ranch worker. To do what her uncle told her, to follow the orders of her bosses at the ranches where they found work.

She dressed like a young man in trousers and shirts, the only clothing she had. Kalen glanced at the warm coat hanging on the peg, a shadow in the faint light. That, the gloves, and the Stetson were the only nice things she owned. And they had been gifts from the family who probably knew she wasn't as smart as they were. Just too kind to say so.

Early the next morning, before Miz Savage or Doreen stirred, Kalen walked up the slope to her uncle's grave. She stared at the mounded dirt, which was already settling. Glancing around in the increasing daylight, she marveled at the view from here. Miz Savage was right. A body could see the entire valley and far into the distance in all directions. Again, that sense of peace that she'd felt the first time she saw the ranch came over her.

Kneeling, she picked up a clod of black soil and crushed it in her hand, then watched the dirt cascade through her fingers to the ground. "I guess you belong here now, Uncle Jed, but I don't. These folks are kind, but . . ."

As no one would hear her, unless it was her uncle's ghost, she whispered, "He'll never love me, Uncle Jed. He'll never marry me." She inhaled a hitching breath. "I guess I better move on."

She laid her hat on the ground and gazed into the distance. "Don't know where I'll go, but I'm leavin' you in a beautiful place." She glanced down at the grave again. "Guess what, one day Miz Savage will prob'ly be close by, too. I know you admired her.

"There's nobody left, Uncle Jed." Tears clogged her throat. She'd not have to worry anymore about findin' him passed out somewhere.

Time after time, once he'd sobered enough to climb onto the high seat, she'd loaded up the wagon and pushed on. Moving wasn't so bad. Besides the two horses and wagon and a few pieces of clothing, all they possessed was one saddle and bridle, a couple ropes, the twitch, a shovel and two threadbare bedrolls.

Tipping her head back, watching a hawk soar on a light breeze, she thought of all she'd be leavin' behind. She'd never had a real, grown-up woman friend . . . until Blair.

And Cameron . . . She smiled. He was a caution, rambunctious, like a mischievous colt. One day he'd find a woman and knock her socks off with his winnin' smile. She guessed it was called charm. And kind, so kind, like his sister and mother.

Miz Savage. Oh, my. Such a lady. She always treated Kalen so nice.

"Taylor . . ." Beyond speech, Kalen bowed her head.

Tomorrow mornin' she'd head out. Didn't make a lick of difference which direction. She just couldn't stay here and long for what would never be.

Nolan squeezed through the fence and straightened. His back creaked like an old hinge. Lord, Lord, he was gettin' too old for this early-mornin' patchwork on fences. Course, it could be barbed wire needin' restretchin'. A heap worse than nailin' up a few boards.

Clay followed him through the fence, a tool belt clanking on his slim hips. There'd been a time when Nolan was as spry and muscular as any man on this ranch, but Father Time was takin' his toll. Though still strong enough to do what was required, Nolan let the younger fellers do the heavier work now.

The missus and the young'ns didn't expect him to do more than direct the hands on the never-endin' tasks needed to keep the ranch in top shape. Taylor, like his pa afore him, believed that excellent stock sprung from good breedin', expert handlin', and clean, comfortable surroundin's kept orderly to do what was necessary.

"Rider coming," Clay said as he released the heavy belt from around his narrow hips. "Kalen girl."

When Nathan and Clay had begun working here about three years ago, it hadn't taken Nolan long to understand that a few cryptic words from the two passed for amiable conversation. Running Wolf had communicated much the same way. Taylor, though not as abrupt, didn't run at the mouth, neither.

Clay buckled the belt to Nolan's saddle. Pulling the slipknot off the fence, he leaped aboard his own horse's bare back. Without another word, he headed farther along the rows of paddocks, checking for loosened wood. If he found any, he'd let Nolan know.

Holding to his place, Nolan watched Miss Kalen ride toward him. He frowned when he saw what she rode. While he was prob'ly the better of the two belongin' to her uncle, the raw-boned geldin' still cut a sorry sight.

As she neared, he saw a bedroll flopping behind the saddle. If he didn't miss his guess, she sat Jed's old saddle, too. He scowled, lifted his hat and wiped the sweat from his brow with his sleeve.

"Miss Kalen?" he questioned. She slowed, then stopped a few feet away. He eyed her somber expression and the equipage attached to the saddle. A sack clanked a tinny sound when her knee brushed it. Cup and plate, he thought. A shovel, rope, and that gol-durned twitch he'd cringed at when he saw it in Jed's wagon. Even though a rifle stuck up from the scabbard, alarm swept him. "Goin' somewheres?"

"Yessir. Hope you don't mind Tom gettin' in the strongbox. I didn't think it right, but he paid me a month's wages less two days."

"Tom can do that when I ain't around. No problem." He scratched his chin. "Less two days?"

Her cheeks reddened. "I haven't been pullin' my share since Uncle Jed . . ."

"That ain't right, and you got no call for leavin'. You got a place here, missy."

She sucked in a shaky breath. He figured she was two nips from bawlin'.

"Miz Savage know you're lightin' out?" He wasn't surprised when she shook her head.

He scanned the gear again. "What you plannin' to eat?"

She patted the rifle and a pocket. "I'm a good shot, Mr. Woodruff. And I'm right handy with a snare."

"That may be, but you ain't got no coffee that I can see, and you got no flapjack makin's. Potatoes, neither."

"It ain't like I'm travelin' across the desert, Mr. Woodruff. There's several ranches no more'n a two-day ride. I can prob'ly find work at one of 'em."

The horse blew and stamped a foot. She patted his withers. "I best be goin'. Old Jim is gettin' impatient-like."

He clasped the near rein but patted the horse's

nose. Neither of Jed's horses was high strung, but from long experience with abrupt handling, Nolan automatically used calming methods.

"Miss Kalen, you can't go ridin' off without a sure place to light. Taylor would have my hide if'n—"

"Mr. Savage don't have a say 'bout what I do. Besides," she added, the bleakest expression in a body's eyes he'd ever seen, "he don't care." She tugged on the reins to lift the horse's head from Nolan's restraining grip.

With no choice left, he released his hold and stepped close to the fence, out of her path.

"So long," she said over her shoulder.

He swore her voice was roughened by tears. And that galvanized him to sprint for his horse tied at the end of the paddock.

In less than fifteen minutes, he pounded up to the house and threw himself out of the saddle. Striding across the porch, he rapped on the door once, but didn't wait to be admitted.

Lael looked up from her daily devotions and blinked when the foreman burst into the parlor, his breathing labored. "Nolan?"

"It's Miss Kalen, ma'am. She's leavin'."

Nolan's scratchy voice and heavy breathing alarmed her. "Are you all right?"

"It ain't me to worry 'bout, ma'am. It's the Barrett girl. She's taken little but herself and rode off. For no reason. We gotta go after her."

"Kalen is gone?" It was hard to take in. And like Nolan, she could see no reason why the girl would leave. No one had mistreated her here. No one would dare. And from the little talk she'd heard, Kalen had done a fine job, whatever the task.

"Ma'am?" Nolan questioned.

Lael gazed off into space. "I thought she would stay if her uncle was buried here. But, puzzling as it is, we cannot hold Kalen here against her will, Nolan."

"Taylor wouldn't let her go."

Lael thought perhaps Nolan was right, but . . . "The earliest we can expect Taylor home is tomorrow evening. Until then, we must abide by Kalen's decision."

For several seconds there was no sound, then Nolan sighed. "Maybe you're right. But your boy is gonna be mad."

One can hope.

Chapter Twenty-nine

Kalen drew in her mount to assess her surroundings. Fortunately, the sun had shown all day, so she had been able to keep to a fairly northerly track. Problem was, she wasn't sure how soon she should turn east. If she missed the ranches, Waco was thataway; once there, she could ask around. Get a better notion of direction and how far she'd have to travel to find work.

By midday she had shed her warm coat, but as the sun blazed toward the horizon, the temperature began to dip. She should prob'ly find a sheltered place to stay the night.

Standing in the stirrups as if the extra inches would give her a better view of the endless, low-rolling terrain, she twisted one way, then the other. Casting a quick glance at the sun, she figured she had about an hour afore daylight deserted her.

Though it was opposite the direction she wanted to go, maybe if she hustled, she could reach the line

of trees that might, she hoped, border a stream.
Could she be that lucky? Only one way to find out.

Since Jim would never be a saddle horse, she
clicked her tongue and lightly tapped the end of a
rein on his rump. He responded like he would in
harness.

She got him up to a trot, and before long she rode
among a few live oaks and straggly sycamores. Sure
enough, she found water. More a trickle than a
stream, but it served to relieve her thirst and Jim's.

After tying him so he could graze, she pulled a
length of twine from her pocket and fashioned a
snare. She'd filched some leftover biscuits from the
Savages' kitchen afore daylight, but she'd finished
the last one midafternoon.

Kalen banked the small cook fire, laid out her
bedroll and slipped beneath the threadbare blanket.
Belly full, she cast a glance Jim's way. Although he
looked half-starved, he was an easy keeper. Both of
her uncle's horses were intelligent enough not to
founder themselves by overeating. Right now he
stood that relaxed, hip-shot way, dozing. While
placid-natured, he would come alive if threatened.
She counted on that.

Peering through the canopy of foliage, she could
see those same sparkling stars viewed from the Savages' house. She wondered what Taylor was doin'
right now, then chastised herself for a fool. She had
to stop this dadburned longin'.

She flipped to her stomach and reached behind to
drag the blanket over her backside. The ground was

too hard against her cheek, too cold. This wasn't gonna work. Wearily she turned back to stare bleakly into the heavens. Not goin' to be a restful night.

Kalen came awake to bright daylight. Throwing her arm across her eyes, she groaned her displeasure at the glare . . . and even that slight movement, jarred her creaking back.

Sensing she wasn't alone, her eyes flew open. She sat straight up and searched the woods. Behind her, Jim's nicker was answered by another horse.

Tarnation!

The blankets fell to the ground as she clambered to her feet. Her blood froze at the sight of three Indians. In the next instant, she recognized Graceful Bird and the taller of the two men.

He scowled. "What you do here?"

Shoot, he prob'ly didn't know her name, but his question meant he'd recognized her, too.

Graceful Bird spoke in their befuddling language. The men walked away, leaving her to face Kalen alone. She waited until her companions were out of earshot. "You go?"

Kalen nodded and began untangling the knotted blankets. The disarray, added to her achin' bones, told her she'd had a restless night. "You're a long way from home."

"Hunting."

So, Kalen had been right. Graceful Bird might not speak English well, but she understood a lot.

The woman jabbed a thumb against her own

white-and-green calico-covered chest. "Taylor mine."

Maybe not. Wouldn't he have asked her to marry by now if he intended to? Maybe Graceful Bird wouldn't fit into the Savage family any better than she would. None of her business, though. And it no longer mattered.

Kalen told herself that, anyway.

Trying her best to ignore the woman, she went about breaking her meager camp. After saddling Jim, she stowed her belongings, tying them on each side of the horse to balance the load.

Just as she finished, the men came back. The one who seemed to be in charge rattled off something to Graceful Bird. Her retort was short, dark eyes stern. They faced each other down. Finally, the man snapped curtly and strode away.

Graceful Bird didn't budge. Instead, she sneered something in Comanche, not at the man but at Kalen. Then in English, she said, "Sound Of Wind soon mate."

Kalen wondered if the woman was trying to convince herself or Kalen, but this time she couldn't let it pass. Not the least bit Christian of her, but Kalen sneered back. "Maybe. Maybe not." With a shrug she lied, "Makes no difference to me."

Eyes spiteful, Graceful Bird only grunted, clearly disbelieving.

Her adversary was right, but Kalen swept up her hat and mounted, determined to hide her anguish. Throat thick she said, "So long."

Paying no attention to direction, she slapped Jim's rump harder than necessary and never looked back.

* * *

Taylor slowed behind his siblings. As they neared home, he allowed Blair and Cameron free rein to race each other to the barn. Traveling with them always made him feel ancient. But then, he had never been as carefree as his siblings.

They were still ragging each other when he rode into the barn, but Taylor chose to ignore them. Their high spirits signaled they were as happy to be home as he.

Jasper appeared and led Blair's horse to her stall to rub her down. Taylor and Cameron took care of their own mounts.

Despite the late hour, Taylor noticed lantern light still glimmered from his mother's upstairs room. She'd had no clue when they would arrive, yet she somehow sensed they would be home tonight. Like him, she looked upon vague premonitions as unsettling rather than fortuitous.

"Thanks, Jasper." Blair threw her saddlebags over her shoulder and started for the house.

"Tell Mother we'll be in shortly," Cameron called.

Instead of simply acknowledging the request, Blair, as usual, had to have the last word. "When she hears *me*, she'll probably figure that out."

As he dragged the saddle from Creation's back, Taylor silently wagged his head. *What a pair.*

A few minutes later, he and Cameron mounted the stairs and paused at their mother's door. One glance at her face and Taylor's gut clenched.

"Mother?" He strode into the room, Cameron dogging his heels. "What's wrong? You aren't ill again, are you?"

"No, dear." She patted the harlequin quilt. "Sit down. I have something to tell you."

Scowling, he cast a quick glance at Cameron, who was equally as perplexed and concerned.

"Kalen rode out early yesterday morning. She has left us."

"Left us," Taylor repeated woodenly. "For a few days, two weeks . . . forever?" *Please, not forever!*

"Nolan came to me when he saw her leaving. He thought we should go after her, but I . . . Taylor, she *is* a grown woman. If she's decided to move on, we have no say in the matter."

Taylor could not speak past his closing throat. Any response was deadened by a roaring in his ears. *Kalen has left*, repeated over and over.

Why would she leave?

I want her.

But she apparently did not want him. He rubbed his chest, dead sure his heart had cracked and half of it plummeted into his stomach. He rose from the bed and walked to the doorway.

"Taylor?" his mother questioned.

At the same time, Cameron said, "You hired her. You can bring her back."

No, he thought. If she wanted to go, he would not stand in her way. "That is where you are wrong, Cameron." He walked down the hall to his room, and closed the door.

"Idiot!" Cameron grumbled. He snapped his attention back to his mother. "Sorry. Not you. It's that stubborn brother of mine. There is no telling what sort of mischief will befall Kalen out there alone on the prairie."

Lael extended her hand. A moment later Cameron took it. "Give him time, dear. He will come around. Taylor must lick his wounds for a while."

"Wounds?" Cameron snorted. "My brother? And for that *while*, Kalen is riding farther and farther away. Into possible danger."

She squeezed his fingers. "I pray God that is not the case."

Taylor leaned back against the door, rubbed his eyes and pinched the bridge of his nose. Damn her to the netherworld. Did Kalen think nothing of their times together?

Sneaking off without a word to anyone. Thunderation! Had Nolan not seen her, no one would have known what happened to her. For that matter, no one knew where she was now or what may have befallen her since yesterday morning.

His eyes adjusting quickly to the darkness, he shed his coat and hung it on the door hook, then strode to the window and lifted the curtain aside. Resting a hand on the wall, he leaned and stared into the night sky.

Still cold, but at least clear tonight. No rain to soak her belongings and maybe drive pneumonia into her lungs. Eyes bleak, he muttered, "Foolish woman."

Spinning, he stomped to the bed and dropped to the edge, pressing calloused hands on either side of his legs. He glared at his boots as if they had somehow offended him. *Kalen, Kalen, Kalen!* wheeled through his mind like the blades of a windmill spinning in a stiff breeze.

His chin lifted as his brother's words rang in his head. *You can bring her back.*

Not giving himself time to talk himself out of it, he grabbed up spare saddlebags, stuffed one side with a change of clothing, his moccasins and a loincloth, retrieved his coat and pounded down the stairs to the kitchen. He filled the other side of the saddlebags with Doreen's canned goods, fatback, bacon and coffee. He'd snitch a coffeepot and utensils from the saddlebags left in the tack room.

On his way to the stud barn, he walked through the main barn and came to an abrupt halt when Kalen's little gelding swung his head over the gate, whinnying for attention. "Spirits," he gritted, tight-jawed, "what is she riding? Don't tell me . . ."

Sure enough, walking on, he found only one of Jed's geldings. *Little fool.* Shaking his head in disgust, he stalked into the stud barn, directly to Comanche Moon.

With swift tosses and quick jerks, he had the horse saddled, and his saddlebags and bedroll secured in no time. He swung aboard and thundered out of the barn.

Unaware which direction she had taken, he rode to the end of fenced pastures, then slowed and began the painstaking search for sign.

He would find her, all right. And when he did, he would bring her back to where she belonged or know the reason why.

Chapter Thirty

Her mouth desert dry, Kalen knelt in the dirt, head hanging as four Comanche warriors surrounding her argued in guttural tones. Why in tarnation hadn't she bedded down an hour ago while she still had full daylight to see where she was goin'?

Oh, no. Instead, she stumbled right into a bunch of Indians. Indians she sure as shootin' had never seen before. And if their angry conversation meant what she thought it meant, they were gonna have her for supper. But first, she'd be violated . . . maybe by all four . . . *before* they skinned her. *Please, Lord, not alive. Let me die first.*

Although she'd give anything not to shake so, she couldn't help it. She knew what folks meant now when they said a body could taste fear. A heavy, rough hand snatched her up by the hair.

"Ow!" She kicked and swung at him. "Damn you! Let me go!"

He did, stepping back to join his laughing companions.

"This ain't one bit funny, you rat snakes!" *Shut up, Kalen. You're just askin' for grief.* But what did she really have to lose? *Oh, Uncle Jed! Taylor . . .*

One of them stepped closer and feinted as if he intended to pull her hair again. When she batted him away, he found it hilarious; he doubled over and slapped his knees, the ends of his greasy hair nearly dusting the ground.

The other three pounded him on the back, laughter rolling out of them. She looked off toward the lighter sky where the sun had set. If only she dared . . . Shoot, she wouldn't get ten steps before they were on her again.

Suddenly, they started yelling at each other. She looked from one face to the next, wishin' she knew what all the loud palaverin' was about. The older one punched the scar-faced one on the shoulder, hard enough to stagger him.

But he came right back, swingin' like he meant to do some damage. No foolin' this time.

And then she heard it.

Hoofbeats.

Faint and growin' louder.

Faint though they were, she lifted her head and saw a rider comin' hell-for-leather straight at them. The Indians, so caught up in their melee, didn't hear him.

She squinted to see in the gloom. Another Indian?

Then her heart nearly stopped. She recognized the big stallion eating up ground. *Comanche Moon!*

"Oh, God, oh, God," she whispered. Taylor was bearing down on them. And suddenly she knew what he intended to do.

She turned, raised her arms and took a running step just as he swooped down. His arm circling her waist, he jerked her off her feet. She lifted her knees and went with the momentum, landing in front of him on the stallion's back.

Letting out a bloodcurdling, triumphant scream, Taylor thundered right through the Indians. They fell back, scrambling to get away from flying hooves.

"Taylor, Taylor! Thank God, thank God," she chanted, twisting to throw an arm around his neck.

Still flying at full speed across the ground, he held loose reins and a rifle in one hand; his other pressed her against his body. She pulled his head down and kissed him . . . hard. Then, over the horse's pounding hooves she heard the chilling screams.

Jerking her mouth from his, she scanned behind them. "They're comin'!"

"Of course." He pulled her arm off his neck. "Turn around, woman, and hang on. We have to find someplace to defend ourselves until I can talk to them."

"Talk to them? Are you nuts?"

In the next instant, he hauled in Comanche Moon so hard, the horse reared, sending both of them sliding off his bare back. But prepared, Taylor landed on his feet. When Kalen staggered back, he snatched her up around the waist and ran like hell for the meager protection of oaks and rocks. He whistled shrilly, a signal to his neighing horse. Barely evading the Indians' attempt to catch his trailing reins, Comanche Moon followed.

"Here," Taylor ordered, and the horse weaved between two large rocks, presenting himself before Taylor like a seasoned warrior. "Good boy." He gave the stallion a slap on his rump as he sidled by.

Taylor dumped Kalen behind a rock. She watched as he pulled a six-shooter from the belt around his waist. That, a loincloth and moccasins were all he wore. No wonder she thought he was another Indian.

"He *is* Indian, dummy," she muttered. But Taylor was an Indian she thanked God for.

Kalen rubbed her backside. The ground was unforgiving, for sure. She started to peek over the rock just as a bullet kicked up chunks that stung her face.

Taylor mashed the top of her head, sending her to her knees. "Stay down, woman!"

In the next breath, he yelled something in Comanche. Another bullet whizzed past, but Taylor didn't give up. Again he bellowed several words she wished to heaven she could understand.

Her head hugging the rock, she watched him talk to the sky, not ready to put her head up for target practice, although the bullets had stopped.

He paused, listening to one of the Indians call back to him. Kneeling, he laid his palm against her cheek. "If you want to live, to leave this place, do as I say. Do not, I repeat, do not let them see you while I speak with them."

"But you—"

"Listen to me! I can convince them to leave only if you remain quiet and do not interfere."

She searched his intense eyes. His jaw clenched as he brushed his hand away from her face. "Stay down." He stood. Showing himself as he holstered the pistol, he stepped into the open. *"Pabi?"* he said, then, "brother?"

His voice faded as he strode away from where she crouched, her every limb trembling. "God, hear me just this one time," she whispered, arms crossed over her head. "Please, please keep him safe."

If he ever hoped to take Kalen away from here, he must make these men believe she belonged to him. In his band and several that he had visited, warriors honored the mate bond if they knew it to be truth.

"Greetings, my friends." He waited for the courtesy to be returned by the one in charge. Taylor was surprised when the youngest of the three stepped forward.

"Hawk Talon," he announced, punctuating his name with a slap to his own chest. "Brother of Howling Coyote."

Not good. More than the full circle of four seasons had passed since last Taylor heard of Howling Coyote's raids northeast of Waco. The chief made slaves of those he allowed to live, captured and drove off every horse they owned.

"I am Sound Of Wind."

When he failed to name important lineage, Hawk Talon smirked. "You have no father?"

Taylor swept his arm high and wide. "My great father rides his stallion with the Spirits."

Like every warrior Taylor knew, Hawk Talon was superstitious. Taylor, himself, would not mention a dead relative's name, but reference to the After World left these warriors mute with fear.

Taylor stepped into the breach. "My stupid

woman lost her way and wandered from camp." He shrugged as if Kalen was of little value. "She carries my babe or I would abandon her."

Privately, he thanked the Spirits Kalen could not understand his words. Otherwise, she would ignore his orders and come out of hiding hopping mad.

Hawk Talon scowled. His companions grumbled among themselves. "She is not round of belly."

"Pieces Of Sky Eyes said she grows quick with child."

All three men stepped back, eyes round. The oldest asked, "The shaman?"

Taylor squelched a grin. Pieces Of Sky Eyes was the most gentle of women, but she wielded powerful medicine. Grown men ran from evidence of her magic.

"She is wife of my uncle, One Bear."

The older Indian leaned forward and squinted at Taylor. "You are called Savage?"

Taylor nodded, uneasy. What had these Indians heard about his family?

The Indian turned to Hawk Talon and muttered something Taylor did not catch. But bless the Spirits, Hawk Talon began to back away, pointing at Taylor. "You go."

All four pivoted, strode to their mounts and swung aboard. From that distance Hawk Talon ordered again, "Go!" Wheeling around, he did not look back as his horse lengthened into a gallop. His companions followed closely.

Taylor narrowed his eyes, wondering what in thunderation that was all about. He watched until they disappeared from sight. The scree of a hawk startled him. Watching the free-flying bird, he smiled. *Thank you, friend, for reminding me to make tracks myself.*

He hurried to the rock where, miracle of miracles, Kalen had actually done as he had told her and remained out of sight. Before they moved from this spot, though, he would make his case, and by the Spirits, she would return to the ranch if he had to hog-tie her.

Crouched behind the rock, Kalen strained to hear, but a bird's cry overhead distracted her. She cast a baleful glance skyward and listened again.

Footsteps? Not boots. But then, Taylor wore moccasins just like the Indians. And heaven help her, Indians could strike quietly if they wanted to.

She hadn't heard much besides a few indecipherable words. Maybe they'd put a knife in Taylor's heart before he could warn her. Heart racing, she crouched lower. What could she do?

"Kalen?"

Such relief washed over her at Taylor's deep voice, she fell against the rock and brushed tears from her cheeks. Tears she hadn't realized she'd shed.

He saw the tears and knelt quickly. "Are you hurt?"

She gave a sharp shake of her head. "No, I just thought . . ." She threw herself at him, sprawling atop him as he fell backward. "God, Taylor, I thought they'd killed you!" Laying her head on his chest, she hugged him.

"Hold me," she pleaded. "I thought you were dead."

Sitting up, he moved her to his lap and wrapped his arms around her shaking frame. "I'm all right, Kalen. Don't cry." He stroked her curls. "Shh."

She jerked back and glared at him. "What are you doin' here?"

This woman was like a chameleon, wilting one minute, spitting fire the next. "Saving you, it appears." He arched a brow. "You left without a word to anyone, Kalen. I . . . We wondered if—"

"We who? I told Mr. Woodruff I was headin' out."

"Nolan is not the person who hired you, Kalen. I—"

"Nobody hired me. You hired Uncle Jed. I got tossed in as an extra for pennies."

"Whoa! Have you not received pay right along with the rest of the hands at the end of each month?"

"Well, yeah, but that was sort of forced on you."

Though she argued with him, Taylor still held Kalen on his lap, still wrapped his arms protectively around her. The fear he had felt when he saw her surrounded by unfriendlies had sent his pulse racing. It had begun to slow, yet he needed her in his arms, needed the reassurance.

"Kalen, nothing is ever forced upon me. I do what I please, when I please. If I had not wanted both of you on the ranch, I would not have hired you."

She focused narrowed eyes on his. "Is that the truth? But you thought I was a kid."

"Not for long," he murmured, his fingers stroking her back as though taming a wild thing.

She shivered.

He lowered his head, lips a breath from hers. "I quickly discovered you are a desirable woman."

He kissed her, halting further conversation or protest. He wanted her . . . now. But he would wait. A plan had sprung to mind. One so full of promise, it made his heart sing.

If only Kalen would agree.

Chapter Thirty-one

They didn't ride far before making camp. Taylor smiled to himself, aware Kalen didn't know exactly where they were. He wanted it that way, had planned it that way. If all went well, he would have her in his arms once again, and this time . . .

Anticipation hummed through him as he watched her scour the utensils with sand, then rinse them in the stream. His gaze traveled over her narrow back and rounded bottom. The coat could not hide her charms. He licked his lips and smiled when she turned to look at him. Perhaps she had sensed his stare.

"What?"

"Nothing. Are you about finished?"

She gathered up everything and walked back to the fire. It had begun to die, and Taylor would let it, keeping only a few coals alive for a morning fire.

"We probably won't do more than coffee in the morning." He hiked his chin at the saddlebags. "You can stow everything but the cups and pot."

She returned to stand across the fire from where he sat. Where he had spread their bedrolls, side by side. Her gaze lit on them, then flicked to him.

"Um, Taylor, do you think we should sleep so . . ."

"Yes. It is cold tonight. We will need shared warmth."

Kalen glanced over her shoulder when a coyote howled. From a different direction, another answered, then another. He saw her shiver as she slowly sank on the far end of her bedroll.

"Huntin' for supper, I guess, huh?"

He nodded and beckoned. "You'll need to scoot in here, Kalen. This is the top of the bed."

She crawled to sit beside him, casting him a troubled look. "Why did you come after me?"

He picked up her hand, looked at the reddened knuckles. Rubbing his thumb over them, he sought the right words. It was now or never.

Glancing up, he brushed the backs of his fingers along her cheek. "I had to find you, Kalen. You took one of my most valued possessions with you."

She blinked, leaned back. "I didn't! Tarnation, Taylor, I took only my clothes and old Jim." She glanced at the gelding placidly eating the oats Taylor had split between the two horses. "Shoot. The Indians didn't even bother to take old Jim."

He clasped her chin and focused on her eyes, which mirrored the firelight. "Kalen, you should have taken the gelding I gifted to you." He laid a finger over her lips before she could speak. "But you did take something I cannot live without."

Her brow furrowed, but she didn't look away.

"You cannot guess what it is?"

She shook her head.

He reached for her hand and turned her palm against his chest. "Feel that?"

"Your heartbeat? Yeah."

"That heart yearns for you, Kalen. If you do not return with me, if you do not agree to be my mate, it will cease to beat."

Her eyes were like saucers. Her mouth gaped. "Wha . . . ?"

He brushed unruly curls from her temple. "You took yourself from me, Kalen. You took my heart. I want to marry you the white man's way. I want to mate with you the Indian way. Now. Tonight."

She wagged her head between his hands. "That doesn't make a lick of sense. Sometimes you hardly speak to me."

"Because I did not want you to have to make a choice between me and your uncle. To have to live like an outcast from the world you know. Long ago I vowed not to mate, not to put another woman through what my mother has endured. But then you came along."

"Uncle Jed . . ." She frowned. "Well, he'd've come around."

His heart beat loudly in his ears. Did that mean she would accept his suit?

"Besides, your mother seems happy enough."

"Mother rarely leaves the ranch, but when she does, I always ride at her side."

"Stands to reason, Taylor. She can't see a thing. She'd get lost in no time."

He chuckled. Then, unable to be near yet not touch her, he picked up her hand and again rubbed his thumb across the knuckles. "That really isn't the point, Kalen. Mother senses when she is not wanted."

Kalen nodded. "She has a sixth sense, all right." She tugged her hand, but he tightened his grip. Giving up, she evaded his eyes. "Taylor, y'all are smarter than me by a long shot. I . . . don't fit."

"What gave you such a notion?"

"When we're just sittin' around shootin' the breeze, your mother uses words I don't even know. It ain't like she's readin' from a highfalutin book."

He laughed. He could not help it. "Kalen, Mother has spent her life reading and sewing. She can do little else. It keeps her mind occupied, but she certainly doesn't mean to sound better than others."

"Oh, I ain't sayin' that! It's just . . ."

He again laid a finger across her lips. "Stop. You are a fine woman. I want you just the way you are."

"What about . . ." She stopped, searching his eyes. "What?"

"I thought you and Graceful Bird . . . She said . . ." Groping for the right words, Kalen shrugged.

He closed his eyes. He should have spoken directly to Grace long ago. Not fair to her or to Kalen. Time to say so.

"Grace has been a friend for most of my life, Kalen. I should have been straight with her. Now, she will be hurt. I am sorry for that, but I love you."

Her eyes widened. "You love me?"

"That is what I have been saying for the past five minutes."

"You said you *want* me." She shook her head emphatically. "Ain't the same."

He captured her face between his hands. "Hear me, Kalen Barrett. I love you now and forever. I want you by my side until I walk in the Spirit World." He leaned in and kissed her gently. "And you? What are your feelings for me?"

"Ask me again."

"Ask you again? Oh." He grinned. "Will you marry me?"

"Yes. Yes. Yes!" She launched herself into his arms, knocking him back for the second time that day.

It seemed a shame to waste it. . . .

The day, bright day sunny, mirrored the day when Kalen had first arrived at the Savage ranch. She drew in her mount and absorbed the tranquil setting. Though brisk and cold today, the sun sparkled off the distant tin roofs. Dozens of horses dotted the pastures crisscrossed by miles of white fences.

She glanced at the man atop the magnificent stallion by her side. He turned his head, the blue of his eyes rivaling God's heavens.

His smile sent blood rushing to her head. He leaned toward her and captured her mouth in a searing kiss that made her weak in the knees. Good thing she was sitting!

Taylor backed off and searched her eyes. "Ready?"

"Uh-huh." With him beside her, she was ready for anything.

They rode at an easy lope until they neared the house. The screen door opened and Blair stepped out, then turned back inside.

As Kalen slid from Jim's back, Taylor came

To the Edge of the Stars

around and clasped her hand. Both moved toward the porch. At that moment, Cameron ushered his mother through the door, Blair close behind. Brother and sister smiled broadly, but Miz Savage merely looked curious.

"Is that you, Taylor?"

"Yes, Mother, and I have someone I want you to meet."

His deep voice vibrated through Kalen like a cat's purr. He drew her with him as he mounted the steps.

"Mother, may I present the future Mrs. Kalen Savage?"

Kalen knew she would remember the contented sense of belonging that washed through her when Miz Savage smiled and extended her hands. The most elegant lady she had ever met pulled her close and gave her a kiss on each cheek.

"Welcome home, Kalen."

CONNIE MASON

The Black Widow

That was what the desperate prisoners incarcerated in Devil's Chateau called her. Whatever she did with them, one thing was certain: Her unfortunate victims were never seen again. But when she whisked Reed Harwood out of the cell where he'd been left to die for spying against the French, he discovered the lady was not all she seemed.

Fleur Fontaine was the most exquisitely sensual woman he'd ever met, yet there was an innocence about her that belied her sordid reputation. Only a dead man would fail to respond. Reed was not dead yet, but was he willing to pay…

The Price of Pleasure

ISBN 10: 0-8439-5745-X
ISBN 13: 978-0-8439-5745-7

DAWN MacTAVISH

Lark at first hoped it was a simple nightmare: If she closed
her eyes, she would be back in the mahogany bed of her
spacious boudoir at Eddington Hall, and all would be well.
Her father, the earl of Roxburgh, would not be dead by his
own hand, and she would not be in Marshalsea Debtor's
Prison.

Such was not to be. Ere the Marshalsea could do its worst,
the earl of Grayshire intervened. But while his touch was
electric and his gaze piercing, for what purpose had he
bought her freedom? No, this was not a dream. As Lark
would soon learn, her dreams had never ended so well.

The Privateer

AVAILABLE JANUARY 2008!

ISBN 13: 978-0-8439-5981-9